Octob

The Dirt-Brown Derby

A PI Frank Johnson Mystery

"A great protagonist, a suspenseful story, a wonderful sense of place. It's all here. An impressive debut by Ed Lynskey. He gets it right the first time out, the atmosphere, the characters. Watch out for this guy!"

—Edgar, Shamus, and Anthony Award-winner Steve Hamilton,
USA Today bestselling author of PI Alex McNight mysteries

"There's a new thoroughbred in the noir world of private investigators. Ed Lynskey's *The Dirt-Brown Derby* is vintage crime—smart, crisp dialogue, a town full of dysfunctional characters, a carefully twisted plot, and a terrifically enjoyable read."

—Nero Wolfe Award-winner Linda Fairstein, *New York Times*
bestselling author of the Alexandra Cooper mysteries

"Ed Lynskey has written a noir thriller that thunders across rural Virginia like a crazed stallion. Incredibly fast paced scenes abound, with crackling dialogue, and violent, unpredictable characters as PI Frank Johnson battles to unravel the mystery surrounding the death of a young girl allegedly killed by her own horse. This is a wild ride, hang on tight."

—-Ed Dee, author of Police Detectives Anthony Ryan and
Joe Gregory series including *The Conman's Daughter*

"PI Frank Johnson is prickly, quirky, judgmental, and persistent. *The Dirt-Brown Derby* is a solid, fast-paced read."

—Barbara D'Amato (Mary Higgins Clark Award, Agatha, and Anthony Award-winner author of Cat Marsala mysteries)

"*The Dirt-Brown Derby* is tough, snappy, and fascinating. Lynskey's PI Frank Johnson explores a crime and a stratified society in a way that grips and entertains. A high-speed read cover to cover."

—John Lutz, Shamus and Edgar Award-winner, author of *SWF Seeks Same*, (1992 movie *Single White Female* starring Bridget Fonda) and *Fear the Night* (2005).

"Ed Lynskey's distinctive voice brings the locale to life."

—Shamus and Edgar-nominee Charles Ardai, author of *Little Girl Lost*

"Ed Lynskey's *The Dirt-Brown Derby* is hard, fast, and unsentimental. P.I. Frank Johnson is a guy you want on your side, and Lynskey is a writer to watch. We're sure to be hearing more from both of them."

—Anthony-winner Bill Crider, author of the Sheriff Dan Rhodes mysteries

"Ed Lynskey is a smart writer who features witty dialogue and clever narrative topspin. His P.I., Frank Johnson, is a recovering boozer with a sharp tongue, a conscience, and a predestination for trouble. A wild church shootout pits true evil against a good doer's darker side. A fun read that informs as well as entertains."

—Charlie Stella, author of *Cheapskates, Charlie Opera, Jimmy Bench-Press*, and *Eddie's World*

"If you want great characters, mysteries that are not the norm, and a work that draws you into the storyline, you will want to read this book. Good job Mr. Lynskey; I look forward to reading more of your work in the future."

—Shirley Johnson, Midwest Book Review

"Praise for *Out of Town a Few Days*: Ed puts Frank into a jumble of places, and a quandary of troubles. And with an attitude, Johnson is constantly finding out the truth in each case. With murder, women, and some choice stories, this book is a must. The stories are all fast-paced, with a well-written style I have grown to expect from this writer."

—Virginia Johnson, Detective Mystery Stories

"This is what the PI genre is about and Frank's swift, violent glimpses achieve this better than most."

—Russel D. McLean, Crime Scene Scotland

"Mystery lovers will welcome a change in their reading habits. I know I did."

—Robert H. Goss, Round Table Reviews.

The Dirt-Brown Derby

A PI Frank Johnson Mystery

Ed Lynskey

Excerpt appears in *Yale Anglers' Journal*, Yale University.

A Mundania Press Production
Mundania Press LLC
6470A Glenway Avenue, #109
Cincinnati, Ohio 45211-5222

To order additional copies of this book, contact:
books@mundania.com
www.mundania.com

Book Design, Production, and Layout by Daniel J. Reitz, Sr.
Marketing and Promotion by Bob Sanders

Trade Paperback ISBN-10: 1-59426-232-2
Trade Paperback ISBN-13: 978-1-59426-232-6

eBook ISBN-10: 1-59426-233-0
eBook ISBN-13: 978-1-59426-233-3

First Edition • July 2006
Library of Congress Catalog Card Number 2006927878

Production by Mundania Press LLC
Printed in the United States of America

10 9 8 7 6 5 4 3 2 1

Dedicated to Heather, with love.

Chapter 1

Sunday 9 AM, April 16th

"No thoroughbred will crush in its rider's head," Mrs. Taliaferro was telling me over the telephone. Maybe it was stress but she bleated her words through her adenoids. "My daughter was murdered."

"Murder is for local authorities," I replied. "As a rule, no PI gets involved in it. Me, for instance."

"My sheriff calls it an accident. So, you can imagine how hard he is looking for the killer. Let's set your retainer at, oh, say $50,000." She paused to let that sink in. "Does that sway you?"

"Look, I've never even set foot in Kaiser."

"Perfect. An outsider is what I need. You fit the bill to a tee."

"What if I say no?"

"$200,000 is my final offer."

Picking myself up off the floor, I said, "Let's talk. 2 PM, your house this afternoon. Agreed?"

"That pleases me to no end." Beating me to the punch, Mrs. Taliaferro hung up.

An hour later, I was en route for Kaiser. Car windows down, I soaked up Virginia's bucolic splendor. After a few miles, the scenery changed. I passed a smoldering tire dump. Later, a road gang—the bulk of them under thirty and black—picked up litter in the divider strip. The sentry dangled long arms off an automatic rifle across his shoulders like the Oz scarecrow. Some things would never change. In a little while, I spotted a trio of stick crosses tasseling on the Kaiser water tower. Today was Palm Sunday. The crosses commemorated not one, not two, but three deaths, a fact usually downplayed.

Kaiser's main drag: a cycle shack, a post office, a hospital, a garage, and an ex-railroad depot that was now a deli. There was a public library in an ex-filling station in which to conduct genealogical research. "Meats Merci" on a rust-pitted sign advertised what I took to be a slaughterhouse. I winced to see sinewy kids on rollerblades pulling crazy stunts on homemade ramps. In low-riding cutoffs and tube tops, legs long and tanned, girls in the bed of a pickup truck waved back at knots of old men in the shade. If this was a foretaste, maybe Kaiser wasn't half bad.

Then I braked to pull into a graveled lot. Moored between two "Farm Use" pickups, I hitched up the emergency brake. Only then did I zero in on them—three toughs in bleached jeans. One wore a torn NASCAR T-shirt and black cowboy boots. Another's belt buckles said "STOMP ASS!" I scooped something off the seat to carry, ranged out, and approached the store casual-like.

The beefy tough, backside against the plate glass, didn't budge. I sensed his three pals shifting to block my line of retreat before I could protect it. A rookie mistake.

"Excuse me," I said.

"Would you listen at this crap, Adam." In a falsetto mocking voice, the tough behind me said, "Excuse me."

"I heard him." Glaring at me, Adam advanced. I noticed his knuckles, two of them armored with rings. "No excuse for you." A run of snickers. Adam balled, unballed a fist. A scar zigzagged over his jawbone. Maybe a razor-thighed whore had sat on his face.

I visualized my hand pulling from my belt.

"You're a real ugly fucking bastard."

The nearest tough slugged my shoulder. "Answer the man."

Was I pissed? Enough to go up a rope, but I didn't bat an eyelid.

"Has a chainsaw got the Pollock's tongue?"

They jeered.

I turned. "Sorry to disturb your post hanging, guys. I'll just fade, okay?"

"Get an earful!" Adam was feeling his oats. "Don't he sound chicken?"

"Why don't we check that out?" A Kabar skinning knife materialized. "Around back in the alleyway."

The piece of metal I plucked from my waistline fended off a punch leveled at my guts. Adam yelped. I was hurting, too, though not as much. I sucked for oxygen and straightened. Shoving past Adam, I charged up the three steps. The .357 targeted at their foreheads froze them. Adam squaring his shoulders tensed as if to make his move.

I lined the .357 on his grubby mouth. "Bring it on." Billy Jack couldn't have uttered it any better.

Adam massaged his fist.

My thumb cocked back the hammer. "Better take a hike while you still can."

Adam's pager beeped. He checked it, then jerked his head. They scattered out of the parking lot before vanishing behind a boarded up house. My central nervous system switched off high alert. I did a quick scan. No cops. Good.

Hovering inside the door, the old storekeeper bowed by arthritis squeezed my forearm. Paint speckled his apron and pencil stubs poked from behind authentic jug ears. I cached the .357 under my shirttail in my waistband.

"Virginia hospitality," I said. "Gotta love it."

"Adam and the Kilby cousins get off on breaking bones. What are you buying?" he asked.

"A Bud tall boy to go."

"Interested in a Lotto ticket? It's a twenty-three million dollar jackpot. Drawing is at midnight and I way overdue to sell the winning ticket."

"Nope."

"Lousy day for luck all around, huh?"

"Playing Lotto is for chumps."

"Pity." He double-bagged a cold one, rang me up, and deposited the change into my still shaky palm. "Anything else?"

"Yeah. I'm looking for a Mrs. Mary Taliaferro."

"Yeah, you would be. Now watch me read your mind. You're a tabloid writer here about her daughter's death. See? Told you I was good."

"Sorry to spoil your record, Carnac. I'm a private licensed detective here at Mrs. Taliaferro's say-so. My name is Johnson."

"You have my sympathy, Mr. Johnson," he said.

"Why? Will she bite off my cock or something?"

He fidgeted, then said, "I'd pass a kidney stone on Christmas day rather than deal with Mrs. Taliaferro. She's a flake off the upper crust."

"About her daughter's death," I said. "You care to break it down for me?"

He nudged the sacked beer across the tile countertop at me. "Thrown off her stallion, she was trampled. It was awful. God never made a finer girl than Emily. Pretty as the day is long. It's her mother who I've got no use for."

"Some say a horse stomping its rider is unusual."

"That's why the stallion is called Hellbent."

"But Emily, as I understand it, was a crackerjack rider."

"That didn't mean squat," he said. "Hellbent was a catastrophe waiting to happen."

"Has murder ever been mentioned?"

The old storekeeper, studying me over horn-rimmed glasses, knitted his white Andy Rooney brows. "I've got nothing else to add, son."

"Then point me to Dakota Farms and I'm gone."

The old storekeeper's pencil scratched a map on a box top. Pickled eggs suspended in a big jar watched us. On the Community News corkboard was a poster for a Suicide Survivors Support Group. Over the cash register, a plaque identified the store credit manager as Helen Wait. Still waiting, I unscrewed the bottle cap; the icy brew tasted vile. Finally, I thanked him for the directions and waded back into April's sweat lodge. No spring to speak of was typical in Virginia.

The three toughs hadn't double backed to slash my tires or sugar my gas tank. I withdrew the .357—hell, the damn gun hadn't even been loaded. Once seated, I decided to play it smart and swung my legs out of the car. I stalked around to key open the trunk lid. Rummaging beneath a spare tire, I took up the tire iron and stashed the .357. I buckled up and stroked the engine, and hid the tire iron by the center console.

To my right down three blocks, Sunday services at the Charismatic Catholic church had disbanded. Parishioners stirring arms and rejoicing inside primer-patched Nissans and Toyotas came on strong. Palm fronds slapped their rapt faces. Rosaries dangled from rearview mirrors. At last, I pulled out and consulting the boxtop map took a side avenue. Sure enough, there it stood.

Every town and city in Virginia had at least one—the ABC Store. Sin tax on alcohol netted the Commonwealth a tidy sum. In observation of the Sabbath, however, the ABC Store was closed. Signs required proof of age and disapproved of loitering. That didn't hinder the tribe of derelicts glaring back at me.

Booze, no matter what day of the week, spelled dire news. At least it did for me. Leaning out the car window, I sent my bought tall boy ricocheting off a parking meter, the glass smashing on a manhole cover. The sheriff's cruiser galloping up behind me must've seen the whole thing.

No red-blue roof light flashed at me. I watched in the rearview mirror, as the cruiser crept alongside a squat, dirty blonde. She strode faster, the angry strides of a woman in a short skirt. After a word with her, the cruiser screamed around me. She shot him the bird.

Yes sir, Kaiser was shaping up to be my kind of town.

Chapter 2

Sunday 2 PM, April 16th

Beyond the railroad tracks, the road snaked between white plank fences hyphen by the occasional horse jump. New asphalt capped the fairway. I straddled the double-yellow center line. Crows flew up from a road kill skunk. Horses grazed on bluegrass combed by breezes, a vista that went on for miles. Which famous writer had said the rich carry the world in their hip pocket? At 8.6 miles, my car crested a knoll and a stone hut popped into view—according to the storekeeper's map, this was my turnoff.

Braking, I eased to a stop. A security guard in high water britches raised a dirty white glove. I edged a few more inches closer to the crossbar. A Virginia state flag flapped above us, its grommets a steely clack against the pole.

"You have business here?" The guard shifted as if to lean on my roof but the road crud there repelled him.

"I'm Johnson." He compared my PI license photo to the warm-blooded me. "Here for a two o'clock appointment."

"I'll dial the residence. Meantime, squat on your thumbs," he replied.

The rearview mirror showed the clown jotting down my license plate number. I saw him through the hut's picture window yak on a phone receiver. He muttered oaths the whole way back to my car.

"Drive straight up yonder. 15 miles per hour. Don't scare the livestock," he said. An electric motor chirred while it withdrew the crossbar.

"My PI ticket?"

"Tell you what. I'll safeguard it until you're outside the gate. Enjoy your stay in my house, er, Johnson." He put on a yellow-toothed grin.

My car's pistons clanged and clacked as I ascended the hill in a low gear. My ears popped beneath the hardy American Chestnuts swelling with sea green buds. Further out, native rock fences, the result of somebody's sweat equity, paralleled the lane. Rounding a gradual bend, I just stared all slack jawed.

To look at, the Taliaferro mansion was big and ugly. Chimneys, one brick and one stone, bracketed the structure. The mansard roof was green-streaked copper and the palladium windows arched. A turreted sleeping porch off the second floor looked like an add-on to me. My attention went to the twin front doors surmounted by a fanlight. The door had brass locks and a shield-shaped knocker.

Beside a red Jaguar even filthier than my own car, I cut the motor. A peacock disappeared around a gazebo and Canadian geese had carpeted the lower yard with turds. Rotted timber, I noted getting out, soured the air. The gardener, dressed as a cloddish Hobbit, doffed a pith helmet to swab his head. My nod was rewarded a scathing glare. Did he mistake me for a Nazi paratrooper?

The yard gate squeaked open. I crossed the brick patio, dodging the wrought iron furniture under Martha Stewart umbrellas. The doorbell button created a buzz. I glanced over at the outbuildings that included tenant cottages and a board-and-batten garage. Metal trashcans on wood skids sat behind it. Rotting mortar needed emergency tuck-pointing. I rang again, then clacking the big knocker felt ridiculous.

"Mrs. Taliaferro ain't about."

Ah, the gardener and I were now on speaking terms. "But she just took my call," I said.

"My wife, Rachel, admits all the visitors." He set down the wheelbarrow.

"Can't be. I have an appointment."

He hatched a grin. "Mrs. Taliaferro holding to a schedule? Not bloody likely."

"I've come a long ways. Might Rachel know more?"

The gardener trudged over the patio past the cast-concrete planters splurging with pansies, Dutch iris, and hyacinths. I stepped aside to let him rap on the door until the inside doorknob jiggled. From under a chain lock, a mousy-haired lady not too tall in silver-wired spectacles blinked out at us. Dave Brubeck's "Blue Rondo a la Turk" leaked out the door.

"Wife, was a two PM visitor expected here today?"

She regarded me with no interest. "Mr. Johnson, the professional detective?"

I nodded.

"Mrs. Taliaferro decided to go shopping for a dress this afternoon."

"Ain't that the hog's nuts?" The gardener threw out a bumptious laugh.

"Ralph, watch your language." Rachel gave her husband a withering look before shifting her attention to me. "Mrs. Taliaferro left me instructions to give you. She reserved Room Seven for you at the Kaiser Motel in town. Inquire at the front desk."

"I left my bags at home."

Rachel fidgeted with her apron hem. "Mrs. Taliaferro will arrive no later than ten o'clock."

"Our employer is, how to put it, wife? Well, impossible to fathom, Mr. Johnson. So don't bother trying to understand Mrs. Taliaferro."

"She told me to tell you that she'll bring your check," said Rachel. "I have to run. My egg timer just went off." The door whapped shut.

"What was she thinking?" I asked half-aloud.

Ralph grinned wider. "Hell, humor Mrs. Taliaferro. For $200,000, I'd grovel like a snake under a shithouse."

I slithered away disturbed that he knew the amount of my fat check.

Bored while holed up at Kaiser Motel in Room Seven, I trimmed my toenails during a TV commercial explaining feminine yeast infection. My temptation was a six-pack of Bud sweating on the Goodwill bureau. My plan was to stay sober, give Lady Taliaferro holy hell, and rack out until sunup. Then I'd haul ass for home. If I was unpaid, so what? Sidelined one day wasn't major. It was 10:10 PM by my watch. My client was ten minutes late. I swiped away the gritty oak pollen crusting my eyes. A headache medicine ad now played on the TV.

Digging under the dirty mattress, I extracted a 9 mil and brightened the pineapple lamp. The .357 remained wedged underneath the spare tire in my trunk. This big, blue beauty was a Ruger P-85 automatic, a double action with a 15-round magazine and fixed sights zeroed out at 25 yards. My preference was a Glock with an extended clip to belch out 33 rounds but that was overkill for this job.

Still, we "NRA gun nuts" liked the high ordnance. A bass-heavy rap tune from a car idling outside made my room door vibrate. Rap artists sporting goofy names like Snoop Doggy Dog, Chuck D, and Public Enemy shot from the hip, called themselves gangstas, and banked gobs of green. Barnum's adage was proven correct.

It was now eleven minutes after ten. I dry-fired the 9 mil as a "Mannix" rerun came on the TV. Another car chase ensued with the attendant fireball crash off a seaside cliff. Mannix looked tired. I felt tired. Kaiser was tired. My client was twelve minutes late. I wanted to leave this dirt-bag motel. What was keeping me? Two hundred thousand dollars is what. I swerved one leg off the bed as a double knock drew up my 9 mil centered on the door.

"Who is it?"

A muffled lady shout said, "Mrs. Taliaferro."

I holstered the 9 mil. "It's open. Come on in."

She slogged in, nudged the door shut with her butt. First impression: I'd waited for this? Her sundress—years ago powder blue when plucked new off K-Mart's sales rack—extended below her knobby knees. Average looks, average build, and average walk. No chinchilla stole over a silk negligee. No strings of chaste pearls. No shockheaded blonde off the fashion show runway.

"Are you Frank Johnson?" she asked.

I recognized that rapid-fire, nasal cadence. Eyebrow cocked in affirmation, I gestured to a high-back folding chair at the foot of the bed, then turned off the TV. Gathering her dress together in her hands, Mary Taliaferro sat down and crossed her ankles. Although the top buttons were undone, she didn't tip much cleavage in her account.

"Is this room your idea of slumming, Mary?"

"Mrs. Taliaferro, please." She acted reassured by the formality. Her opalescent polished fingernails clicked. "I concede it is crass, our meeting here."

"Where were you this afternoon?" I asked.

"Everywhere and anywhere. I wasted the entire day driving hither and yon. Middleburg, The Plains, Marshall, Markham, Orleans, Arcola, Upperville, Hume, Delaplane, Paris..."

"Why?" I asked.

"Johnson, as I explained to you over the phone, my daughter died a few days ago. Staying home right now distresses me even though I'm by nature a very private person."

"Not too private. Your maid told me where to meet you."

"Rachel has been in my employ for years. I trust her implicitly." Mrs. Taliaferro removed a pack from her purse, tapped a cigarette out to her lips, and applied a match. Her smoke made me crave a toke. "Was your day so horrendous?" she asked after her next exhalation.

"First, your security guard took my PI license. Second, your congenial gardener welcomed me. Then I traded whispers with your maid through the keyhole. Most of all, I'm tired and sick of playing footsie with you."

"Oh, Rachel can be melodramatic." Mrs. Taliaferro smiled briefly. Twin teardrops tracked through her rouge. "See this? Well, do you? I've been bawling my eyes out. It can't go on. Will you help me, please?" It wasn't so much a request as a plea.

Dry up and knock off your crying, I thought. Then, aware of her drawing out a checkbook, a disgust galled me. "No ma'am, sorry I can't but I'll recommend a top-flight agency. I've known them for years. Not me, though. I apologize for any inconvenience."

Sobs underlined her whisper. "Emily died on Thursday. My life has been a living hell since then. You don't know how much." Her sentence trailed off. More tears. "Please reconsider. Mr. Gatlin spoke highly of you."

With the invocation of Robert Gatlin, a self-made billionaire lawyer who I worked for on occasion, I had a softening of heart. Gatlin and I had briefly discussed my coming. Only, I wasn't going to bring him up if she didn't. But now she had and I was on the hook.

"Fine," I said at length. "Start from the top. You allege Emily was murdered. Why?"

She composed herself. "Because no true-breed horse will choose to crush a human."

"The pony was coerced?"

"The murderer bashed in Emily's skull, then staged it as if her thoroughbred was death's agent."

In my ignorant opinion, the story was outlandish and improbable. Approaching it from a different angle was worth a try. "Did you or your daughter have enemies?"

Mrs. Taliaferro flicked ash to the carpet, inhaled, and vented smoke through a pained sigh. "Like me, she was warm and outgoing. Very well liked by all who knew her."

I pressed the point. "Any suspicions about her killer's identity?"

"No one specific," said Mrs. Taliaferro. "Are you, then, interested in taking my case, Mr. Johnson?"

Never once did Mrs. Taliaferro's luminous green eyes wander from mine. She hadn't dodged a question or fudged an answer. Her grief was raw. That was understandable. All told, my gut reaction was inclined to believe if not feel sorry for her. Besides, I was penniless and Gatlin had put me on the firing line so how could I refuse her?

"Make that out to Franklin Johnson. As for autopsy results, police reports, forensics reports, crime scene photographs, interview list, videotapes, et cetera, who do I consult?"

"Sheriff Pettigrew." She butted the cigarette in an ashtray on the TV, creased and detached the check with a crisp rip.

A $200,000 check was signed in red by Mary Taliaferro. Folded in thirds, I put it under a spare car key kept inside my billfold.

"I've learned the hard way that a standard contract greases the skids." I removed the documents I'd filled out on my typewriter back home and handed them to her. She inscribed both without reading a single word. I filed away my copy behind her fat check.

"Mr. Johnson, you've got a real knack for fixing messes. Mine, I hope, isn't any different."

"I have some ideas. Set up a hotline for tips, for instance. Offering a reward can sometimes flush out useful information. But it's your money, not mine."

"Money is never an impediment."

"I'll drive out first thing in the morning. We can discuss it then."

"I want this son of a bitch brought to justice. And to die before my eyes." That vow made, Mrs. Taliaferro tied on a paisley scarf, her sandals clopped out the door, and she dissolved into darkness.

In my dreams that night, dirt-brown mustangs and palominos mounted by skeletons stampeded behind my eyelids. They were ghost-riders, every lowlife felon and scammer I'd ever clashed with. A few rotted in the grave. Most however were locked behind bars. Uniformed prisoners I'd escorted to Riker's Island while an Army MP leered at me.

One desperado I'd helped arrest and convict for manslaughter in upstate New York had been released early, despite my impassioned letter of opposition to his parole board. The vengeful bastard wouldn't back off, not for a second in coming after me. I jolted awake in a cold, prickly sweat.

The pineapple lamp on full blaze, I tuned in to a Susan Cabot flick. She was gorgeous, "a beautiful woman by day—a lusting queen wasp by night." Ms. Cabot's skull, I recalled, had been caved in by a barbell that her son Timothy wielded. The year? 1986. Macabre trivia did the trick and I fell back asleep, if you could call it that.

Chapter 3

Monday 9 AM, April 17th

"The word I get is your dick got knocked in the dirt." Sheriff Pettigrew tapped a pencil eraser tip on my PI license.

Here in his office I sat fascinated by a millipede doing a can-can dance on his pencil sharpener. With a gold braided neck chain, a salon tan, and a trim mustache, the early middle-aged sheriff personified my idea of a lounge lizard. Riot gauge Mossberg shotguns bristled on a rack behind and above him.

"Everything local, swings back to me." he said.

Miss July—Pettigrew's vintage 1982 Playboy calendar girl—beamed above us, how I pictured a nubile Faye Dunaway in a nudist colony on Independence Day. "This swung back to you flat-out wrong," I said.

"The climax has you drawing out a handgun. Tell you what, I'll be a nice guy and pretend I never heard that part." He tossed me the PI license. Cloying Aqua Velva came with it. "Because if I didn't, I'd have to cuff and stuff you right now."

"My gun permit is valid."

"No doubt. What caliber?"

"A .357 inside an evidence safe welded to my trunk." A half-truth cut close enough although I'd half-planned to install the evidence safe.

"Leave it there. My brother Stanley Pettigrew works in the Taliaferro gatehouse. He tells me his bitch of a boss hired you." Pettigrew reared back, hands grasped behind his head. A languor informing his eyes was deceptive. The millipede had wiggled under the desk calendar.

"My client entertains grave doubts about her daughter's death," I said. "She paid me to tidy up inconsistencies..."

Sheriff Pettigrew rolled his head. "How do you mean, inconsistencies?"

I went on. "And, to nail down my point, I agreed to do it."

"Big waste of your time. My investigation is a done deal," said Pettigrew. "Emily's death was ruled an unlucky accident, plain and simple."

"Experts say a horse rarely tromps on its rider," I said.

Unimpressed, Pettigrew scraped his palms across wavy, sandy hair. "Just as many experts say horses are unpredictable. A lot like people are."

"Uh-huh."

"Rich folks on their mounts aren't immune to gravity either. Ask that Superman actor."

Cheap shot, I thought but said, "You finished investigating in three days. Mighty efficient police work."

"Not that amazing. Emily Taliaferro's case was cut-and-dried."

"My job, then, shouldn't cause you heartburn."

I felt Sheriff Pettigrew's dislike of me intensify. He realigned his Elk's Club tie clasp. "What job?" His snake eyes avoided mine.

"My job is to ferret out the truth about Emily's death."

His frown seethed but his voice kept low and even. "Johnson, don't show up in my county and tread on my toes. Because I can bury you deep like anything that's dead and stinks."

"You might like to rethink that threat," I said.

Pettigrew's eyes, blue and blunt, now fastened on me. "I don't care if Robert Gatlin is your shit hot attorney. You have two days to wind up things and scram."

"Your police files might give me a leg up," I said.

Boots shuffling wood, Sheriff Pettigrew rose to his feet. That was my cue to do likewise. "As I recall saying, the official report will be issued in a day or so. I'll ask my girl Friday to airmail you an autographed copy."

"You mean sent by Pony Express."

Pettigrew's upper lip curled. We didn't shake hands—that was too civilized. My impulse was to smash in his nose except I'd end up with a thuggish cellmate. AS I ducked into the mid-morning sun, a squat, dirty blonde bumped against me with a surprised grunt. She was the one Pettigrew had wolf whistled at earlier from his cruiser. I assumed she was his "girl Friday" here offering her services bright and early Monday morning.

I like to get a worm's eye view of the crime scene or, in this case, what remained of it days after the fact. I retracied my route to Dakota Farms. Gawks left and right at my client's endless acreage dizzied me. The word "Dakota" resonated in me as the New York City apartment building where John Lennon was popped. A young fellow sitting at the gate, waffle-sole boots propped up, waved me through. I drove up without my car self-destructing and joined the Jaguar parked in the same berth as the day before.

Beyond a birdbath and lawn sprinklers, Ralph slung a five-pound sledgehammer busting up a stone moongate. He threw the sledge by a morning glory trellis and greeted me now unhooking the gate. He trudged over, and intercepted me on the patio, but I was fresh out of friendly.

He said, "You're now one of us. Welcome aboard, sucker," he said.

My thumb jerked over a shoulder. "Is our boss lady available?"

"No. Rachel chauffeured her to Robin's Mill. The Artists Guild sponsors a big annual gala and Mrs. Taliaferro is their champion."

"She's not much of a homebody," I said.

"Not since Emily died. I hardly see her anymore myself. You can put her mind at ease, though. That's a godsend."

"Was Emily murdered?"

Ralph's neckless head swiveled about to me. "Only her grief-stricken mom figures it that way. Emily's spill off the horse was a fatal accident. Nothing more. Now it's up to you to convince her."

"I'll keep that in mind. Did you see your sheriff process the crime scene?"

"He did a cursory sweep of the woods after they carted Emily out like a burrito. It was a terrible sight."

"This morning the sheriff ripped me a new airway. What's his vendetta with Mrs. Taliaferro?"

"Paybacks. Her wealth funded his opponent's last election. A damn Republican. Pettigrew squeaked out a victory. By then the bloom was off their, um, friendship."

The cagey manner in which he'd uttered it led me to ask, "Friendship?"

Ralph licked his lips. "Look, Johnson, get this straight. All I do here is the landscaping. Mulching and mowing and weeding. I don't tell tales out of school."

I motioned with my head . "Flashy Jag. You drive it?"

Ralph dealt me a stare. "Pierre, the trainer, does. Mrs. Taliaferro gives him that much free rein, believe it or not."

"She loves her ponies," I said. "Is her husband a polo enthusiast?"

"Not unless it's from the bottom of the Atlantic Ocean," said Ralph. "His plane, a Cessna, vanished in the Bermuda Triangle during the Gulf War. Those dangerous prop planes should be outlawed."

"And his billions couldn't rescue him." I shook my head. "Tough sledding."

"Pierre is at the stable. Mrs. Taliaferro suggested that I introduce you two." Ralph slid off his goatskin gloves as we walked away from the mansion. I gathered the pair of them didn't get along.

"Does Pierre live here?"

"Yeah, the same as Rachel and me. Except we're on the back hall and Pierre's room is at the end of the central corridor."

"Sweet."

"Yeah, especially for Pierre, our hero of the hour. He found Emily dead."

"That's why he drives the Jaguar, huh?"

That wisecrack earned me a scowl. We remained on a paved lane leading to the stable, a low, long brick building. The wrought iron weathervane of Chanticleer favored a southwest wind, the same direction as my home. Swallows knuckle-balled by lightning arresters on the spires. A yellow barn cat scampered by us at the doorway. Ralph followed me inside. A columnar ashtray with a chrome top and black body served as a doorstop to the tack room. Neat's-foot oil and saddle soap pungent, I sneezed. Spick and span marble parquet floors had Ralph mincing steps. We hustled by a dozen vacant stalls lined with fresh clean straw with alfalfa bales stacked chest high in the corners.

Shoulders slumped against a pillar, Pierre was hosing out a stall. He was blade-thin, a Gumby physique towering six inches over me at six-two but with tiny feet.

Ralph cuffed him on the shoulder. "Pierre, meet Frank Johnson, the detective here looking into Emily's death."

Pierre's wet right hand clamped mine. "Mighty proud to make your acquaintance," he said.

"Same here," I said. "You keep a clean barn."

"All in a day's work," he said.

Ralph's snort piled on his disgust. "Tell Mr. Johnson about Emily that morning."

"Well, every Thursday morning she took out Hellbent for exercise. Like always, I helped her tack up. She was partial to a new bridle path her mother had had just laid through the woods. Only this Thursday, the restless horse later galloped up alone. No Emily. Freaking out, I searched down the path to find her lying on the ground, raced back here, and yelled to her mother who'd walked down looking for me. She phoned 911."

Ralph cut in. "Rachel and I in Kaiser followed the EMTs home."

"Well, Emily lay all limp. No breath, no pulse, her skull mangled. Skin off the bone. Blood everywhere. That's it." Shivering, Pierre resumed spraying down the stall, finding comfort in his routines.

I shouted over cascading water. "Mrs. Taliaferro told me to scope out the spot. She sent me to you."

He stopped spraying and the nozzle clinked to the floor. "She did?"

Bending the truth didn't pique my guilt. "'Pierre should guide you' were her exact words."

Ralph with impatience half-raised a hand. "Be seeing you, Johnson."

"Yeah, go plant some pretty pansies." Pierre did a limp wrist.

Ralph stiffened. "Shelton, I've had about enough of your giving me shit."

I interrupted them. "Hey, both of you quit with the jawboning. Ralph, head on back to the yard. Pierre, lead me to the damn bridle trail."

"Screw you both." Ralph wheeled and left us.

"Arrogant asshole," said Pierre.

Pierre and I began plodding through a pasture shin-deep in winter brown grass. He calibrated his long-legged gait to match my slowness. Beggar-lice adhered to our trousers. It was a sticky, hot day but still too early in the year for marauding deerflies and rubbing on DEET. I'd have to get new clothes in town as these had grown rank even to my nose. Also a pair of sunshades.

"Pierre, you're the professional," I said. "Was Emily's death a riding mishap?"

"Aye, it was. And that horse warrants a bullet smack dab between its devil eyes."

"He's that rambunctious, huh?"

"Hellbent shied and bolted. Emily lost her stirrups and flew headlong to the ground. In pure panic, the stallion scrambled over her. Those iron-shod hooves, the rear legs in particular, turned into piling hammers."

"She wasn't geared in a riding helmet?"

"Who, Emily? Get out of here. That girl was nothing but a free spirit."

"Were her saddle, bridle, or bit damaged?" I asked.

"No sir. We don't use faulty equipment."

"Mrs. Taliaferro insists foul play was involved." My gaze perused his face. Not a muscle tweaked although he took his time framing a response.

"That my good fellow, is the mother in her speaking. Her reckoning with maternal guilt," he said, at last.

"You're definite it was the horse that killed her?"

"Look, I named that nag the first morning he arrived here. After he kicked out his trailer panels, I asked, no I begged Emily, to ship Hellbent back to Kentucky. No dice. She was smitten. I'd scouted and photographed better prospects but she wouldn't have anything to do with them. For her, it was Hellbent, and let the chips fall where they might."

"Was Emily over mounted?" I asked.

"Anybody on Hellbent is. Except of course maybe Zorro," said Pierre.

I pointed to a graveyard encircled by a wrought iron fence across the chopped cornfield. Three big, gaunt trees brooded over the headstones. "Whose old family cemetery? The Taliaferro clan?"

Pierre scoffed. "It's not for folks. Taliaferro race horses are buried in that plot. Go figure. The rich do live different."

"People with more dollars than sense," I said to concur with him.

"Well, I'm going to be cremated," said Pierre. "I asked to have my ashes scattered across the Aztec's pyramids near Mexico City. Why, I don't know. Because it's sort of exotic, I guess."

"H'm. Exotic."

We approached the ten-foot swath to a bridle path hacked through sumac and locust trees to virgin oaks a few yards further on. I waited while Pierre checked his rabbit gums baited with turnips and apples but no luck. Understanding the lure of bridle paths as I did was easy. A young friend that I deer-hunted with back home, Chet Peyton, enjoyed a good living from mashing his Allis-Chambers bulldozer to carve them out of forests. Affluent girls at private schools such as Mary Baldwin, Randolph Macon, and Sweet Briar delighted in cantering over hill and dale exploring Chet's new serpentine trails.

"Pierre, what all can spook a horse?" I asked him.

"Bear, lynx, a timber rattler. Minus blinkers, a slip of shadow at the corner of its eye will startle him. Something as simple as a wasp can sting its nose."

"Maybe this time Hellbent really saw the devil."

The dark sarcasm didn't evade Pierre. "Satan has hooves, too."

We were now in the oaks. "Do others use this trail?"

"Youngsters from town troop in for picnics and whatnot," replied Pierre.

I asked the next logical question. "And the older kids?"

"Their wild rave parties, or so I've heard, take place down the road in a field. Mostly a wallflower, I never go there so I don't really know."

Emerging from the stand of oaks, the trail took us into a stumpy clearing, descended into a shallow ravine, and passed underneath a giant holly tree. We halted. Rusted hulks strangled by honeysuckle and Virginia Creeper were components to a donkey engine. Mining operations, possibly for iron ore, once fueled hardscrabble men's ambitions. The Piedmont was larded with played out mines drilled and dug into mountains and creek banks.

Pierre gestured to a disturbed patch of dark, wet ground. "That's where Emily fell off." Stooping, he righted a white wood cross staked by the trail, apparently his makeshift memorial to the late Emily.

"Boy, that was a march and a half, Emily had some endurance." I said.

"Emily was a natural athlete. She once rode in a steeplechase with a hip pointer." In grave, tender silence, Pierre placed a berried holly branch beside the white cross.

"Was Emily old enough to compete in shows?"

Pierre choosing action over words, sought inside a back pocket for a wallet chained to his leather belt. He flipped to a photograph and handed it to me. "Two weeks shy of sixteen, she was damn near ready. Emily was on her way to Bryn Mawr, too." His voice swelled with pride.

While admiring her blonde pluck, I could measure some physical resemblance to her mother. "I'd say Emily was a poised, young lady full of spunk. True?"

"I agree. Who'd ever take a notion to kill her?" Pierre spat.

"The great horned owl is the only predator that will devour a skunk," I said.

"...meaning?"

"Meaning every wild thing has at least one enemy." I purposefully dropped his wallet, and Emily's portrait slithered out the plastic folder. Recovering it, I read the girlish writing on the back:

To Sweetest Pierre,
My "Duke Longman,"
Love Always,
Emily

Pierre grabbed back his wallet and Emily's headshot. "Anything else, Johnson?"

I got up to prowl about the holly tree. "Give me a second to set it straight in my mind what happened here." On the opposite side of a fallen log, my eyes landed on a slingshot. I glanced at Pierre. He was retying his work boot. After swaddling the slingshot in a clean handkerchief, I stuffed it beneath my sweatshirt.

Pierre's face twisted in anger and impatience, for no apparent reason. "I have to get back to work." Our talk was completed. I thanked him for the A-plus effort showing me around.

We hoofed it to the stable in silence. I snaked down their little mountain in my car and at high noon roared off to Kaiser.

Chapter 4

Monday 12:30 PM, April 17th

Taken from the old storekeeper's larder, I washed down beef jerky with a cold Royal Crown soda. I'd been obligated to fast and eat fish for lent, so beef jerky was welcomed protein in my diet. Just the same, I had a thirst for a mid-day beer. Outside the store at a cafeteria table, I bought a box each from the Girl Scouts peddling do-si-dos, samoas, and thin mint cookies. I could subsist for an eternity on their refrigerated thin mint cookies.

Sizing up a new metallic-blue Ford 150 pickup truck parked at the curb, I knew I had to have one sometime in my life. Until such time, the thin mint cookies had to do. I realized I'd forgotten to buy my sunshades but said screw it. The Post Office was next door and I gave myself a little pep talk. Here you go, Johnson. What's say we try and alter our luck for the better?

The slingshot was made from inner tube strips, cord, and an Y-shaped willow branch. Was it some kid's plaything dropped along the trail? I had a contact who might do me a good deed. A forensics scientist at the state laboratory in Richmond, Darl Adkins had bailed out of our small town of Pelham, Virginia, withering along I-81.

No shock to those who knew her best, Darl had graduated from VPI with top honors. We shared two avocations: cats and crime fighting. That was enough to nurture a casual friendship. Scribbling a cover letter, I reassured her my tomcat still tolerated me. That led to my request for her to process any latent prints on the slingshot. I carefully put both items in a business envelope addressed to Darl's home. The postmistress was shameless to bribe with my box of cookies.

"Please stamp 'URGENT' on the front and back," I said. "Make double sure it goes out with your next pick up."

"What the devil is that important?" she asked.

"It's hush-hush. Key evidence in a murder investigation," I said, mysteriously. Before I stapled the flap shut, she peeked in to see the slingshot. "It's for my nephew," I said. "Won't his mother, my dear sister, love it?"

We exchanged knowing smiles over my joke not really a joke. Any criminal investigator with half a brain would agree what I had was a long shot, but every once in a blue moon they too paid off. I went back to my parked car.

It limped on its way west through town. Out of both side mirrors, I frowned to see the black exhaust the tailpipe reeked out. The tire dump fire coming into town had smelled better. Kaiser boasted the one motel, a throwback to the 1950s. Neon tubing tracked along the guttering. I docked at the lobby shaded by a retractable awning striped like a zebra and let myself inside. The proprietress with an annoyed glower saw it was me again. The fat lady was busy weaving dried yarrow stalks into a floral arrangement. Her lank, silvery hair was swept back into a ragged ponytail. Her nutria teeth nibbled on sunflower seeds.

After spitting out the hulls, she asked, "How are you hitting 'em, slugger?"

"Is there any hope for a clean towel, a new soap bar, or even a TV with a vertical hold that actually holds?" I asked her.

"Fresh towels will be out in a jiff," she said. "I can hear the wash on its spin cycle."

"Meantime, mind if I have a peek?" My Andy Jackson sparked a glint of interest in her eyes.

"Have at it, slugger." She plucked away the $20 banknote and twirled around her room registry, a loose-leaf binder. Riffling its pages, I skimmed her guest list—Jones, Doe, and Smith were popular surnames. My roving eyes, however, kept tripping over "Duke Longman."

"This Duke Longman is like the Energizer Bunny," I said. "He stays here almost every other night in Room 3. It must be a standing reservation for him."

She reacted. "Hey, this is a free country the last time I checked the Constitution."

"Not that free," I said. "Minors, under-aged, jailbait—does that mean squat to you? It sure doesn't to Duke Longman."

"I can't pretend to know about that. Mr. Longman arrives late. My night vision is crummy. He ponies up the cash and gets a key. Beyond that, it's none of my affair. Or yours either, I should hasten to add." The peeved proprietress tossed aside the unfinished floral wreath.

"You pocket your nickel. What else in the world matters, right?"

She blanched but not so much. "Didn't I see Mrs. Taliaferro tiptoe from Room 7 late last night?" Her accusation, glib and dangerous, threatened to expose my client's confidentiality so I clammed up.

"I'll drop back by to get the clean towels." The door handle I shoved was broken.

"Nellie Chaise stars on the Adult Channel 66."

"So?"

"So go pound your pud, bop your banana, or whatever it is you men do. Just stay off my case, hear sweetheart?"

I skipped Nellie's panting on Channel 66. Her skin-deep acting was a desultory con anyway. Alcohol and tobacco abstinence made killing time a drudgery. The room felt like a kiln. I went out, fished a trusty hooligan bar from my trunk, and pried at the stuck casement windows. The top one cracked. Standing there hot and disgusted, I felt the incinerator's smoke tingle my nostrils. Beyond the green baize curtains, mufflers on a vehicle or two rumbled by. I stretched out on the swayback bed.

I couldn't relax. Professional guilt piqued me to get cracking and earn that $200K windfall in my wallet. Pierre Shelton cast long shadows in my mind. He'd acted tight and keyed up on our excursion to Emily Taliaferro's crime scene. What did I know about him?

Pierre was the last individual to see Emily alive. Such a person was surprisingly often the killer. He raced the snot out of a Jaguar, courtesy of Mrs. Taliaferro. He pampered their prized horses. Emily's mug shot with its mushy endearment had to count as a private trophy. The Kaiser Motel was his sugar shack.

My spotlight next swung to Emily Taliaferro. What had I gleaned about the victim? She was an angelic face, a moxie spirit, and an avid equestrian. Type A personality wired her. Her mother never stinted her whims. Last but not least, Pierre had brought her here six nights by my tally from the motel registry. Finally, I knew brutal as it was tragic, her homicide was undeserved. But then what murder is ever deserved? Mrs. Taliaferro's fat fee vaguely rankled me.

Was it reasonable to try and fit Pierre as Emily's killer? It fit better than the glove did on OJ. I scratched my knee. Murder was a crime of passion. Room 3 where Pierre and Emily had played whipped up plenty of libidinous passion. Further reflection suggested Pierre's discovery of Emily's corpse along the bridle trail was a bit too rehearsed. As a minimum, Pierre (a.k.a. Duke Longman) owed me an explanation.

Sheriff Pettigrew might give up some background information on Pierre. I jabbed a toothpick about knee high between the door and the jamb. Upon my return, I'd know if anybody waited inside uninvited. The sheriff's office was walkable, but I drove over and parallel parked with only my front fender hanging out.

Sheriff Pettigrew sat at his desk typing when I shunted my caboose into a chair. Ben Franklin reading specs perched on his nose lent him a wise, scholarly air. I couldn't stifle a sheepish grin. Sunbeams from the slanted shades highlighted duffs of air-borne lint. I sneezed. Clearing throat phlegm, he hunted and pecked slower and slower until his arms froze and his fingers stopped on the space bar.

"Johnson, does my endeavor at honest labor amuse you?" he asked.

"No," I replied.

"What can I do to be rid of you?" He removed the reading glasses and folded them up to put into a shirt pocket.

"What did your background investigation of Pierre Shelton reveal?"

"Pierre? He's an outstanding horse trainer."

"Does he have a history of violence? Has he ever been pinched?"

"No and one arrest. Attempted second-degree rape. 11th grade. Charges were dismissed."

"Didn't that hoist a red flag, sheriff?"

"Relax, Johnson. It was consensual. He and some teenybopper were forking inside a VW of all places. They hid out behind a Kroger's Food Store late on a Friday night date." Sheriff Pettigrew rolled the yellow sheet of paper from the typewriter to snow pak out a typo and then sign off. "No harm, no foul. We've all been there, right?"

"Did the girl's parents file charges?" I asked.

"Then just as fast dropped them. Let's keep it real. Five will get you ten, the girl was a slut. Off the record, most are flirts. She'll grow up to strip in a gentlemen's cabaret. Or else turn tricks up on D.C.'s 14th Street. Naturally I'll deny ever having made such a characterization."

"Naturally."

"Now my turn with the questions. Is your handgun under tight wraps?"

"Absolutely, sheriff."

"Good, leave it. On the Taliaferro crap, any dramatic developments?"

"Not too awfully dramatic."

The baton now in his meaty hand tipped toward the doorway. "Fantastic. Make tracks. You sour my stomach."

"Chew on chalk sticks," I said. "They work wonders for me."

"Yeah well, you keep your nose clean."

My next stop in town was the same store. The old storekeeper, bless his gout, unearthed a pair of dungarees, a package of three boxer shorts, a clutch of white crew socks, and a couple of cotton plaid shirts. All about my size, too. Back at the Kaiser Motel in Room 7, I stripped, broke out my own soap bar, and showered in hot, then fast cold water. A shave was bliss. I tucked the clothing sales receipt into my wallet—a business expense on Income Tax Schedule C. April 15th had come and gone. Overextended and owing money, I hoped the forgiving folks at the IRS would buy my hard luck story and grant me an extension. I was doing God's work by helping to stamp out evil, after all.

A new man, I stepped outside my door. The mid-afternoon sunlight fell into my eyes. As expected at this early hour I saw no cars in the parking lot. An ice machine gurgling in a kiosk behind dropped a lug of cubes. An obese maid thrashed a pillow with a Ping Pong paddle.

Ignoring me, she next waddled behind a Hoover vacuum. Pennies and beer tabs clattered up her attachment. Cursing, she switched off the Hoover and bent down. I moved fast. Her pushcart was a trove for clean towels which I pilfered to go stow in my room.

Seeing the room phone reminded me. Chet Peyton, between bulldozing prospects, was babysitting my one-eared, scar-ravaged tomcat. His lineage sprang, I suspected, from feral lynxes stalking Virginia's foothills. Some kind of a pet.

"How's the Shithead?" I asked Chet Peyton over the connection.

"He's king of the manor," said Chet. "You making do okay?"

"My case is all dead ends and I'm brain-locked."

Chet laughed. "Ginkgo biloba and ginseng are the brain herbs that make you smarter."

"For you maybe. I'll stick to burgers and fries, thanks."

Chet's levity quit. "If you get jammed up, Frank, call me. Gerald can watch the damn cat. Or we'll both swing on up to join you. Gerald is a monster. Getting laid and hard liquor haven't yet taken the edge off him."

"You're at the top of my list." We talked some more, rang off, and I took a quick walk downtown. The Kaiser Savings & Loan stood catty-corner to the black folks' launderette. Segregation was a relic of the past but the races still kept largely to themselves. I headed over into it and the busy bank lobby disabused my notion that the hamlet was completely comatose. A high school-age teller who was a young Mariah Carey look-alike scrutinized my check. Her name pin read "Miss Carole Dawson."

Carole's confusion cleared once she'd fathomed the string of zeroes. "Oh, no wonder. It's drawn on one of Mrs. Taliaferro's accounts."

"I'll also need a checking account to keep it in."

"Mr. Morgan, our senior manager, will have to handle this transaction. One moment, please." Her murmurs on a red phone extension summoned him.

An old lady behind me plopped down a canvas tote bag. Her time was more important than mine, but I didn't budge. My mischievous smile further incensed her.

A light bulb popped on. "You're that detective," said Carole. "The one brought here for Emily's death."

Nodding, I slipped her my last business card. "Were you friends with Emily?"

"We had Algebra and U.S. Government together. I still cry. We miss her."

"Emily was special. Did she date?"

Carole crooked her finger, and I leaned in to her whispers. "My boyfriend told me she was crazy about an older man. I can relate to that. You see, my boyfriend is older, too. Keep that under your fedora, please."

"Absolutely, Carole. Any idea who Emily was—"

Mr. Morgan barged in primping his fish lips as Carole explained my request to him. She slipped back to me my business card saying she had a photographic memory. Morgan whisked me over to a green desk in an alcove too near the elevator. After spinning a chair about on its leg, I straddled it ass-backward.

"This is certainly a hefty balance for a mere checking account," he said. "Do you think it's prudent?"

Pudgy fingers stabbed the keys to a quaint adding machine. I was tempted to request that he put everything in paper money. Except then we were talking about some weight. Uncle Sam had issued no bill larger than a $100 Benjamin Franklin in 20 years to curb money laundering by drug traffickers. It was a brilliant strategy with stellar results since drugs were no longer a pox on our society. Right.

"A checking account will be fine."

"All I mean is you could do better. What's more, I can help you if you let me."

"Thanks, but no sir. Checking it remains."

Becoming a royal pain, he persisted. "My institution offers high yield CDs. FDIC insured. Competitive rates of return on your principal."

"Does fast service come bundled with your competitive rates?"

The florid banker pouted over my rejecting his best intentions. Nonetheless, I owed Mr. Morgan a debt of thanks. I schlepped out the bank's revolving door, and resolved to keep a sharp eye on my pile of money. Brassy sunlight hurt my eyes. The odd girl was dusting off shelves in the local drugstore near the pharmacy counter, when we crossed glances. I'd been putting on various sunshades and cringing at the hoodlum results seen in the carousel mirror.

Twirling a ringed finger, the odd girl beckoned me. Always a good sport, I followed her out and up one block across a busy intersection. We entered Sally's Nails ("Walk Ins Welcome!") flanked by an antiquarian bookstore and the Bluebird Bus Terminal.

Sally smiled and complimented the odd girl. "As always, your hands look exquisite. Really, dear, they should star in TV commercials for fingernail polish, dishwashing detergent, or the world's finest cubic zirconium jewelry."

"You're nicer than Goldilocks," the odd girl said.

"Who is your pal?" Sally wiggled her penciled eyebrows to signify me.

"Why, this is none other than Frank Johnson, Private Eye," the odd girl said. "He and I crashed the high school prom once upon a cruel time."

"Hello, Sheila," I said. "Speaking of cruel time, where does it go? And how did you ever wash up in Kaiser, of all places?"

"We'll knock over old times tonight over dinner at the Boomerang

Tavern. Can you make it?" asked Sheila.

I agreed to meet her there then.

After leaving Sally's Nails, I ducked into the antiquarian bookstore. Any Gold Medal detective pulps (John D. McDonald, Charles Williams, or Gil Brewer) would enliven my nightstand reading. No Gold Medals but I stalked past book rack after book rack of dog-eared ladies' romances and cozies that would never fall out of favor.

Memoirs took up one entire aisle, both sides. Everybody and his brother had written a book about how it felt during their fifteen minutes of fame. I'd tried reading a few memoirs. Christ but did other folks live colorful lives. Incest, bestiality, fratricide, betrayal, and dozens of aberrations were trotted out for us to lap up like hungry drones swarming the honey pot. I mean, how did they ever survive all that trauma? The sordid story was all. But, it was all bullshit.

I detoured around the Charismatic Catholic church and strode toward the Kaiser Motel. Small world after all, I mused. To hook up again with Sheila Hamilton, daffy as ever but she was ever so beguiling. Our dinner date was guaranteed to make my day.

The proprietress thudded on the plate glass window to catch my attention. She hit her forefingers together, ragging me with a "naughty, naughty" sign. Wasn't she special, a national treasure? The telltale toothpick in Room 7 was absent. Hence, an intruder had intruded. I toed the loose door to have a careful look inside. Straddling the threshold, I squinted into shoals of dimness. Lamplight and cigarette smoke etched Mrs. Taliaferro's silhouette. Leaping up, she tore into me, screaming and slapping.

"You abysmal detective," she said. "I hope you're satisfied! How could you let this destroy me again?"

I rebuffed the attack. "Whoa, lady. What are you saying?"

"Pierre, dead, shot in the chest." My client's eyes speared me. "It's your fault!"

My allegiance, quite suddenly, vaulted out the window. "My assignment was to tree your girl's killer," I said. Then, somewhat more rational and calmer, I added, "Did you notify the sheriff already?"

Trembling chin belied her fierce exterior. "Stanley Pettigrew just went for him."

"Then the sheriff will go planetary before you know it." I crossed the room to close the door as Mrs. Taliaferro, her sobs pouring out in dry heaves, retreated to the bathroom for solace and repairs.

A siren blurted. The wail earsplitting loud, Sheriff Pettigrew was on the hunt. His blue-and-white cruiser—the overheads flashing and the police pursuit engine sounding like canned thunder—barreled into the motel's lot. Tires skidded up dust and gravel from the stomped on brakes.

I found Mrs. Taliaferro swaying on the edge of the bathtub. Pale and frazzled, she quivered through the shoulders. I helped her to her uncertain feet, and escorted her from the room.

"Relax a little," I said. "No arrests have been for murder. Yet."

"Halt, Johnson!" Sheriff Pettigrew hollering stepped up on the chassis and chambered his .38 to point over the car roof straight at my nose.

My shaky hands stayed in plain view. "I'm standing right here, aren't I, sheriff?"

"Hands up," he said.

Both Pettigrew brothers and I were at the Dakota Farms stable. Mrs. Taliaferro had lingered behind in the squad car. The stable's overhead lights were unsparing on the gaudy murder sprawled at our feet.

Sheriff Pettigrew hitched his trousers, squatted down, and tested a wrist. No heartbeat. A neat but fatal hole and a vicious black smear splotched Pierre's shirt. Stanley forked Pierre over but no exit wound showed. A push broom Pierre had been working poked out from under a leg. The stall's fodder rack and feed box were both empty. Bits of straw lay scattered everywhere. It was obscene and the smell putrid.

"Was Mrs. Taliaferro the one who rang you up at the guard shack?" Sheriff Pettigrew asked his brother.

"Exactly. I then raced up here. She was hysterical. The damn scatterbrained woman. I kept telling her an ambulance or doctor was pointless. Pierre was dead as lead."

The grim sheriff frisked the dead man, twisting his pockets inside out. "A key ring, a penknife, a few dimes, nickels, quarters. Oh—well—what's this? No billfold."

"Was it a robbery?" My look went from one, then to the other brother.

"No thief came in a vehicle. Not a soul came through the gate," said Stanley.

"You sleep now with one eye cocked open?" I asked him.

His glare acidic, Stanley said, "Screw you, Johnson."

The sheriff was testy. "All right, enough. Give me a little room to think, will you?"

Whinnies and pawing sounded from the stalls to our right. Pierre had been cleaning them when the killer put in an appearance. The rest of the horses were going without dinner tonight.

"We got paid yesterday," said Stanley. "Couldn't Pierre have gone to Kaiser and cashed his check? I know that he carries a wad. Not that I'd steal from him."

"Easy enough to verify. That might account for the missing billfold." Sheriff Pettigrew sharpened his glance about us. "No murder weapon, expended brass, or other extraneous objects."

"Smallish diameter." Stanley put a pinkie at the wound to compare diameters. "What, a .22 or .25?"

The sheriff grunted. "Either one for sure. At close range, too." They arose and transferred callous stares in my direction.

"Mine is a .357, unfired, in my car trunk."

Sheriff Pettigrew snapped. "Consider it confiscated! Your license revoked!" Anger stroked a slight lisp in his enunciation.

The MF-slur for him stalled on my tongue.

Ever eager, Pettigrew egged me on. "Out with it, Johnson. Dare you. Man, I'll slap you in cuffs for insulting a sheriff. Give me the slightest provocation to do it."

I pasted on my best professional impassivity.

"Windwood is in Saint Pete fishing." Stanley licked his thumbs before nipping on a silver booze flask appearing out of nowhere.

"You'd better call Joyner then. It's a goddamn emergency, too. I'll expect preliminaries tonight." The sheriff's eyes locked on me again. "Johnson, just why do I think you are in the thick of this shit?"

"I'd better pry my client out of your cruiser," I said. "And try to soothe her jitters."

"All right, then. You've one hour to come in voluntarily," said the sheriff. "Don't make me send the posse after you."

In a little, the tableau put Mrs. Taliaferro perched on a burnt orange divan, me on a hassock. Sketch in the square-hewn ceiling beams, paisley curtains, yellow wallpaper and carpet, and potted conifers. Her den promoted quiet talk and contemplation. She'd lit another cigarette, had the first smoldering in the onyx ashtray. She dabbed the corner of a handkerchief at her eyes like women do to preserve their mascara.

"Where's your staff?" I asked.

"Rachel and Ralph on Mondays zip off to West Virginia," she replied.

"Why?"

"It's their day off. They like to lose playing at the ponies and return home stone broke."

"What, you're home all alone?"

"So what? How else will a grieving mother ever learn to fend for herself?" she asked.

I admired her courage. Her wet bar fully stocked was my old oasis. A saucer held fresh-sliced lemon wedges and green olives amid the cocktail hour stemware and ice bucket. "Drink, ma'am?" I asked.

"Please. Double bourbon, neat, on the rocks."

Fixing her order, I had half a mind to defy my AA vows for a Whiskey Collins. Didn't Satan tempt Christ in the desert, but He just said no? I did likewise.

"My eternal thanks." Over the crystal-glass tumbler, she expressed mild shock. "And the bartender has a club soda?"

Aware my hour was fleeting, I jumpstarted her narrative. "You said Pierre was at the stable and..."

"The A/C here had conked out. It grew hot and stuffy. So I dialed Pierre on the cell phone. He sometimes pretends not to hear. After making a beeline to the stable, I hollered for him. After no response, I looked around. Seeing him that way was horrible." More bourbon did marvels restoring her composure.

"Who was here this morning?" I asked.

"Just Pierre and me. Stanley insists the gate was down all morning. No day laborers checked in."

I didn't underscore how that made them both prime suspects. "Pierre's billfold was missing which suggests theft as a motive."

She gave a pained sigh. "All this has happened at Dakota Farms. What's next?"

"You should be more security conscious," I said.

"I've read about our murder capital, Washington, D.C." She sipped her bourbon too fast. "That's why I employ a full-time security force."

"Still, any random killer could've slipped in off the main road," I said.

Taken aback, she said, "Up until a week ago, I lived in calm splendor."

"Your security is too lax. For starters, I'd suggest cameras, motion sensors, and the whole shebang. You here alone is dangerous, too."

"Okay then, as my detective, you can move into a spare room here. I have plenty of free space. Rachel will get you settled." That under duress she could formulate a practical plan amazed me.

"Whatever you say. Deadbolt the doors, latch the windows, and keep the exterior lights on. Some deputies will process Pierre's crime scene. In the interim, the sheriff expects me at his office."

"The sheriff is a jewel of a jackass," said Mrs. Taliaferro, her declaration emphatic.

She accompanied me through the two-story foyer to the door. Her wool clogs moved noiseless over the carpet where my eyes stayed pinned. I hitched my stride. An edgewise shot at her lush posterior netted me assurances she'd worn quite well. Her jeans and collarless blouse accentuated an allure I'd overlooked chronicling earlier in the smoky, hot motel room. The difference was striking.

Mrs. Taliaferro toggled on the foyer's cathedral lights and sidled close enough for me to count the ginger freckles cresting her high cheekbones. "Mr. Johnson, I wish to thank you," she said. "Your help is immeasurable. Listen, I apologize for throwing my tantrum back there."

I wanted to kiss her on the lips. No, better put, I wanted to jump on her bones. Just as impulsive, the lust ebbed. Self-restraint weighed in. A second later, my former self--the wary, weary detective--returned. Mary Taliaferro was first, foremost a client. Goofy, huh?

I trained my idle gaze on three photos on the gate table leg. A tall man smiled in each, a protective arm around a youthful Mary and adolescent Emily. Wide-shouldered and copper-tanned, he was what some women qualify as rugged. This was, I presumed, Carl Taliaferro, her late husband. While I pictured his Cessna's fatal buzz into the Atlantic Ocean, Mary Taliaferro stirred her shoulders. Had I intruded into her haunted past? With a wan smile, she ushered me out the door.

"Good night, Mr. Johnson."

"Bolt all doors, ma'am."

"Right, I'll keep a closer watch on my home," she said.

Grinding the car motor to life, I switched up my high beams. Stanley at the gate conjured his Ali Baba magic to retract the bar. All four of my windows rotored down. Spring peepers tweedling in the jack pine made my sortie into Kaiser a pleasurable one. My allotted hour had expired, but I blew by the sheriff's ill-lit office. His squad car—supercharged by a hog-block engine on chrome-spoked wheels—was eye candy to impress Kaiser's voters.

I knew the Kaiser Motel sold sex fixes. Newer model pickup trucks grazed in front of room doors. Pinpricks of light filtered through the drawn curtains. Orange neon letters blinked NO VACANCY. Discretion was vital. No questions asked, lucre exchanged hands, and services were rendered. Everybody went away happy.

Midlot, I notched a U-turn back to the street and berthed at the motel's curbstone. I noted a frumpy lady dodder by, a fat dachshund on a leash and a baggie of turds in her other hand. I saw through a chink in the lobby drapes, the proprietress sat slumped against the refrigerator snoring.

Pea gravel scuffed underfoot to Room 7. I twinkled a penlight's beam inches from the sill. The toothpick was intact. Jungle grunts came from Room 5 or 6. I wanded in my passkey, a ruby light burped. Nudging the door, of a mind to grab the 9 mil and split, I flinched as a torpedo hissed by my ear. Missing, the blow instead clubbed me on the shoulder. I staggered as the doorknob whacked against the drywall.

Pain seared through my clavicle. The mercury vapor streetlamps cast us in fuzzy shadows. I dodged a phantom fist and bulled my clumsy way through the threshold.

A puppet, my assailant, dangled inches out of my range. I smelled violence. My upper cut didn't connect. Off balance, I righted myself into a Sugar Ray crouch and wove in closer. He slugged away. Tracers of pain skewed through my midsection. This exceeded any roughing up—it was for all the marbles. A half-moment later, I lost him in the weak light. His radar, however, had a bead on me.

His sap just missed clocking my temple where the skull runs thinnest. Dazed, I swayed. Sandwiched between the door and my attacker, I went with what felt instinctual.

Somehow my legs propelled me upright. I gave it my last ounce of strength. My right cross thumped into banded gristle—his solar plexus wasn't jelly. Garlic breath burst from his lungs. Yeah baby, he registered pain. I wanted to hurt him more. A lot more.

My left fist arrived too late—again, I diced at only air. Our dance was finished. He sprinted by me. Frenetic footsteps padded on the concrete apron by the kidney-shaped swimming pool.

My hot impulse was to pursue but it was too late. He vaunted over a cyclone fence, and vanished. Kneading my shoulder, I recorded a snapshot of his height and stature—tall and beefy. That was all I had. I never saw his face. On a side street, an engine rumbled to life. Getaway tires burned rubber on the paving as he roared off to the west. Breathless, I leaned in the threshold.

The nearby headboard banging quit. A squeaky door spilled out a bright wedge. "What's all the fracas?" a voice asked. "I lost my stroke."

"Oh, your sister just left for more condoms."

"No kidding. Your sister eats me raw." His door clicked shut.

He was mistaken. My only sister was dead.

After flipping on the pineapple lamp, I tilted its shade to angle light on the bed. My heart ticked harder. I forked up the mattress, and groped all underneath it. I felt an irregular section I had cut from the mattress.

Christ Jesus, yes, and I thank you.

My fingers curved around the polymer grips. Better than that, the 9 mil packed all of its 15 rounds. Some consolation since my sloppy technique had almost burned me. That was bad. Lesson learned: windows as well as doors were entry points. I ducked into the john. At eye level was an open window with plenty of wiggle room.

I sat on the commode. Clammy night air blew down my neck. Jeez. A whippoorwill yipped. Where was I when The Big Man doled out brains? I composed an ad for the Today's Detective web site. WANTED: a sidekick to watch PI's back. Must be sharpshooter. IQ must exceed the PI's 75 scored on a good day.

I felt revenge and rage boil inside me. A Zippo lighter lay on the toilet tank top...should I torch this hellhole? No, that seemed too radical, too hardcore. It was smarter to retrench. A hasty room search yielded nothing. The maid had mooched all my brew—six crushed cans clinked inside a drawer with an edge worn Gideon Bible. She'd unwittingly done me a favor. I crammed my soiled clothes into a drawstring gym bag.

It was time to eject. Trotting, I followed my assailant's lead. The lit swimming pool was a heavy, green gravy. I scrambled up the cyclone fence for a toehold, hoisted myself to the top, and dragged over it. Landing hard, I felt pain needle both knees. Right then from Room 7, hearing an angry voice got me to chuckling. Sore as hell, the proprietress was spouting off.

"Johnson, damn you! Look at this mess! By god, that man has gone wild. Hog wild."

Chapter 5

Monday 10:30 PM, April 17th

I avoided the motel, and cut to the sidewalk intending to circle the block. Along a row of forsythias set to a paling fence, I explored taking a shortcut. A Doberman loped off a rear deck, pinned back its ears, and growled like a garbage disposal. Exterior lamps flared on. A lady whistled between her fingers. Hurrying, I retreated to the safer, darker side of the street. No vehicles scuffled by and I took no special pains to conceal the 9 mil held at my side. At last I found my car.

I zipped along Main Street to the sheriff's office. Light glimmered from under his door sill. Coasting up, my bumper tagged his. I stashed the 9 mil in the fake vent, then fetched the .357 from out of the trunk. The dent in his bumper, I noted, was a nasty lick.

Pettigrew's first words when I walked into the room were, "Johnson, is your watch broken?" Cordovan loafers disappeared off the desktop. He slid something into a drawer. Tie now off and collar unbuttoned, he acted a bit flustered. The fresh heat of a perfumed lady on him was undeniable.

My knuckles, bleeding and sore, burrowed into my pockets. "My client is upset."

"Mary Taliaferro is a prime murder suspect. That'd upset me, too."

"So is your brother Stanley," I said. "Don't rush to judgment."

"Stanley is not in trouble. I have a few questions for her."

"Mrs. Taliaferro intends to cooperate fully," I told him.

"Good. Tomorrow. Nine. Have her ready. I'm driving out to Dakota Farms."

"What's Joyner's status on Pierre's autopsy?" I asked.

"What's it to you? Tomorrow you're a fart in a monsoon, remember?"

"Because my client will want to know when I return tonight," I said.

"Tell her that Joyner dug out one .25 caliber round. Time of death was between 2 and 2:30 PM, but no later than 3 PM. No other trauma was observed on the corpse."

"How does a puny .25 cut down a man?"

"The bullet drilled the heart," the sheriff said. "Pointblank range at a center mass, it wasn't a difficult shot to hit the right spot."

"When will Emily's autopsy report be available?" I asked.

"In due course," he replied. "Now fork over your piece."

Manufacturing a frown, I placed the .357 on his desktop. "My alibi for Pierre's murder is airtight. I was with you and at the Kaiser bank all afternoon."

"Yeah. I checked already." After unloading the .357, the smug sheriff gave the it a sniff test before padlocking it in a filing cabinet. I heard an unseen sneeze. Our eyes looked over at the shut door to an interview booth.

"Gesundheit," I said.

He ignored me. "Your permit?"

I palmed open the state-issued gun permit for his inspection. He reached for it, but my wallet snapped back. "Nope. This goes where I go." I gestured with my head. "Or else I'll shake out what's behind Door Number One."

Shrugging, Pettigrew tapped a Masonic ring on the desktop. "The motel manager called here bitching about a trashed room. Yours. What gives? And don't play me for a moron."

"You know what I know." Nearing the door, I paused. "From here on I'll be staying at Dakota Farms."

"By tomorrow, you best be a fading memory. Or I'll come to shake you out."

A dirty, pink bra lay by a desk leg. I grinned and he guessed why. He pointed to the door. A sudden draft slammed it harder than I'd intended. The ten-minute hike through the night air raw as kerosene flushed Pettigrew out of my system.

The Boomerang Tavern was what my granddad dubbed a "roadhouse." Like him, I despised mobs but cherished gin. Dimensions narrow and crude, this honky-tonk was no exception. Bowling trophies lined its gilt-edged mirror. Smoke swatted my eyes spotting Sheila near a "Star Wars" pinball machine. A Nashville hat act, on the jukebox, was ladling out what passed for C&W music these days. Pioneers like Merle Haggard, George Jones, Lefty Frizzell, and Hank Snow were names only in here. I preferred them, even if they were from my daddy's generation.

I signaled Sheila to commandeer a wall table, then wended my way through the revelers. An elbow jabbed me at a painful spot high in the ribs. I looked into a Kilby's wicked grin.

"Excuse me," he said.

Stepping by, my boot heel impinged on his toes. He winced.

"Sorry," I said. "Force of habit. I crush all the roaches I see."

"Watch your back," he advised between gritted teeth.

Waving to a waitress bussing tables, Sheila saw me walking up. "What made you late?" she asked.

"Mrs. Taliaferro found Pierre dead, shot in the chest once. Stanley ran her into town. That's where I got sucked into it."

"Make mine a bourbon and water," Sheila told the waitress. "A club soda and no ice for this gentleman. An order of nachos and hot wings, too." The waitress left, and Sheila asked, "Was Stanley Pettigrew all smiles?"

"Why?" I asked. "Were Pierre and he at odds?"

"Well, neither of the Pettigrews will ever win a local popularity contest." Sheila glanced over to the bar and back with again a wistful sigh. "Living in Kaiser for five years is a long, long time."

I laughed. "It can't be the end of the world."

"Maybe not," she said. "But you can see it from here."

The solicitous waitress brought our drinks and grub. I excused myself while Sheila ordered herself another bourbon and water, her first down the hatch. A hand-lettered sign guided me to the Bloke's Room. Through the kitchen door wedged open by beer pallets, I beheld a skanky brunette balanced on the edge of a table, her jeans spilling undone.

Sheriff Pettigrew, the man on his knees, couldn't see me. Eager hands braced on his shoulders, the brunette coached him into her. She darted a look over at me and smiled some kind of lewd. When I came back out, the kitchen door was barred. I slid into our booth. Alcohol had lubricated Sheila's analytical processes.

"Doesn't Pierre's death alter the complexion of Emily's?" she asked. "Has the same crazed killer now struck twice?"

I pointed to my busted head which she'd overlooked commenting on. "No, struck three times if you lump this in."

"All I'm asking is are their deaths related?"

"It's probably too early to determine," I said.

"You can't connect any of the dots?"

"Don't I wish. But maybe you can shed some light on something. Was Emily Taliaferro so terribly sweet and innocent as those singing her praises say?"

"Teen-age girls brazen through rebellious streaks," said Sheila. "As for Emily, what? Yesterday she was a mall rat and skinned her knees playing lacrosse. She was a daughter typically spoiled by a rich mother. Where are you headed with this, Frank?"

"Emily and Pierre did the bone dance at the Kaiser Motel. A half dozen times but more wouldn't surprise me."

"Debutante and horse trainer. I guess it just goes to show that opposites can attract." said Sheila.

"What's really frustrating is I don't have a clue to act on."

Sheila pursed her lips. "Have you questioned Emily's mother?"

"Not quite yet, She's a bit overwrought."

A jukebox tune polluted my ears. Garth Brooks tried out a Kiss song. God spare us. I scooted across the pine seat. "Speaking of which, I promised Mrs. Taliaferro to return early tonight. I'm boarding at her stable now."

Sheila's reaction was deadpan until her lovely jaw protruded a quarter-inch which, I thought, denoted jealousy. She then invoked an old joke. "Under cover work, eh?"

"What? Aw, don't start. Mrs. Taliaferro is a client. I work for her. End of story."

Sheila rolled her glassy eyes. "Famous last words."

The silence between us grew awkward and surly until Sheila giggled. "Frank, don't be such a tight-ass. Come on. I'll pay and then you can walk me home."

We entered the night, our elbows linked. Sheila wore gladiator sandals with leather thongs laced up her sexy calves. A reflex from the old days, she patted the small of my back.

"Don't fret, Moll," I said, jokingly. "My gat awaits me in the flivver."

"Righto, Mister Knuckles," she quipped in return.

Kaiser at night was serene. No sirens shrieked, no gunshots popped, and no choppers hovered. Citizens had set out their recycle bins. Kids had chalked a hopscotch grid on the sidewalk. A Neighborhood Watch van crawled up and away. In the stairwell by Sally's Nails, Sheila released my arm with reluctance I was thrilled enough to hope.

"Our apartment is one floor above us. I'd invite you up, but moms are sticklers for prudish house rules."

"Then quick, kiss me," I said. "And I'll hop off happy as a horny toad."

She did.

While hopping back to my car, I went back in time. Our cohabitation was how I'd broken into the PI business. Sheila had deemed I lacked a basic ambition and purpose in life. Maybe I did, maybe I didn't. The PI trade, she figured, was at least a steady one. At her badgering and with Lawyer Gatlin also twisting my arm, I passed the exam and was issued a private investigator's license.

In due time, my persistence and patience paid off with solid results. It made me sought after. My client list was bottomless even in an overcrowded profession that included every retired sergeant major and beat cop. At the same time, I grew lousy for company. Fatigue kept me in a morose mood. Sheila accused me of becoming a tough guy caricature, self-absorbed and emotionless all the time. She also wanted a family which to me flew in the face of common sense. On that hollow note, we'd parted ways.

The sheriff's office was dark and empty. My car roared by the Charismatic Catholic church. I heard its denizens stomping and singing loud enough to splinter the rafters. Monday night's prayer warriors were bleeding the Lamb Everlasting. I goosed the gas pedal. Onrushing wind flushed the discordant music, secular and religious, from my ears.

My mind went back in time. It was an old story. Alcohol addiction started with a beer now and again, but to groove with my older pals, I hit the harder stuff. Bourbon bottles bloomed in paper sacks. Following my dad from a quarter century before, I was a big wheel making booze the axle on which to turn I drank before, during, and after school. Then the drill was to out drink anybody anytime anywhere, what transformed me into a full-fledged alkie by age 15.

Any alcohol would do. If less than 86 proof, the drink wouldn't fuzz my mind and that was a bum rush. My mom and dad before their untimely death rattled in their own shaky orbits. I didn't blame them. At school the teachers pulled their hair out trying to understand me. Well, at least one did.

Mrs. Charles—young, pretty and very pregnant—turned me on to "Literature." She was gushing with ideas. I liked to read books, even the meaty ones. She chucked every William Faulkner novel at me. I liked, even related to, one or two like *Sanctuary* and that bastard Popeye with his roll-your-owns, sulfur matches, and fire from Hell. And Joe Christmas in *Light in August*, the working fool always at sweat labor in a bustling sawmill.

One morning in April, a substitute teacher usurped our homeroom. He was swarthy with bushy black hair and a Jersey dialect that wise guys on TV used. Years later, through the grapevine, I learned that Lieutenant Charles had diddybopped over a Claymore mine along the Mekong Delta. I had felt sorry for Mrs. Charles.

Alcohol ripped out my heart one rainy night. I'd gone to bed early because something bad I'd eaten hurt my guts. After much threshing about, I kicked off the fitful sheet and fell into a sleep.

Furious fists thumped on the front door. I bolted upright, my heart a trapeze hanging high in my throat. More knocks thundered. Semi-alert, I swung my feet over the bed's edge to the floor and started walking.

I snicked off the deadbolt lock and twisted the knob. Lo and behold, there behind the screen slouched a sheriff deputy clad in a long, yellow slicker. The porch lamp beat on his enlarged eyes. A suety white hand scraped over his lips.

"Are you Frank Johnson?" he asked me. My sleepy half-nod was perceptible but he needed a vocal confirmation. "Well are you, son?"

"Yes," I said. "W—w—what's this about? It's—like, what?—two-thirty in the morning."

He was the paragon of diplomacy and tact, what they must teach at the academy. "This is about your parents," he said. "When's the last time you saw them?"

"A few hours ago. They went out, dancing at Glendale Country Club. Can't you wait until daylight to speak with them? I mean what's so important?"

"Can I duck inside out of the rain?" he asked in a different voice. He stepped through the screen door. Once in the foyer, water dribbled off the slicker onto my mom's pine-plank floor. He took off the snap-brim hat wrapped in waterproof plastic and smacked it against his leg. "Whew, it's raining like a mule pissing on a flat rock out there."

"My parents?" I said to remind him.

"Son, there's no smooth way to break this, so I'll shoot from the hip." Even now, those words resonated with great power. Smooth. Shoot from the hip. He came out with it. "Your father and mom tonight were T-boned and instantly killed. At Manley's Corner. By a drunk. A CPO driving like gangbusters back to his base in Norfolk. Only the booze didn't get him there. He's a sobbing mess in our custody and flat out admits to everything."

Grief pounded me low and tight. I gulped. Then, the deputy sloshing water like a damn duck asked, "How do you feel?"

Both my parents had been killed by a speeding drunk only hours ago, and he asked me how I felt...

I braked approaching the floodlit gate where Stanley Pettigrew flagged me down. Staggering up, he stabbed a flashlight into my sleep-deprived eyes. My right hand groped beside the gearbox except no tire iron. Stanley was mangling his customary quid. His hair was mussed and his collar askew. The reek of alcohol on him could blister my car paint.

Stanley garbled his words. "Justwhointhehellareyou?"

"I'm Johnson, remember?"

"Gimme the password." His flat hand slapped my car roof.

"Stanley, just step aside. Let me through. Okay, bud?"

"What is it, the password?"

Stanley screamed for an attitude adjustment. Switching off the engine, I tapped the fake vent and scooted out on the passenger side. From across the roof, Stanley blinked. Clenching the 9 mil, I choked its barrel end. I tramped around the car through its high beams. Bat Masterson, I learned from watching old westerns, had perfected how to deal with belligerent drunks.

"Spread-eagle against the grille, you big bowlegged mother." Stanley's drawn revolver wagged at me.

Straight kicking, the tip of my boot whapped his gun hand. Stanley screamed and threw up his wrist. The revolver fell to the pavement somehow without discharging. His fist missed me by a mile. Sidestepping and heaving the 9 mil, I unloaded smack on his head. He threatened to topple forward, reared up, then sank backward with a groan. He sank into unconsciousness.

Whippoorwills cheered me towing Stanley by the ankles to prop against the rock-and-mortar wall. Once conscious, he'd rave at the axe embedded in his skull. I tamped out his bullets, and seeded them along a drainage ditch. After attaching his revolver to the flagpole's halyard, I sent it clattering up the flagpole. The slapstick silliness left me feeling good as the motor chirred to retract the gate's bar.

I crested Mrs. Taliaferro's hilly driveway. My headlights showed me someone had moved the dirty Jag. A tin dragon lantern streamed out light on each corner of the patio. Brass footlights outlined the slate walkway. My hip mashed against the chime button. A neon horseshoe glowed over the lintel, its open-end down, not up. Any good fortune washed down and off the horseshoe. The inside door knob rattled and the door opened for me.

"Is that you, Mr. Johnson?" asked Rachel.

"I believe I'm supposed to sack out here now."

"Yes, that's why I've been up waiting. Come in."

Rachel ,wearing a poplin housecoat, stepped back to let me inside. The foyer was also cold enough to hang a ham. She herded me up a floating staircase which branched at the top into a trident of corridors.

"Do I go left, right, or straight?" I asked her.

"Straight," she said.

My new lodgings, behind the fourth door, right-hand side, seemed like the lap of luxury.

"Swell. I'm too pooped to pop," I said.

"Feel blessed, sir. Your room is grander than mine." Rachel's complaint drifted with her down the corridor.

A terrycloth robe, "Taliaferro" emblazoned across its shoulders, dangled from a hook in the private full bath. A vase of cut white lilacs on the bureau smelled good. After caching my 9 mil under the soft mattress, still fully clothed, I flaked out. I read the first few lines in a magazine about Virginia wineries before sleep claimed me.

The next morning—it was Tuesday—after showering, I examined the impressive shiner from my duking it out in my motel room. What abuse this job dished out. Following my nose, I found the chef kitchen. I poured myself a glass of grapefruit and pilfered the *Washington Post* off the zinc countertop. I sat at a wrought iron table on the patio to soak up the sun. What was Sheila doing? I wondered. Gazing far afield, I watched a purple haze rise up from the pasture. The big, black stallion cantering across it had to be Hellbent.

"Ahoy, neighbor." The salutation was masculine.

"Morning," I said.

Ralph the gardener rested his gold mug and *Daily Racing Forum* on the patio table. He was, I noted, a southpaw. "That robe was Mr. Taliaferro's. Rachel is under strict orders never to dispose of his things. You're nowhere near big enough to fill his shoes, though."

Maybe he didn't intend to, but Ralph got under my skin worse than a case of chiggers. I yawned extra loud.

"Nasty news about Pierre," said Ralph. He wasn't too choked up about it.

"The nastiest. Were you at yesterday's races?" I asked.

"We whisk off early every Monday, come rain or shine."

"Did you win any tri-fectas? Maybe retire and go loaf on a beach sipping pinã coladas."

"Very funny. I putter in the petunias and my wife plays the maid here. What do you think?"

I changed the subject. "Were Emily and Pierre in deep with each other?"

Ralph sniffed. "Pierre had no hang-ups about robbing any cradle."

"Like your hemorrhaging money at the racetrack?"

"Go climb your thumb, Johnson."

"Hey, joshing. Being at the track does give you a jim dandy alibi."

"Yeah, well I toe the line." Ralph bolted to his feet and his fingers mashed into fists. "Pierre's dying will break few hearts. He was a grade-A prick."

"Careful, Ralphie boy. That hostility won't sell with the sheriff."

"He can go climb his thumb, too." Ralph stamped off the patio.

I could envision his biceps straightening horseshoes. Or the surly SOB might sling a sap in a dim motel room to my punch out my lights.

Scanning Thomas Boswell's column chastising greedy baseball team owners and petulant multi-millionaire players, I went through the kitchen. Rachel, huddled under the pots rack, pared apples, their peelings falling into a colander.

"Were the ponies kind to you?" I asked her.

Rachel just continued scraping the knife. Ralph, I supposed, had spread his good cheer all around.

My dirty clothes had been laundered and neatly folded. These amenities were making me soft. Once dressed, in haste, I very nearly collided with Mrs. Taliaferro at the stairhead.

"Why, Johnson," she said. "We should chat. Follow me."

We took the central corridor and hung a fast right. My glance swept over the rich lady's sewing room: mannequins, spools of thread, and pinking shears. A lady's left glove, Aigner I believe the brand to was, lay on the Singer sewing machine. She and I sat.

"Johnson, Johnson. Stanley telephoned me this morning all in a snit." With a disapproving headshake, she regarded my black eye. "What antagonizes the both of you?"

"No bad wrinkles we can't iron out for ourselves, ma'am."

"Please see to it then."

"Right away, ma'am."

Mrs. Taliaferro's voice, like her cheekbones, seemed strained. She wandered through the valley of the dolls, I suspected. Her eyes glinted as she stared off into space for a moment. A friend of mine, a cocaine fiend, had developed that same vacant stare.

"How did things go with the sheriff?" Mrs. Taliaferro asked me.

"He verified that a .25 capped Pierre."

"Y-y-yes, but will he harass Dakota Farms any longer?"

"He could be here any minute," I said.

Mary Taliaferro gnawed at her cheek lining. "I have to fly out to La Jolla, California, for a ribbon-cutting ceremony. The Cordon Bleu is a new fine arts museum three which I helped to fund. My late husband and I lived there for a good number of years before coming back East. Anyway, our flight out of Dulles Airport leaves at 10:00 AM sharp."

"Our flight? Your philanthropy is commendable," I said. "But your sense of timing sucks."

Unfazed, she issued further orders to me. "Pack an overnight bag. Our limousine driver to the airport will arrive within the hour."

"I don't think so."

"What say?" I heard the angry, hot blood streaming through her veins.

"No, as in I ain't budging a muscle and neither should you."

Oh, did she ever wield a temper. "Johnson, I pay you good money to expect your complete loyalty!"

"Two murders hang over us. No, you gut it out here or else I resign and you can have back your money."

To my utter amazement, she caved. "All right...I'll contact the curator and beg off, say that a family emergency has cropped up."

Mindful of my precarious status, I next did a bit of brown nosing. "And I'll intercept our good sheriff on the patio."

"A splendid idea," she said.

"Also, let's go ahead and install surveillance cameras at the main gate."

"M'm. I better first discuss it with Stanley."

I camped out, over the next half-hour, on the patio studying the AL box scores. It was all a bit corny. Here we were straight off an L. L. Beane catalog cover. Ralph mulched azaleas. Rachel baked apple pies. Mrs. Taliaferro sipped her morning sherry from a big glass goblet. I watched Hellbent. The ebony stallion, frothed in sheeny sweat, had cut a high-speed rut about the perimeter of his pasture. In his dirt-brown derby, he ran in literal circles looking for a way out of here. A new fellow who Ralph knew in town, James Martin, was to be our new Pierre and he'd have his hands full dealing with Hellbent.

Sheriff Pettigrew was punctual. After conquering the hilltop with horsepower leftover, he got out of his Crown Victoria cruiser. He barked a little into the car radio and latched the door. He squatted at the side mirror to tweak a snap-brim hat and fuss with his necktie's knot. With a flourish, he hooked a baton on his gun belt. He bounded toward me seated at the patio table. He walked tall and when seeing me feigned shock.

"Honest to God Johnson, you run into more hat racks."

"No oftener than your brother does," I said.

If he cared or knew about my prank at the guard house, Pettigrew showed no reaction. Instead tipping his head, he said, "Does that god damn horse's motor ever quit?"

"Just my unfanciful opinion, but maybe rich folks rile him."

"Yeah? Well, I manage them fine."

I nodded. "It shows, too."

"You said that right."

"Did you bring along Emily's autopsy report?"

"Why bother? You're shipping home today. Remember? We struck us a deal and you're going to stick by it, too."

"Well sheriff, that depends on my client's wishes, now doesn't it?" I said at same the instant that Mrs. Taliaferro, the full effulgent sun behind her, materialized on the patio like stepping out of a cabana.

Sheriff Pettigrew's gaze roved over and affixed on her. I, too, did a double take. Sheathed in a gauzy lavender dress, Mrs. Taliaferro strolled over to us. A nylon half-slip obscured her bottom hemisphere. A vision from the waist up, though, she withheld no secrets. Those pair of rising erotic details smote you in the eye.

Sheriff Pettigrew gushed. "Why, good morning, Mary. Feeling sprier, I sure hope."

"Quite, sheriff. Rachel is chauffeuring me to a garden show." She was pulling on a pair of white gloves. "It's a Middleburg gala I sponsor every spring. I'm running late, too. Rachel! Where are you?"

Despite his obvious annoyance, Pettigrew switched on his charming deference. "But see here, Mary. Here I've driven all this distance to record your statement of events over Pierre's death. Maybe we can do it over a cup of tea? It won't take long."

"Why? I've already rendered my version in your squad car. Yesterday as I recall it." Her words stung cool and curt. "Johnson here has been assigned to assist you."

Smirking, I acknowledged Pettigrew's sidelong glance.

"Yes, I understand, Mary," Pettigrew said. "But, you see..."

"Sheriff," she cut him down. "You'll direct any questions to Johnson. And that's that. Rachel, where are you? I'm late and I'm getting unhappy."

Rachel, digging out a key ring from a purse, in a powdery blue suit, came out to the patio. While skirting Pettigrew, they were cool to his dour expression. Rachel engaged the automatic garage door opener prior to their settling inside the BMW. Mrs. Taliaferro, while they rode around the driveway's first bend, waved a white hankie out the window. She was, I swear, taunting the sheriff.

"You managed that rich lady just fine," I said.

He twisted about spearing me with a pointing finger. "Knock off with the sass, huh? I've a hard enough job to do as it is."

"Are you rethinking the cause of Emily's death?" I asked. "Perhaps it was murder like with Pierre."

"Hell no! Johnson, I've damn little time for you." The sheriff marched to his cruiser, revved up his gas hog engine, and streaked below for his dutiful brother to let him out of Dakota Farms.

Chapter 6

Tuesday 9:15 AM, April 18th

Since Pierre and Emily had slipped around a lot behind people's backs, their stealth needed wheels. Stalking by the trashcans on the skids, I sized up Mrs. Taliaferro's garage front. The faulty door mechanism had left an 18-inch gap through which I wormed. Inside, I coughed on the gas fumes. My eyes focused on old snow tires piled beside a pneumatic jack underneath the jalousie window I found glued shut. Boxes of Christmas ornaments lay on a decrepit orange sofa. The dirty Jag in the last of four bays, was also locked. With a Slim Jim from my MacGyver satchel, I flipped up the doorknob on the passenger side.

That fragrance, what was it? Again, I sniffed—Charlie perfume? Sure. My knees pressed to the concrete floor hurt. The Jag's bucket seats were velour thrones. I inventoried the glove compartment's contents. Owner's Manual, DMV Inspection slips, penguin ice-scraper, road flares, Upperville horse show ticket stubs from the previous autumn, tire gauge. But I found no calfskin wallet on a chain like Pierre's.

I found under the lambskin floor mats, rolling-papers and a half-empty MD 20/20 bottle. My penlight probing ashtrays showed them wiped clean. Too clean. The crime scene lab weenies could vacuum up any hair, fabrics, and fluids later, but right now I played to score right out of the box. Flattening my face to the carpet, I directed my beam under the bucket seat.

"Oh yeah, come to papa. What's this? Can't be. Sure enough, it is."

The white paper bag I held contained a used home pregnancy kit. I plucked out my forceps. The sales receipt was from a Middleburg drugstore, Roger's. Now I was cooking with gas. No, I was ranging ahead of myself. It could be the kit wasn't even Emily's. Pierre had plenty of other girlfriends. Anyway, she wouldn't be so careless to need this sort of kit, would she? Hell, she was a kid. It was still worth chasing down. I tucked the receipt into an envelope, crawled back outside into morning sunshine, and jumped into my own crate. Ralph had told me Middleburg was about thirty minutes away. I'd make it in twenty. Hopefully.

Creeping before the gate, I squawked my horn. Stanley from inside the hut activated the crossbar to withdraw. I avoided trading scowls with him. Headed east not west for this trip, Middleburg took me away from Kaiser. I jotted down the mileage for possible reimbursement. Not two miles down the hardtop, I realized that Mrs. Taliaferro's plans also involved Middleburg. Excellent. I'd also tail Rachel, the light-footed, jazz-loving, and meticulous housekeeper. My impression was that she played Mrs. Taliaferro's confidante.

My foreign car clocked forty miles per hour, its thin tires hitting thirty on the curves. I slowed it down a little. First weekend back home, I'd go car shopping. For not a bling-bling new model but a plain jane to blend in. Some car manufacturers, I knew, were selling hybrids. Those seemed right up my gasoline alley. It'd feel righteous to dip into my 200 grand and pay off the car dealer in all cash so they could stick the finance charge.

My fidgety fingers snared a pack of emergency Marlboros held in velcro straps behind the sun visor. My tongue and gums sued for nicotine. I resisted and they got nothing. The time had come to make some changes in the life of Frank Johnson. I balled up the pack of cigarettes to throw out the window.

A short stretch beyond a played-out phosphate quarry, I passed by a new gated community. Cookie-cutter McMansions were ghettoed inside the islands of paranoia and snobbery. Granite walls topped with jagged jar bottoms kept out the riffraff. It was great, if your groove was to live in a ghetto. Me? I liked to live without borders. But hey, to each his own.

I surfed to NPR news to hear the run-of-the-mill shit about suicide bombers, race riots, and predatory lending. One news report told how banks in the Washington, D.C. area no longer hired security guards. It was more cost effective to have bank employees hand over the money when armed thieves demanded it. Robbers were having a field day. How many bank customers and employees ended up shot? I had to wonder.

Seeking something more up-tempo, I fiddled with the dial until a song froze the dial setting. This big voice belted out lyrics nothing like I'd ever heard before. A shock jock came on and said the crooner was Pearl Jam's Eddy Vedder. Pearl Jam and Eddy Vedder. Well, well. I'd sample deep cuts from their CDs at Borders. We bachelors, young and old alike, loved our music and stayed on the lookout for enjoying new kick-ass tunes.

My first trip to Middleburg bewildered me. It sucked me into a rat maze of residential streets. I saw dual clean, even sidewalks. I didn't see any chain-sawed reindeers, white-washed tractor tires abloom with jonquils, or bowling balls to spiff up front lawns. Ticky-tacky was a no-go here. High property values ruled. A couple million got you in a realtor's door much like a cover charge paid your way into an exclusive disco.

Serendipity is what got me to the brick Safeway on the main stem. I dropped anchor. With Mrs. Taliaferro at the Community Center over one block for a while, I had time enough to run my errands. A BMW's car alarm tripped a staccato of obnoxious horn blasts. A horse groom squatted sunning his prune-pitted head. We exchanged slight chin nods. I went by Hockman's Radio Shop (out of business), Magpie Café, and the Odd Fellow's Hall. Lengthening my stride, I turned to make a street corner.

A candy-cane barber pole twirled beside a tinted door. No doubt I could've bugged Sheila to style my shoulder-length shag. Being a sultry morning, though, that mane couldn't bake my neck a second longer. Cowbells tied on the door handle clanked as I shoveled inside to a dim coolness. I favored a ladder-back wood chair with my ham hocks.

The customer ahead of me was sprawled out horizontal in the one chair. A pinstriped bib covered him. Hairy, knobby hands protruded from under its edge. Stropping a straight razor on a leather band, the barber bald as a cue ball gave me a crooked smile. Slap-slap. Slap-slap. Slap-slap.

He finished with his sharpening the razor, and scraped its keen edge through the hot, white cream on the customer's face. His motions slow but expert, the barber liked to talk. I sort of listened. To me, a man shaving another man smacked of fag's stuff, but, hey, again to each his own.

"Bill, how do you like this weather?" asked the barber.

Through the shaving cream, Bill muttered. "It's hotter than a popcorn fart. Influenza weather, I'd say."

"Plenty of flu in the air, yep." The barber wiped off shaving cream on a towel before resuming his ministrations.

"I just got over a bout of influenza," said Bill.

"You don't say." The barber took up the leather band again. Did he wink at me? Steel flashed. Slap-slap. Slap-slap. Slap-slap. He honed it extra sharp. An involuntary shudder rolled through my shoulders.

"Boy, this spring those peeper frogs could wake the dead," said Bill.

Déjà vu. My mind pulled up a hardboiled story I'd recently read called "Five O'clock Menace." Its author? Hammett? Chandler? No, more modern. Bingo, Bruno Fischer. The story also had a barber giving a shave.

Bill shut his eyes in a relaxing bliss. "This afternoon I'm headed off to pick me a mess of cress."

The barber in his crisp, white smock took a moment to wink at me. "Is that so? You spend a good many afternoons fetching cress, huh, Billy boy?"

"Times are tough," said Bill.

"There you go. Times are very tough. Water or winter cress?"

"Winter cress." Bill coughed a little. "Excuse me. My allergies are acting up. I know where the tastiest cress is mine free for the taking. Wild and free."

I struggled to recall just how Fischer's story played out.

"Hey bud," the barber said to prompt me. "Does the taste of cress make your mouth water?"

"Sorry," I said. "I'm a steak and potatoes man."

Bill's raised brows let his hard blue eyes land on me. "You don't know what you're missing, man."

"That's my loss, I guess."

"Well, you'll never get a better shave than here." Smiling, Bill shifted his attention to the barber. "Say, where did you learn your trade so good?"

"At the state pen," said the barber. Bill's shoes twitched up.

"The shit you say. What were you in the pen for?"

"Aggravated assault. Now I'd like to ask something, Bill, if it's not too personal."

"Sure thing." A moment ticked by. "If it's not too personal."

"How long have you been fucking my wife?"

A dry chuckle in my throat, I was set to laugh. Except no laughs came. The hush grew eerie.

"Ouch!"

A slug of blood—gaudy red against the white shaving cream suds—juiced the razor's edge. Stirring, Bill managed to wheeze out, "Um, Jesus, Jesus, Jes—..." A trailing hiss gurgled to hoarse gasps.

"Next!"

Snapping away the bib, the barber pointed the razor at me. His finger then crossed lips his to make a hush sign. He'd get no argument from me. I dropped the *Field & Stream*, stepped out into the lunch-time horde, and fixed my eyes front and center. In Fischer's story, the barber didn't go with impulse to slit the customer from ear to ear. Times had changed.

Half-block down another side avenue, a beautician shop advertised Men's Haircuts, $14. I went through its glass door and at the counter signed in on a clipboard. Dangling icicles twinkled over the cash register. Conversation percolated behind a silk screen.

"Howdy-do," I sang out. "Are you folks open?"

The sprite chattering abated. Heels clinked over tiles. A sandy-haired, tanned-faced lady tying on a black plastic apron over a denim dress sauntered up. She checked the clipboard.

"Well...ah, Mr. Johnson, hello. I'm Vi. What can I do for you today, sir?"

"A regular man's haircut, please. Nothing too fussy. Trim up front. Taper to the collar. Square off the sideburns but hold off on any mousse or fruity shampoos."

Vi scratched her elbow. "You're easy to please. Why don't you get settled by the sink?"

I scooted down in a chair with my neck hitched in a notch to hang over the sink. Goose bumps pimpling my spine, I kept a wary eye on Vi but saw no straight razor appear.

"I'm letting the water warm," she said. "We're shorthanded. Are you off today?"

"Just in town," I said. "Thought I'd get my ears lowered."

"A good haircut makes good things happen to you." Vi with her gift of gab had to moonlight on a psychic hotline.

"That's the way I heard it told, too."

Hot water jetted out and stout fingernails scrubbed my scalp. Once she finished, I tingled down to my balls. Vi spread a towel on my shoulders and sponged my wet hair as I sat up. We walked over to her fashion chair by an illuminated mirror.

"Do you work on a horse estate?" Vi draped a black plastic sheet over me and fastened it at the nape of my neck. A young man shambled up to the counter. A Vietnamese lady clad in black came out from behind the silk screen and took him right on. From their labored dialogue, I gathered the young man was mentally challenged.

"No," I told her.

"Well, I was born and bred on a horse farm. Steady your head please, Mr. Johnson."

I grew curious. "On a farm in the vicinity?"

Vi's electric clipper, grooming at my ears, buzzed. "Not an awful distance away. It was in Fauquier County, near a whistle stop called The Plains."

"The Plains. I've been through there." I smiled. "It's small, nicer than most towns."

Vi's hand nudged me. "Bend your noggin down for me, please."

A pound of my locks littering the floor was grayer than I remembered. "Can you help me with a question about horses?" I asked.

"Be glad to if you agree to quit bobbing your head," said Vi.

The young man at the work station was telling a strange, gory tale about the barber shop down the street. The Vietnamese lady laughed. "Will a horse stomp its rider to within an inch of his life?" I asked Vi. "I've always wondered."

"You've got a cowlick." In the mirror, Vi's scissors pointed it out to me. "I kept your hair longer there by design."

"You're the professional," I said.

Vi's electric razor, shaving the nape of my neck, prickled. "About your question. If ever agitated or panicked, any damn horse will turn on its rider." She combed bangs into my eyes and snipped them downslope.

"No ma'am, other direction. My part tacks to the right," I corrected her. "I'm talking about a thoroughbred."

"The same goes for a thoroughbred." Vi undid the black plastic sheet to peel away and shook off my hair snippets. The hand mirror she canted at several angles divulged the neat hairline she'd sculpted.

The young man, trimmed and happy, went ahead of me. He paid the Vietnamese lady, then fanned out the one dollar bills in his hand. "Take out your tip," he said.

"How much?" asked the Vietnamese lady.

The young man shook the money. "As much as you like."

Vi interrupted. "Why, honey, we'll take one dollar. That's fair. Now fold up the rest of your money and put it inside your pocket. Be seated until your brother arrives."

I tipped her a twenty on twelve fifty (hey, I had two hundred thousand dollars in the bank!) and strolled into the sun. Too damn bad my confusion about Hellbent's role in Emily's death had only multiplied. Yellow brick sidewalks, both sides of the street, teemed with the Beautiful People. They came primped in paddock boots, breeches, and jodhpurs. To the Beautiful People, I had to look like a day-tripper, a dabbler, and an interloper. Middleburg swarmed with insects like me.

Without much effort, I tuned out the Beautiful People. I liked knocking along a Main Street USA without bumping into another damn Gap, Banana Republic, Starbucks, or Barnes & Noble. No Lord & Taylor, Bloomies, Saks, Macy, or Nordstrom conspired to snare my credit cards. The Beautiful People patronized their own posh shops.

Roger's Drugstore at of Main and Delta Lane was quaint. Inside, I saw an authentic soda fountain, a green marble counter, and tiers of adventure-hero comic books. Ceiling fans rippled flypaper strips. I toyed with a Shakespeare Fishing Rod and Reel, appropriated from the window display.

"A nifty rig, it has a super smooth drag. I use one myself every afternoon I can steal away to Mott's Landing. You know it, above the falls?"

The gentleman attired in a green pharmacist's jacket had to be Mr. Rogers, early-to-mid fifties. Well fed. Family man. Also, I recognized, a wimp.

"Sucker fishing is in season. A bamboo pole with a 12-pound test line at the river's side is what I call paradise."

He put on a rubbery smile. "How might I assist you? I'm stocked up in Viagra, Rogaine, and Grecian 5 Haircolor."

"I'm plenty healthy but have a father's dilemma." I palmed my PI license at him. His eyes widened. "You see, my daughter procured a female gadget at this drugstore." His intelligent eyes recognizing the sales receipt absorbed the subtleties of my meaning.

He protested. "Those home pregnancy test kits can be bought anywhere. I must sell dozens of them."

Emily's photo, the one her mother had given me, duplicated the headshot I'd seen fall out of Pierre's wallet. "Does she look familiar? My daughter is a minor." My acidic tone stressed the final word.

"Any such purchase by a minor is legal," he said in defense of himself. "Besides, she may've picked it up for an older girlfriend."

"I don't care. As her dad, I'm interested in how she ended up with it." I elevated to my full height to intimidate him. "Let's say your cooperation right now will aid me as a cop plus give yourself a civic pride."

"All right then. But this way please." He steered me by the elbow out of earshot of a middle-aged lady browsing the Ziggy greeting cards. "Your daughter and this tall, lanky guy traipsed in here that afternoon. Sorry, no video—my camera crapped out last Christmas and I never had it repaired. Your little girl brought that kit straight to my cash register."

"What type of auto did they come in?"

"A sports car. One of those low-slung two-seaters. You need what model? Give me a second...a Jaguar, yep. It had to be a Jaguar."

"All right," I said. "From here on, we're cool. But this stays confidential, hear? Now ring me up for the fishing gear."

Relief softened his pinched face. "Absolutely, sir."

Outside Roger's Drugstore, I looked left and right before stepping off the curb. A young man strode toward me. With horror, I recognized his type—a cheap suit in a bad haircut toting a Bible. At the last second, I executed an about-face. Why was I always a magnet for every evangelist nutso? It was too late to run or hide. I had to stand up and take my lumps.

"You—the big guy—wait up." His reedy holler attracted the attention of passersby. "Yes, you. May we talk, sir?"

Footsteps snapped into a smart trot before a tap came on my forearm. "Sir, a moment of your time, please."

To stop was an irritation, to ignore him a public spectacle. "Okay but I'm in a hurry. Have it out, brother," I said.

Hoisting a pamphlet at me, gray eyes singular in their intensity, he said, "Blessed are the poor in spirit, for theirs is the kingdom of heaven. Mathew 5:1."

Pushing it back, I replied, "If there's a Hell below, we're all going to go. Curtis Mayfield, 1970." Two teen-age girls in short knit jackets and Capri pants giggled at us. I was Rowan; he was Martin. Rowan and Martin on Laugh-In, we were a chuckle a minute.

He shifted his hearing aid toward me and lectured in shrill concern. "Your wrongdoings won't be forgiven! Hear me?"

"Woe rules me; this world sucks; and I'm going to Hell in a rowboat. Okay, got it. Thanks for your concern just the same." I sidestepped him now loping over to accost a new sucker.

I went inside the public library. Middleburg hadn't upgraded their microfilm newspaper archives to the digital age. I sighed. The air war to Operation Desert Storm kicked off on January 16, 1991 at 6:38 PM EST with the cease fire on February 27th called by Bush Senior. That was the timeframe for my research in the Middleburg scandal sheets and gossip columns. Mr. Taliaferro had died, according to Ralph, during the Gulf War. Having a little trouble, I struggled to thread the spool of microfilm through various knobs and slits of a viewer new when JFK took office. In exasperation, I hunted up the research librarian.

More practiced, she aced it while snickering under her breath. I was a fast learner, though. The Middleburg newspapers were weeklies so my research clipped right along. The fuzzy obituary I rolled up on Mr. Taliaferro was short and not so sweet.

LOCAL HORSE ESTATE MILLIONAIRE
DIES IN BERMUDA TRIANGLE

MIAMI, Jan. 25 (Friday)—Carl Taliaferro, 32, aboard a Cessna 6-seat charter aircraft en route from Nassau to Miami International Airport never arrived at his destination. A massive air and water search was launched late on Friday evening by the U.S. Coast Guard after being alerted by Mrs. Taliaferro.

After concluding a business trip with hotel entrepreneurs in the popular tourist city of Nassau, he boarded the airplane with plans to make Miami and join his wife and friends. No further radio transmissions were heard from the Cessna upon taking off from the island resort. No debris wreckage or other sign of the missing aircraft was uncovered.

After three days of exhaustive effort, a Coast Guard official said, "We had to call off the search. To be honest, no one gave Mr. Taliaferro and his pilot much chance of surviving in that choppy sea for this long."

Middleburg joins in expressing collective sorrow over the loss of one of our stalwart citizens and extends heartfelt condolences to Mrs. Taliaferro and their only daughter Emily.

Memorial services have yet to be finalized. The grieving family has asked that all sympathy cards and letters be mailed in c/o Dakota Farms.

"Mr. Taliaferro was a leading breeder of champion horse racing stock," said Ralph Phillips. "I can't imagine this place without him directing our daily activities. He was a great man to have known and to have worked for."

Mrs. Taliaferro could not be reached for further comment despite repeated messages left at her lawyer's office.

Other than verifying that the old boy Carl had taken a fatal plunge into the shark-infested Atlantic Ocean, the obituary didn't reveal much else.

The photograph of Carl Taliaferro bore Emily's nose and eyes. I paused over reading the Ralph Phillip's quote again. Short and perfunctory, but it somehow rang false and hollow. I stuffed the microfilm reel back into the cardboard box. Maybe I was reading too much into the quote.

The cartographer's shop next to the Safeway was now open. I found a public pay phone on it's outside wall. Those cellular telephones were no more private than blabbing through a megaphone. Underlining the directory phone listing, I dialed Sally's Nails and was elated to hear Sheila's voice.

"Did Mrs. Taliaferro diss the sheriff?" she asked.

"She walked out on him and went to Middleburg."

"Middleburg? Where are you now?"

"Same place."

"Give it up. What did you find?" Sheila's homing instinct was uncanny.

"A sales receipt for a home pregnancy kit I found inside of Pierre's Jaguar. The drugstore owner confirms Emily with Pierre bought it on March 31st."

"Three days before her death," said Sheila. "Was she pregnant? Have you reviewed her autopsy report?"

"I haven't any idea and I'm not allowed to read the autopsy report. Sheriff Pettigrew thinks I'm homebound even as we speak."

"You're giving up?" Her disbelief was genuine.

"I'm no quitter."

"Oh, hells bells. My 10 AM for a pedicure just breezed in. But she's a great tipper, so I'd better go. Can you drop by this afternoon, say around two?"

I agreed to and hung up. While gazing at Holy Land maps, it occurred to me that Pierre's wallet and my tire iron were both missing. Theft of the latter bugged me. Who'd rip off a tire iron? My next heartburn was about my package in the mail going to Richmond. I'd call Darl Adkins, my forensics friend, in the next day or so and tell her about it. I'd play a little hardball, with Pettigrew, and get my hands on Emily's autopsy report.

I happened upon Mrs. Taliaferro's BMW foraging by a fire hydrant along Main Street, with a parking ticket tucked under a wiper. Further on, the Middleburg Community Center was a pink stucco building fronted by four white columns. Flowers and fragrance inside it enveloped me. Mrs. Taliaferro, true to form, gossiped with a knot of old socialites. They flocked by tiered rows of asparagus ferns and a stone cupid spurting water out its navel into the fountain. A flimsy wrap made Mrs. Taliaferro more presentable this time. I didn't espy Rachel.

Downstairs was an eight-lane duckpin alley. Husbands in red

suspenders, gleeful to flee the garden show, bowled over the waxed maple lanes. A few bowlers routed balls in the gutters. Pins exploded and I saw balls racked along the return troughs. Rachel wasn't at the snack bar or the lockers. I conned the desk attendant into checking the ladies room for my absent-minded grandmother. No Rachel.

From across the alley, I glimpsed Rachel's dodge out of a side door. I evaded a coot balancing a tray of beers and exited the same way. A crushed white gravel path twined uphill to an amphitheater. I sprinted to a hollyhock hedge. Down in the front on the outdoor stage, an antsy Rachel paced. She craned her neck peering into the backstage, then plopped down on the bottom step.

Noon. My stomach pinched. A towhee scratching under a crepe myrtle startled me. My head prairie dogged up over the hollyhock hedge. Rachel's head jerked around as if footfall amplified an intruder's brisk entrance. I recognized the man as Adam, the tough from my first day in Kaiser at the store. He handed a pleased Rachel an envelope. Odd. Straining to eavesdrop, I heard (or imagined?) my name uttered. Adam's gaze in my direction sent me ducking down.

I next watched Adam wave as he left Rachel who rejoined the garden show. That didn't seem promising, so I tailed Adam walking on rangy legs. Risking detection after the hollyhock hedge petered out, I jogged to stay up with him. Plunging into a traffic circle Adam defied honking cars squealing tires to brake for him. Was he taking evasive action to elude me? No, I decided, such aggressive stunts were his style. At a pickup truck sporting an orange camper shell mounted to the back, he stopped, unlocked the door, and reached in to retrieve a sheet of paper.

Adam blitzed through narrow alleys and behind shops. I allowed a half-block cushion. Twice he whirled and twice I pancaked to the scummy pavement. Broad daylight didn't help me. The riot gate, a piece of cake for him, I could mount only by a running start. We pushed beyond posh Middleburg. Circumventing a sea container by the feed store silos, he loped up a railroad embankment. I tripped and dinged up my shins on its creosoted crossties.

After I straggled through a barbed wire fence, a hand shaded my squint from the sun. Adam's point of entry into the distant loblolly pine trees was not so far off. He hurried his pace. Once engulfed in shadow, I figured he'd slow down. In fact, I relied on it. If he neglected checking his rear, I'd breach the field unobserved. It was a comforting thought to start me off.

Two groundhogs, pudgy from feeding on buttercups, chortled at me. Thistle burrs flayed my calves and lactic acid seared my thigh muscles. The squawking I heard was a red-tailed hawk trying to rebuff the aerial assaults by three crows. My lungs, creaking with air, played in and out like secondhand accordions. At the woods' edge, I slumped against a defunct Dodge towed there for a rusty oblivion. My legs cramped so bad I debated whether to go back. By the sun, I gauged Adam was trucking due west, then also invaded the shaggy pines.

A few yards in, I intersected an old logging road skirting a sump. Whiffs of what I took for skunk cabbage intensified but I didn't dare sneeze. May apples and mushrooms studded the pine duff soft underfoot. Sunbeams between boughs broke up the natural shade. My instincts told me Adam was more at home in these woods. He could double back, deploy behind a tree trunk, and make the first shot count. The afternoon before, I recalled, had inaugurated spring gobbler season.

Game Warden to Adam: "What do you have to say, son?"

Adam: "Visibility sucked, sir. Plus which, Johnson wasn't wearing regulation blaze orange."

Game Warden: "Yep. That was damn dumb of him."

Adam: "Fatal hunting accidents do happen."

The logging road ran along a saddle of rocky ground. My eyes scouted the trees. The afternoon was mild, reassuring, and almost normal. I sensed Adam was pressing forward and cared little about where he'd been, but why be sloppy again? I darted from trunk to trunk, bent on looking and listening.

I squatted cowboy-style for a breather behind sawdust pyramids near a plank shed. Sawmill work was one summer job I'd never let myself forget. It liked to have worked me to death. Sparks spewed from the steel blades biting dirt, bark, and embedded wire. I scooped away sawdust day and night from the endless exhaust. I put those thoughts aside and resumed my chase.

Less than a quarter mile later, the logging road fizzled to a deer trail that then dwindled to a rabbit path. I saw, through a fissure in the pines, vultures swoop for dead meat but my legs not quite that tired plodded on. Halting at a loblolly's carved-out roots, I aborted my tail job. The path, curving, ascended into cat briar and staghorn sumac, a torturous snarl inhabitable by humans. I'd misjudged Adam. He'd split off somewhere, perhaps on a shortcut out to the highway. I was famished. Worse still, it was another dead end.

Backtracking, I'd stick to the trail and make better time. That bucked me up. A glint of sunray caught my eye. Forests are larded with glass shards of jars and whatnot trashed in old cisterns, wells, and cellars. Good thing I studied closer what lay before me. One pace more would've been dire.

I bent aside a sassafras sapling. My stomach clenched. Yes sir, damn dire. A steel bear trap yawned its 12-inch jagged jaws. A linked chain ran from it to a metal stake driven into the ground. I lobbed a chunk of quartz on it. Whap! Its jaws could shatter my ankle. The trap was illegal as were what I noted sprouting there—marijuana seedlings. Adam was an herb entrepreneur. Fanning out, I discovered ten marijuana plots. For shits and grins, I sprung all the bear traps.

That explained his excursion into the woods. Local pot farmers had grown ever more cunning to thwart DEA detection. They tilled fewer herbs in more remote sites quite often booby-trapped. Bear traps, however, were to deter rivals from poaching more than nosey narcs. Most cannabis cultivators were blue-collar families outlawing together for tax-free bonanzas and on the side probably blowing a little reefer themselves.

Trekking back, I plucked off a sheet of paper snagged on a berry prick near the piles of sawdust. The page was a map, albeit a crude one. I smirked. The route? Why it was where I'd just come from. Unbelievable. Adam had documented where his pot patches were located.

While starting my car on the first crank in Middleburg, the same thoughts I'd had earlier hit home harder. Yo, hot stuff. Guess what? That just now was a bone-headed move. Suppose Adam had a hunting accident? You'd freight to Loudoun County Hospital in a meat wagon DOA. Freaking, I had to make sure that the 9 mil was still inside the fake vent. The lesson learned was while on this job, go armed.

An elderly man in a brown derby braked his Caddy for me to pull out into the street. We exchanged nods. No BMW was at the fire hydrant. Mrs. Taliaferro had smelled enough roses and returned to Dakota Farms. Beyond Middleburg's corporate limits, I mashed down the gas pedal, making for Kaiser. Sheila was off work in five minutes. I could call ahead with a cell phone, and explain my delay. Wireless technologies, then, did have certain advantages.

I hustled by Dakota Farms. Pants rolled up to his knees, Stanley Pettigrew waded in the drainage ditch after his bullets. Sidesplitting laughs shortened my trip on to Kaiser.

Sheila was still touching up an old lady's permanent. She returned my wink in the mirror. The light hanging over Sally's station was turned off. A young mother in jumbo curlers rushed over to smack her brat emptying the water cooler on the floor. I went inside.

"Sally had a dental appointment." Sheila inspected me in the mirror. "Who styled your hair? Briggs and Stratton?"

"A lady over in Middleburg. Is that okay by you?"

"It's not a very professional cut. Sally would never hire her to work in this shop."

"Next time you're my barber. Can we drop it?"

"It's a bad haircut," said Sheila. "Bad."

I sighed. "Good thing then I don't have to look at it."

I grabbed a mindless magazine off the pile, and collapsed in a seat. Britney Spears was this year's "young thang" in a midriff. Fatigue sifted into my head sagging to my chest in a mind melt. The magazine slithered between my hands and fell to the floor. Up from my subconscious bubbled lyrics to the musical "Sweeney Todd" that Sheila and

I had once seen at the Kennedy Center.

"Are you ready, sleepy head?" Sheila massaged my shoulder.

I stirred. After Sheila secured the door, we bustled down the street to the fat man's deli and squeezed in seconds before the door sign was flipped around to "CLOSED." I put in our orders for two ham-on-ryes slathered with mayo, potato salad, and root beer to go.

"Is life treating you fair?" I asked the fat man.

"It is now. I was an electrical engineer when sixty-hour work weeks dealt me a monster heart attack. My cardiologist said quit my job or die." His hand's flourishing motion swept over a few stools and the shellacked countertop. "This is what I now call my new downsized life."

"It becomes you." I paid the fat man.

"Thanks," he replied. "Next lunch and it's on the house."

We ate outdoors sitting on a rock wall. "Was your afternoon a flop?" Sheila asked.

"So-so. After talking to you, I tracked down Mrs. Taliaferro at the community center. Her housekeeper Rachel hooked up with a punk ass named Adam. I followed him into a nearby piney woods."

"That was brave of you," she said.

"Adam grows a little marijuana guarded by bear traps."

"That makes sense. He's a major league doper," said Sheila. "But Rachel Phillips? Not bloody likely."

"Are Adam and Rachel related?"

"Every soul in Kaiser is somehow or other related." Sheila crumpled a paper napkin. "This is yours, a xerox of Emily's post mortem report."

Surprised, I accepted it. As ever, Sheila was resourceful.

"I can tell you this much," she said. "Emily wasn't pregnant."

Sliding the report under my shirt, I said, "How did you get...no, wait...don't tell me. I might be subpoenaed to give testimony and end up incarcerated for perjury."

"My friend works for the sheriff, but we'd better forget about that," she said. "So, you have a double homicide. What now?"

"For the moment, let's disregard Emily's murder," I said. "Who then possessed a motive to kill Pierre?"

"Ralph Phillips for one," said Sheila. "You say he hated Pierre's guts. Maybe words between them heated up, Ralph flipped out, and teed off on Pierre."

"Okay, I'll buy into that. Also always at Dakota Farms, Stanley Pettigrew had ample opportunity and means."

"It's no secret his brother has a thing for your client. Maybe Sheriff Pettigrew sized up Pierre as a rival."

"Sex plus money equals murder. A classic formula."

"A serial killer off his nut is another possibility." Sheila hopped off the wall down to the sidewalk. "Verifying four alibis for Pierre's murder—the Pettigrew brothers, Ralph Phillips, and Mary Taliaferro—go on tomorrow's docket."

"Sure, babe. I'll polish that off before lunch."

"You're too uptight to think," she said.

Sheila stood within an inch of my knees, her fingers crooked in my belt loops. My earlier fantasy on the breakfast patio returned. Spring peepers, out in spades on this night, serenaded us. I peered behind and around. The coast was clear. The fat man had closed up and gone home in his convertible. Our first kiss was juicy as they come.

"Mom is at her sister's," Sheila whispered at my ear. "Aunt Ida in Paw-Paw. It's time to fish or cut bait, Frankie boy."

"I brought along my pole," I said.

"I'm surprised to hear you talk like that," said Sheila.

"It's part of my irresistible wit." My fingers undid a couple top buttons and rustled inside Sheila's blouse. Her breast scooped from a push-up bra overfilled my rough palm. Her nipple crystallized. Shuddering, she leaned in.

"Shouldn't we exploit your mom's kindness?" I asked.

"Um, I vote yes," she muttered between butterfly kisses. "After all, it's the first night Mom has been gone in five years."

"I can't hold out until next time."

"Nor can I." Her thigh nudged against my center of gravity. Her hands fumbled at my zipper but not for long.

"Bonsai!" I acknowledged her expert grasp. My next thought summed it up best. This was what Sheila and I boiled down to—lust.

"Quick," she said in an excited whisper. "To my walk-up."

"Yes," I said.

We groped by the Bluebird Bus Terminal. A night owl bundling newspaper stacks on the loading dock clapped at us. Sheila raced hobbling on one foot to take off a sling-back shoe, then its mate. The tail hem of her blouse broke loose of her wraparound skirt. I heard a wolf whistle. Sally's Nails came up at last. That vacant boudoir upstairs was ours to colonize.

I pushed in the door by its handle. We poured through, a wedge spinning into the stairwell flooded by harsh light.

Her eyes opened wild. "Last one up fixes breakfast."

"You're on," I said.

We surged upward. I tripped and my hands caught on the stairs. I floundered getting up. Sheila's red skirt hooked on the railing end. Seams ripping, her shirt fell off her twisting haunches. I winced. Sheila hated tears.

"Um, oh shit. Screw it," she said, already three steps ahead.

Our marathon to the top was on. Her pink half-slip maneuvered below snakebit hips, fluttered straight down her athletic, tan legs. They were naked without hose. She stepped up. My blood pressure lifted as did my eyes. Pearl snaps on her blouse, one by one, spurted apart, then the one restraining each sleeve.

Sheila jerked her shoulders. The blouse slanted off them. A fragile triangle of panties hovered a few inches from my nose. Inside and out, I battled delirium. At that instant, a dog yapped. A woman's sleazy murmur peaked from the hallway one floor below us.

"Who's there? Answer me or I'll call the cops."

Sheila, mortified in mismatched bra and panties, said: "Good night, Mrs. Dompkowski."

The grumbling Mrs. Dompkowski clinked shut her door.

A bra strap falling off one shoulder was ultra white. The strap didn't bite into her flesh. Her body moved tight and toned, not one ounce of cellulite. I picked up her blouse and half-slip. We bunched at her apartment door. Sheila stopped. "Damn." She'd left her keys inside. She borrowed my shirt to put on, and went downstairs to see Mrs. Dompkowski, the building superintendent. After their testy exchange, she hurried back with a master key and we went inside. I heard a TV running. My impatient hand toggled on the light.

"Don't bother," she said, now naked from the waist up. The girl's navel was pierced. She once complained one breast was smaller than its twin. To me though, they looked plenty. What did confuse me were her new stretch marks.

"Sorry. Too late," I said. "You wanna do a joint first?"

"A joint? Shit. No time. Strip, damn it!" She threw on the deadbolt and a swivel catch at the top and bottom.

We ran a sack race through the kitchen and a hallway, to her bedroom. Shucking jeans, shirt, and boots, I was excited as she was. At long last my monastic hiatus had ended. Later there was an exhausted but pleased fade to black until I snapped awake. A window draft chilled me. Luminous dots on my Timex read 3:30 AM.

I dressed and retrieved Emily's autopsy report. The object I kicked was my wallet. I was paid to be at Dakota Farms, not to goof off here. Sheila twisted onto her side and garbled a question. I did my best not to disturb her, and stooped to kiss an ear. It tasted salty.

I went down into the featureless streets. Some bums, in an abandoned lot, stoked a burn barrel using wooden skids they pried apart and broke up. They shared a hearty laugh. I scratched my chin stubble, wishing for a cigarette and whiskey bottle to go join their party.

That I didn't was a pity.

Chapter 7

Wednesday 4:00 AM, April 19th

After departing Kaiser, I streaked on my way to Dakota Farms. Along the country road came a pinkish dawn. Muscular yearlings raced side-by-side along a creek bottom where very pregnant broodmares grazed. The same young fellow, inside the stone hut, as two mornings ago was pulling sentinel duty. Head on the counter, he slept beside a boombox radio. A horn solo jolted him to lunge out to my car. I rolled down my window the rest of the way.

"Hi, bud. It's me, Johnson, the private investigator."

"Mr. Johnson, oh sure, yeah. You're cleared. Drive on up."

"Call me Frank," I said. "Mr. Johnson was my granddaddy's name. All quiet?"

"The traffic flows in, the traffic flows out. That's all I know."

"Are you keeping a log?"

"The form is on my clipboard."

My eyes went to his hip. "Are you armed?"

"Yep, a .44 Magnum. My dad's. Security cameras are on order, too."

"Do us both a favor and stay sharp. A killer is on the loose."

"You can bet I will."

I let that go.

My car went up the hill. Before my dousing the headlights, I glimpsed the garage door at its half-wink. Emily's sales receipt went in the fake vent. I used a light touch to shut the car door, and my ears perked up. What was that noise? Hooves battered the turf. There were snorts. Eyes looked like the dots on a domino and a starlit shadow moved like a sleek shark. Hellbent, constrained by a paddock, wanted his freedom.

A house key Rachel had given me undid the twin door. It was too late for a catnap. I'd wake up snarling at everything. I stretched out in bed, I glared at the far wall between my toes. I couldn't sort out my sentiments about Sheila and me. Like before, she was fun, but what did that really mean? I could only imagine a cryptic note taped to her bedpost.

Dearest Sheila,

Thanks bunches for last night. Now fix your own damn green ham and scrambled eggs.

Love like always,
Frank

That settled for the moment, I worked around my billion-dollar brain what little I had on either murder. The dripping shower bugged me. I sprang up, ratcheted down the handles, then brushed my teeth. A shave came next, followed by twenty push-ups. First flipping on the swag lamp, I next pulled out a memo pad and listed Sheila's four leading suspects for Pierre's homicide and their respective alibis.

Ralph Phillips W/wife Rachel at racetrack in West Va.
Sh'riff Pettigrew W/me part of afternoon
Stanley Pettigrew Worked at guard shack
Mrs. T Was in mansion, found corpse at stable

My client and Stanley vouched for each other. Well, sort of. Neither had been within eyeshot of the other. I'd buttonhole Mrs. Taliaferro at breakfast. Ralph I could question while he worked in the yard. The Pettigrews would be harder nuts to crack. That left what? Sheila's wild card, a serial killer lived in Kaiser. A somewhat farfetched theory, I'd hold it in reserve. My heart see-sawed for a beat. A serial killer? Why not just swim to an island ruled by cannibals? A dark fantasy where I shot Charlie Manson through the swastika tattooed on his forehead shook me.

Emily Taliaferro's autopsy report was clinical text I skimmed through twice. The nub of it stated her death was by blunt force trauma. Probable instrument, wonder of wonders, was a horse hoof. I flicked on a penlight and prowled sock-footed into the hallway. All was quiet. I peeked into various rooms. Speed drove me. Six rooms reeked of stale mothballs, a giveaway to no recent human boarders. Whatever supernatural forces lingered in them, I'd no mettle to question. Faster, I padded over to the middle corridor and my first locked door.

I used an Allen wrench and a self-made pick, and scrubbed the tumbler. It was a quick-and-dirty technique to apply the right torque and align the pins. The lock clicked loose. I went in and pushed the door closed. Dawn's light leached through the mini-blinds into a young girl's bedroom. I turned on a gooseneck desk lamp.

I first saw a pair of lace-up jeans draped over a chair back, and a sheer tank top on the seat bottom. Teen-age girls weren't bashful about advancing their God-granted assets. Then again, neither was this one's mother. I picked up a studded denim hat to find a pair of chopper sunglasses under it. This Emily was all too cool. She'd been, I could see, a live wire to pal around with.

What was I after? Any periscope into a dead girl's mindset would make my day. The bedcover was a pink satiny material, similar to a casket lining. By strange coincidence, Emily's CDs included Sheryl Crowe, Jewel, and Natalie Merchant, my own preferences in that genre. I discovered that a fruity shampoo was one of Emily's beauty secrets. Another one was a plastic tub of body butter that to sniff was anything but real butter. A Charlie perfume bottle reminded me of the Jaguar.

So far, so good.

On a cluttered closet shelf, I ran across a tennis racket as well as photos of a younger Emily and her tennis coach at Camp Pocahontas. The feather haired and flamingo legged Emily was smiling. An eight-by-ten glossy of an older Emily stood on the nightstand. She eschewed the heroin chic of teenage runway models in favor of a fresh, natural appearance. In spite of that, her strained smile said that something very much adult had haunted her. Couldn't an unwanted pregnancy disrupt a teenager's equilibrium?

A sealed box of deodorant tampons lay on a cloverleaf-covered sweater in the first drawer. Shamefaced, I averted my glance. Hiding places were becoming scarce. Between the mattress and box spring, I mined pure gold. A daily journal was titled "Be A Bad Girl." No smiley faces adorned it.

It was 6:05 AM. My retreat was overdue. I stowed Emily's journal at my back and slunk into the hallway careful to secure the door behind me. Dishes clattered over talking downstairs in the kitchen. Too risky to pore over Emily's journal, I stored it under my bed, then showered. A mirror over the pedestal sink showed my raccoon eye was blending in with my blackening scowl. I put on my clean clothes and boogied downstairs.

Mrs. Taliaferro at the table spread marmalade on a triangle of toast. Imperial in a burnt orange bathrobe, her eyes dogged me to the silver coffee urn. Rachel poured me a mug.

"Black, please," I said. "No sugar or cream."

"Johnson, honestly. Invest in a decent wardrobe, please," said Mrs. Taliaferro. "Don't I pay you enough? You show up at my breakfast table looking like a hick."

"Morning to you, too, ma'am," I replied.

"Ralph was up at the crack of dawn. I'm grateful at least one man slept inside this house last night," said Mrs. Taliaferro.

Ignoring her dig, I asked, "How was your garden show?"

"To show you how vain I am, I couldn't decide on Midnight Blue Dahlias or Ming Yellow Gladiolas. So, I snapped up both."

"Ralph can set them out this morning," Rachel said.

"No," replied Mrs. Taliaferro after Rachel's sneeze. "These I'll tend to myself. I've taken up gardening for how long now, Rach?"

"Since Ash Wednesday." Rachel sniffed.

"Poor Rach and her allergies. She had a sneezing snit coming home from Middleburg. Flowers in the car, I suppose, didn't help it."

"The antihistamine I took has unclogged my nasal passages," Rachel said.

"I once had a poodle," said Mrs. Taliaferro. "The little mutt had allergies, too. But now you can't play our sick puppy, can you darling?"

"Excuse me," said Rachel. "I should start the day's laundry."

Mrs. Taliaferro's viperous smile approved. "Yes, please do."

After Rachel left the kitchen, I seized my opportunity. "Sorry to rehash this. After you found Pierre dead, did you telephone Stanley?"

Mrs. Taliaferro's raised brows assented.

"From the stable telephone?"

"Yes, just as I said before," she replied.

"Bear with me, please. To extend that timeline," I said. "Stanley next drove up to the house, then raced to you in the stable."

"Precisely."

"Hustling to Kaiser, you then made a beeline to my motel room. Why?"

"I couldn't think of what to do. I was displeased at your laxness and had a room key so I let myself in." She crossed her arms.

I went on. "Why didn't you just phone the sheriff?"

Mrs. Taliaferro's underlip protruded. "As I explained already, I was too upset to think straight."

My questions turned harder. "Pierre drove your Jaguar. Why?"

"He was a valued employee," she said.

"How do you mean, valued?"

"Pierre was a much sought after trainer. Lending the Jag was how I kept him happy. I needed him for my business plan. Next spring was to be my breakout season."

"Horses then are Dakota Farms' lifeblood?" I asked.

"Yes. My passion is to re-establish a racing stable beyond my late husband's grandeur."

Next came my zinger. "Was your daughter, for the lack of a more discrete term, promiscuous?"

"No." Mrs. Taliaferro unfolded her arms.

"Pierre and Emily may've been lovers. Did you have any knowledge or suspicion of that?"

Her palms slammed the tabletop. Mrs. Taliaferro leapt up, her livid eyes spearing me. "You denigrate my fifteen-year-old daughter! You're an evil man."

I remained impassive, letting her surge of rage dissipate. "My preliminary findings are often off-target."

"Oh hell, listen at you. Never mind. Just get out of my sight. Go. Yes, go." Her husky whisper deflated me.

I felt like a semi-heel, and skulked up the steps. However within the next few minutes, I'd broken out Emily's journal. The girlish scrawl matched that on her picture in Pierre's wallet. I read her entries. A bright kid emerged. Horses, clothes, music, Beanie Babies, and boys consumed her roughly in that order. That seemed about right to me.

Emily wrote about her joys and sorrows at horse shows in Middleburg, Warrenton, Upperville, and throughout the Virginia hunt country. Her purple prose regaled how her own mount, Hellbent, was destined for "a greatness of mythic proportions." She dreamed of riding horseback off to the wilds of Venezuela and Australia. I decided against questioning Mrs. Taliaferro about her daughter's journal.

Her diary ended with a single ominous sentence: "I don't know who to trust anymore!!" A row of skull and crossbones was drawn beneath the line. What had instigated that? Had Pierre dumped her after the pregnancy scare? Snapping her journal shut, it crossed my mind how nothing about Pierre came up. Emily had been cagey not write about their tryst. I wondered what maternal wrath such a discovery would incur. Grounded for life. No MTV for eternity.

Or perhaps the rich, decadent mother wouldn't object. Had her lively outburst downstairs in the kitchen been a smokescreen? I grunted. Suddenly I wanted to be done and out of here. I went out and put Emily's journal back in Mrs. Taliaferro's shrine. Business elsewhere beckoned.

It was a dandy day—sunny and less humid. Ralph was kowtowing to his tulip bulbs. I walked past a sundial, down several steps through a sweet hyacinth zone and up to under a weeping willow tree. Its busted branches lay as ground debris. Ralph dumped in coffee grounds into the tulip bed.

"What's doing?" I asked.

"You tell me, Sherlock," he replied.

"Where do you crash up in Jetsam, West Virginia?"

"Chewink Motel." Grabbing hold on a crowbar, Ralph elevated himself upright.

"Do you own a .25?"

"That earns you a hands-down no. Look, I'm busy here, Johnson."

Well, Ralph could go tiptoe through the tulips with but I went over to my car. I drew up the dipstick under its hood,—one quart low. My penlight searched under the passenger seat. No oil cans but a tire iron. Kicking myself, I tossed it on the passenger seat. My car after some grinding spluttered to life. Thick, black exhaust reeled out of the tailpipe as I drove away. A hard hat up on a cherry picker was attaching a security camera to the flagpole. Stanley Pettigrew's free hand checked his gun holster as I swerved onto the main road. That tickled me.

Ralph Phillips had let slip that Mr. Taliaferro's parents lived in Potomac, Maryland, a fashionable enclave just outside of Washington, D.C. Battling the Ebola virus appealed to me more than puttering into any city. Just the same, Mr. Taliaferro's death intrigued me enough to head in that direction.

The Bermuda Triangle had a fabled history of yachts and jets blowing off the face of the earth with no trace left behind. Was Mr. Taliaferro's alleged plane crash simply a continuation of that motif? Or was he some, cagey bastard who orchestrated a vanishing act a la D.B. Cooper? Certainly Mrs. Taliaferro could've drove her husband to pull such a stunt.

I made it as far as Manassas on I-66 before smacking into the traffic tangle. I heard a radio announcer guffaw about the morning gridlock. Funny stuff. We crept northeast, car-length by car-length. One lady driving an SUV in Lane Four flossed her teeth at the rearview mirror. A girl verging on panic applied her makeup. Her eyeliner couldn't etch a straight line. What a cool time to listen to all of the books-on-tape that sat on my to-be-read pile back at home.

Many chewed and slurped their convenience store breakfasts. I fell in that category. A suit-and-tie in an Audi read a Bill Gates memoir. His type of reading and not mine. A subspecies of commuters suffered from a hand-in-the-ear disease. I saw that they jabbered on their cell phones. Who with? The other drivers. What about? Bitching about the gridlock. I wasn't so much bemused as disgusted.

At I-495, a suicide alley better known as the Capital Beltway, I scooted over to the Bethesda ramp to the Beltway and skirted Tyson's Corner office buildings armored in tinted glass. I crossed the Cabin John Bridge. The Potomac River was a drab, water-starved moat. An immediate right off on a ramp was my exit. After four turns, I ended up in Potomac, Maryland.

It was a nice neighborhood. Gobs of green kept things tranquil. My broke-dick car gave the finger to all the pristine Mercedes and Cadillacs. At the right home address I'd looked up in one of the phone directories discarded at the curb (there was only the one Taliaferro listed), I found a vacant parking slot on the cul-de-sac.

The Taliaferro residence was what upscale developers called an English Tudor. Crouched in the knees, I had a sightline to the Potomac River. One of the perks of wealth, it occurred to me, was to live in proximity to water. Apparently, this sliver of a river view satisfied the Taliaferros.

A flagstone walk ran at an angle over the emerald lawn to a solid mahogany double door. Azaleas raged in rancid reds and pinks. A mockingbird darted away from me into the vine-covered pergola. The chimes sounded, their door opened, and a bespectacled lady with gray pin curls poked out her head.

"Yes?"

"I'm Frank Johnson—"

"Soliciting is prohibited," she said. The door flew toward me.

My hand obstructed its path. "No ma'am, you've taken the wrong idea. I came to speak to Mr. Taliaferro and yourself."

"Concerning?"

"Concerning your son, Carl."

"Who are you with? *The Washington Post?* My husband is retired and no longer active in those government affairs. Go away. Leave us in peace. Please."

"No, I'm not the press." I paused. "I'm a detective. Only to talk, I promise you. Five minutes and no more of your time. You've nothing to lose except to get rid of me."

Her tall, lithe profile tucked around the door. "Okay, only you'd better make it snappy."

Their circular two-story foyer was lit in brilliant harshness. My eyes flickered to deal with it.

"Wait in the kitchen," she said. "I'll go rouse my husband. The au-pair's room is now his office."

I sat at the oval oak table while noticing a copper tea kettle collection on shelves over the center aisle.

"Mr. Johnson?" A man's baritone filled the room. "I'm Rusty Taliaferro. My wife said you came to talk about Carl."

He was half a head taller than me even if with the stooped shoulders. He exuded gray sideburns, mustache, eyebrows, and longish hair. His teeth were capped or he wore dentures. A hearing aid clipped over an ear. A hawthorn cane aided in his balance. Man, I couldn't wait to join AARP.

I handed him my PI license like a penitent driver does to a disgruntled highway patrolman. "Private agent. Mrs. Taliaferro, Emily's mother, employs me."

"Oh Lord." His sigh was a pained one. "What the devil has her in an uproar now?"

"She questions the official disposition of your granddaughter's death," I said.

Rusty Taliaferro wrapped both palms atop his cane and lowered himself into an oak chair opposite me. "That fool woman will undo me yet. What has she put you up to? Chasing down phantom killers? She has killers on the brain."

"Well, she claims Emily's riding mishap wasn't accidental," I said.

"Naturally, naturally." He rolled his eyes. "What mom wants to believe their daughter fell victim to a random occurrence of ugly misfortune? We both loved Emily but we're also resigned to accept what tragedy befell her. Life goes on."

"I won't belabor that point. Forgive my intrusion, but it has a direct bearing on my case. Did you ever entertain suspicions that your son's death was anything but what the Coast Guard ruled it as?"

"You mean like somebody sabotaged his plane? Never for a second," he said, strain in his words. "Carl died much in the same tragic vein as Emily did."

The CIA emblem was blazoned on a commemorative plate among the copper tea kettles. "Did you work for the government before retirement?" I asked.

"Thirty-seven years overseas," he said. "I was an embassy official."

"More like a CIA operative," I contradicted him. "Don't bother putting me off. The Freedom of Information Act will make checking it quick and easy for me."

His posture stiffened a trifle. "You're all bluff, Mr. Johnson. Those papers are sanitized. All names and positions have been blacked out. What are you really fishing for here? Level with me or get the hell out of my house."

"Only to confirm the cause of Carl's death," I said.

Nodding, his head sagged to his hands still grasping the top of his cane. His words spoke to the limestone floor. "To the best of my knowledge, Carl perished over the Atlantic. His Cessna ditched in the sea with his pilot. They sank to a watery grave. Motor trouble, foul weather, for whatever reason. Neither was seen or heard from again. Never."

I stood up and without a word walked out of their house and lives. A feeling in my deepest gut told me Rusty Taliaferro was an old man speaking the truth about what had broken his heart.

The jaunt back was long and boring despite the little traffic to deal with. In Kaiser, I docked at a pay phone kiosk. The cord wasn't snipped and bubblegum didn't jam its coin slots. A breeze swatted a hank of hair over my forehead while I buzzed the state crime lab in Richmond.

"Hey Johnson," said Darl Adkins. Her cheeriness was refreshing.

"Did my packet arrive in the mail?"

"Affirmative," said Darl.

"Results, please."

"Hold on. First things first. Does this render us even-steven on all prior obligations and favors?"

"Wouldn't you know it? You ask me that every time. Okay, I hereby absolve you of all prior debts and favors. Tell me something good, please."

"Sorry," replied Darl. A gay laugh, then: "Just funning you. I did tweeze a jot of fertilizer from the wood grain in the slingshot."

"Fertilizer? More specific, please."

"Your basic nursery fertilizer having a 12-6-6 analysis," said Darl. "It's the stuff sold at garden centers and nurseries."

"Would a kid with a slingshot play in fertilizer?"

"Not my two girls." Darl laughed again. "I feel blessed if they go out to the street to bring in the morning paper anymore. Damn

Internet."

"The Internet is a cesspit," I said. "Thanks a ton."

"Johnson, you know we love you down here. Any time you need help, ask away!" Darl's end disconnected.

My swallow constricted. Generic fertilizer was available at any one of a half-dozen stores in Kaiser or Middleburg. Did knowing that aid me? Canvassing each store was laborious. Why couldn't Darl find a palm or fingerprint, even if it was a partial, on the slingshot? I had yet to uncover one thing that could be branded as a worthwhile clue.

I burned oil along Main Street and hammered a hard left before stopping. The sign in Sally's Nails stated "CLOSED FOR BUSINESS" but I craved that girl in the first flat upstairs on the right. I removed the 9 mil, as an afterthought. From here on, I was being just plain smart to carry it with me.

It was queer. I had a load of time to think ascending those same stairs. I'd circled back here, in the spirit of a prowling tomcat. Sheila's red skirt still hanging on the balcony's end signified my boundary. Daylight showed off the flyspecks and ammonia fumes filled the stairwell. Midnight was more romantic—it blotted out the ugliness.

Listening at the peephole, I went numb. Something suddenly felt too creepy. It was too damn quiet. Sheila by nature was a whirlwind of activity. I whipped out the 9 mil. One-Mississippi, Two-Mississippi, etc. marked a five count. No noise came from inside. My fingers rolled the white porcelain knob. It twisted clockwise and the door (unlocked!) inched free. The 9 mil led me inside.

My logic was pretty basic--to shoot any trespasser on sight. Stalking through the kitchen to the bedroom to the bath, I found I was alone with my paranoid self. Sheila's bed was a hamster's nest. Dirty dishes waited in the sink beside a can of Bon Ami. I pawed through her clothes strewn down the hall. Her purse zipped shut was on the dehumidifier. No note was pinned to a pillow and no corpses lurked behind the shower curtain in the claw-foot bathtub.

I went into the bathroom. Clothespinned to the shower rail, three bras dripped dry. On the toilet tank lid was a cosmetic tray. Mary Kay. I ran a visual inventory. Liquid mascara, liquid eyeliner, liquid foundation...Sheila hadn't packed any makeup, I deduced.

Her unexplained absence tripped my panic switch. I paced the hallway. Be reasonable, I fumed. She stepped out to buy an egg timer. Calm yourself. You left without offering her a reason. So, consider it tit-for-tat, Mr. Tomcat.

The wall telephone over the electric range scared up a dial tone. Only one Ida Hamilton was listed in Paw-Paw, West Virginia, Directory Assistance informed me. When I reached Mrs. Hamilton, I asked her if Sheila had been in touch.

"Sheila did call earlier. She's due at work in a couple hours. But Wednesday morning means what comes first? Why, good old

Jazzercise."

I felt relieved. "A natural worry wart, that's me for you."

"She works out in the Catholic church basement," said Mrs. Hamilton. "She's turned into a physical fitness freak."

"I remember now she told me about that," I said. "Don't let on to her that I called. I fell stupid enough as it is."

"Sure, Frank. Just remind Sheila to vacuum," said Mrs. Hamilton. "I'll be home early tomorrow."

"Consider it done," I said, eyeing the general discord around me.

After locking up at Castle Hamilton, I scuffled down the stairs and went forth to find my Sheila. I saw through its broad windows Sally's Nails was a dormant commerce. Curling irons, pigtail cords, and spiky brushes cluttered the pink tables mounted with makeup mirrors. At the end of the block, I saw Sheriff Pettigrew tool by in his muscle car. A leopard tail tied to its whip aerial was a fancy touch. Smoked-glass windows hid his pretty boy face. He knew that I was in Kaiser. Let him go piss on ice. My concerns with him went on the back burner. The ten-minute walk to the Catholic church would do me more good.

Entering the crosswalk, I came armed. Adam hadn't counted on that when he sprang at me by flinging open the door to the orange camper on his pickup truck. The element of surprise, though, gave him the initial edge.

"I'll kill you," he said.

Adam hoisted a commando knife, its double-edged blade jabbing to gore me. I lost my footing and paid the price. He scorched my forearm, tearing for arteries, knuckles, and ligaments. The knife spalled a garnet from my ring. Blood. I assessed the injury wasn't a showstopper. My other hand was pulling from behind. When my fingers clawed out the 9 mil, the hammer snagged in my shirttail. I yanked and the weapon ripped loose.

"You scum," he said. The commando knife sliced within a cat's whisker.

I screamed. "What are you pissed about?"

"Payback," he said.

Feinting, I went right. He went right. Slinging deep from the waist, I whapped his face with my barrel end. It went crunch. His jawbone unhinged. Adam bleeding was also stupid and fearless. That psyched me out. His face white, Adam charged me. Swish. His commando knife slashed to do a tracheotomy. I crouched underneath his swipe. This hand-to-hand combat was calico cats and gingham dogs mixing it up. Adam wasn't played out. He faked left and plunged right, his knife cutting low.

Enough was enough.

I chopped at Adam and got lucky. The 9 mil's front sight cracked his right temple and sent him to the canvas. Not too soon, either. I ran a damage assessment. My fingertip probed the slash mark on my arm. Ouch-damn-ouch. No stitches were required. I knotted my torn-off shirtsleeve into a crude tourniquet. The bleeding soaked through fabric but didn't get on my clothes.

I was amped on adrenaline. Clutching Adam under both armpits, I dragged him into an alley. Falling from garbage cans, mangy rats scattered. Christ. My skin crawled. We were in our basest element.

A concussion was Adam's gravest injury. He'd log in some face time at the orthodontist, too. I righted his head. Bloody clots coughed up. I gasped for wind. Staring down at Adam, I had to clear up our misunderstanding. This scrapping in motel rooms and now on the street was a bummer.

Oyez, oyez, Alley Court was now in session. The 9 mil served as the judge's gavel. Adam gurgled. I explained to him THAT he would reply "yea" or "nay". If any response failed to ring of truth, the gavel pounded on his head. That was fine by Adam.

"You're kin to Rachel Phillips?" I asked him.

Head up and down signified a yea. So far, so good.

"I'll take a guess and say you cover Ralph's gambling debts?"

That solicited another yea.

"This ends our tiff. No mas. Have we got a deal, Roberto?"

His third yea satisfied me.

"An ambulance will be by in a little. If the EMTs ask, tell them you did a Humpty Dumpty off a Kawasaki. Hear me?"

Adam nodded that he did.

Chapter 8

Wednesday 8 AM, April 19th

I huffed up to the Charismatic Catholic church. Some wag had inscribed a peace symbol in the porch concrete before it had dried. Inside while the lavatory faucet gushed to hot, I pissed a bloody red. Bad news. The 9 mil's slide action still racked. Good news. Adam's head wasn't as hard as a barbell.

The piece stuffed into my waistline chafed my skin. A leather holster, not a shoulder pouch but a hip-draw, was a necessity. A First Aid kit in the rectory provided me with dressing and tape. I untied my shirtsleeve, soaped down the gash real good, and rinsed it. The wrapped on gauze made for a slipshod bandage that got me to laughing.

Rummaging in the coat closet, I didn't expose any priests buggering altar boys only a paper bag of donated clothes. Several U2 T-shirts fit me but I decided on a tie-dye. A guitar instrumental swelled out of the basement. The Jazzercise ladies were in high gear. I called 911 and reported Adam's mishap. The dispatcher insisted on my name. I could hear her fingertips typing into the computer.

"Johnny Sparklebreath," I replied before hanging up on her.

I sat on a picnic table, under an oak's shade, and flexed my legs. Downstairs came a mellower song. The Jazzercisers had cycled into their cooling down phase. They'd soon be finished. I idly thought about assuming an alias and retiring abroad. I'd become one Tommy Elmhurst in San Miguel de Allende, Mexico.

I'd hide out in a hotel lounge playing a black baby grand piano. My tip jar burgeoned with pesos. I yearned to play Duke Ellington but the hotel guests requested only Elton John, Barry Manilow, and Billy Joel.

I reflected on my case. One, a .25 had dusted Pierre. Who in Kaiser owned a .25? Was Sheriff Pettigrew on that? Doubtful. Two, where was Pierre's missing wallet? In the killer's coat? Three, hands dirtied by fertilizer, somebody had dropped the slingshot where Emily was killed. Had the slingshot hurled a projectile to scare Hellbent and pitched off Emily?

An ambulance squalled by me.

Four, lust had united Pierre and Emily. Did that target them for death? Five, what was with Mrs. Taliaferro and Sheriff Pettigrew's tug of war over Emily's death? Six, four suspects and four alibis. Wait, was Rachel also a suspect? She probably merited further study...

"Uh hi, Frank. Why are you here?"

Caught unawares, I flinched. Sheila buttoning a jacket over her green leotards, cocked her head at me.

"I was in this neck of the woods so..."

"You called my Mom in Paw-Paw, didn't you?"

"Your apartment door was unlocked." I joined her tramping over the grass to the street. Her duffel bag hit against our legs. We stopped to let the other Jazzercise ladies go past us.

"Okay, so I'm absent-minded as all get out what happened to your arm?"

"I was cut in a knife fight," I replied. "Occupational hazard."

"You should be more careful."

We walked silent, the morning hot. Sheila doffed her jacket. Those green leotards had to be electroplated on her.

"Can you rearrange your shifts today?" I asked.

"Sally will if I grovel enough. What's up?"

"Ralph told me about their motel in Jetsam," I said. "That's his alibi for Pierre's murder. I want to check it out."

"You can more easily verify it by phone."

We strode through the crosswalk. "At first blush, I'd agree with you except the check-in time isn't until eleven," I said. "Pierre was killed between 7:30 and 8:30 Monday morning."

"Meaning Ralph had enough time to murder Pierre and drive to Jetsam," said Sheila. "Rachel can't corroborate their story."

"No. He'd lie and she'd swear to it," I said. "So, let's make a day of it at the Races in Jetsam."

"Only if you change out of that T-shirt. After a shower, I'll phone Sally." Sheila remembering her key this time let us into their apartment. Some minutes later, warm water was spewing on Sheila's scalloped backside when bringing the baby oil, I parted the curtain.

"Ooo," said Sheila, "that's so, so nice, baby. Ooo."

"Let's roll," said Sheila.

That said, our raid to Jetsam started low keyed enough. Sheila drove first and her built-in radar got us through all of the known speed traps. I dozed clear through the Panhandle. Drifting in and out of naps, I overheard her fiddling with the radio knobs. She once keyed in Hank Williams yodeling the workfolks' blues. The transmission was clear and strong.

Ole Hank wasn't singing on a TV commercial selling air-conditioning or frozen pizza. He was the real deal. No schmaltz twanged from his catgut strings. Codgers at the Grand Old Opry claimed not one phony bone invested his body. Hank, not Gene Autry, not Roy Rogers, was the true original singing cowboy. However, he didn't ride off into any golden sunset on happy trails.

Alone in a '52 Cadillac's rear seat one bitter winter night while traveling through West Virginia, his heart quit. A farewell lyric, a hypodermic needle, a gin flask, and a handgun lined his pockets. I hadn't been born then, but I grew up spinning his records bought at white elephant sales for less then 79 cents a piece.

The steel pedal guitar put out an erotic vibe. Did Sheila go with it too? She was humming the Williams' ballad about a soldier boy forsaking his sweetie on Lake Pontchartrain. Sheila and I became the romantic couple in that song which spelled out the word l-o-v-e. Did I want a wife? That notion slapped me awake. Then I took note of a road sign we passed reading "Virginia Is For Lovers." Was that prophetic?

A truck stop a dab over the West Virginia border was our first pit stop. A Peterbilt bumper sticker read, "Sniper Bar & Grill: One Shot Is All You Need." The first dollar earned in such a bar had to be off a kid named Charlie Whitman. It was August 1, 1966. Charlie, a Marine sharpshooter and Eagle Scout, went up into the Texas Tower. Ninety-six minutes later, his bullets killed 13 and injured many more. Two shotgun loads to the skull stopped Charlie. Post mortem results showed a tumor on his brainstem. The Sniper Bar & Grill wasn't really my kind of place.

Sheila tapped me on the head. "Hello? Is anybody home in there? I said I'll get the gas and you get directions."

I went inside the truck stop and asked the clerk.

"Chewink Motel? Why, it's only on the other side of Assville," she said over the restaurant chatter behind us. "I'm only kidding! It's three miles north on your right."

I bought some extra-strength aspirin and in the car swallowed four tablets with a 7-Up. Battling Adam had taken its toll on me. Missing his orange camper shell parked on the street also irked me. Sheila ambled out a few minutes later toting a paper sack.

She laughed. "Call me a slave to local fashions." Inside was a lipstick tube, Bain De Soleil suntan oil, and two goofy gnomes carved from pieces of anthracite coal. She also splurged for five State Lottery tickets.

"You're so too smooth," I said.

A not-too-lucky rabbit's foot rubbed on the five tickets but she didn't win a cent.

"That'll teach you," I told her.

Before long, we came in on Jetsam's fairway flanked by hardware stores, public schools, and a community hospital. Church steeples buttressed a middle-class respectability. Then we clomped over the railroad tracks. The Chewink Motel was a sister of the Kaiser Motel where I'd stayed. Its 1950s splendor had long since vanished. Moss furred cedar shake shingles on small cabins. A weed-infested lawn needed bushhogging and its blacktop lot was weather-blasted. A maid lounged against a lamp post before lighting up a cigarette and blowing smoke at us. Sheila squelched the engine and dropped the keys in my lap.

"Lord, Lord, Lord. Frank, I wouldn't kennel my dogs here."

"We're not with AAA rating hick motels," I said.

"Fine, you go run the hotfoot," said Sheila. "Give me back the keys. The radio will amuse me."

I was annoyed but she had a point. It was my case so I made for the lobby. The old man wearing a bathrobe sat in a sling chair. An oscillating pedestal fan stirred the air. He stared at my PI license.

"I've always wondered if you can lose that license?" He nodded at my wallet going back into my hip pocket.

"Sure, by committing a felony or unethical practices like smashing in the teeth of reluctant witnesses."

"Say, where's you Glock or Sig?"

"Never mind about that. Does he look familiar?" I showed him Ralph's photo. "It's a right sorry likeness. He now has sparser hair and is paunchier with a little chin wattle."

"I ain't at liberty to dish dirt on my guests," said the old man.

"This is official." A twenty went under his hot water bottle.

"Official business is the one exception." He stabbed the photo with a thumbnail. "This yo-yo is a regular here. He breezes in on Mondays without fail. He and his better half, that is."

"Which cabin is theirs?"

"Seven. Always. Like in craps."

"Did he blow in this past Monday?" I asked.

"They arrived noonish and checked in. Then split for the racecourse to loose their shirts."

"Mind if I poke around in Cabin Seven?"

His wave dismissed me. "Sure, go break a leg."

Bopping her shoulders to the radio, Sheila cheered me on through the windshield. Tramping over the pea gravel path, I supposed the cabins once allured honeymooners. Sunlight slanted on a jumble of Burma Shave signs rusting away under a swayback shed. My granddaddy had memorized their jingles like dirty limericks.

Cabin Seven's door stood all the way open. The maid inside was singing a Trisha Yearwood hit. Interrupted by my raps, she looked up. Her muscularity was sexy if you liked female bodybuilders.

"Hi, hot stuff," she said.

"I'm a private cop on a case."

"And I'm a Rockette in Radio City you carry any proof of your claim?"

Again, I encountered a grudging tolerance of my license.

"I'm finished cleaning in here," she said. Bundling up soiled linen, she strutted to a cleaning cart. "Don't forget and lock up. Mr. Fogg will cuss me a new asshole if you don't. Then I'll do you the same favor."

"Promises, promises." My grin came before hers.

I saw typical motel accommodations. The bouquet was Pine-Sol; the bed was spongy; and the décor was rustic. Carved acorns topped the bedposts. A big-chest bureau huddled cattycorner to the bathroom. An oval mirror revealed in this light more gray hair than I preferred.

Alarm clock, face down, ticked off the seconds. Despite the fragrant lilacs in a vase, a sleazy disgust tingled my molars. Inch by inch, I combed over the unvarnished log walls but didn't find any eye of a sneaky spy. I was rolling the tension kinks from my neck when I spotted it.

"Frank, my man, you're way overcomplicating things," I said under my breath.

I kneed the bed nearer so I could climb up on it to reach the smoke detector. It wasn't up to code. It was a fake hiding an old video camera. The power and video cables threaded back into the ceiling. I now had some leverage. I marched back to the lobby and startled Mr. Fogg busy trimming his bunions. "Say hey, pappy." Clenching some shirtfront, I hoisted him up to my eye level.

Mr. Fogg's eyes spun in their sockets. "Have you lost your mind?" he asked me.

"I'm hip to your moviemaking."

"Huh, moviemaking? Put me down. Talk sense, man."

"Eenttt. Wrong response, Mr. Fogg."

I heaved him over the countertop. The man's scrawny fists flailed and a few smacked my bruises. Mr. Fogg sank his dentures into the shank of my hand. Agony raced in spurts to my biceps. I bounced him off the filing cabinets.

"Wait a second." He cowered, his hands over his head. "Wait."

"Cabin Seven, last Monday." I poised, threatening to kick him. "Put on that video."

"All right! Back off! Hear?"

I let him rise and retie his bathrobe. He brought up a crate and pawed through the tapes. He shoveled one into the VCR player. The video came on the monitor but it lacked audio. The date and time stamps in the upper right-hand corner were Monday, April 17th, 12:00 PM. Two people, Ralph and Rachel Phillips, invaded Cabin Seven. He was oafish, she was prissy. Ralph lugged a fat suitcase. Rachel pointed. Ralph deposited his cargo on the bed. Arms astir, she then reamed him a new one. I couldn't read lips from the top view, but she was yelling, livid about something. The video then fuzzed out to snowy static.

Mr. Fogg explained. "Up in these parts, we get a lot of power outages."

I thumbed the VCR's Eject tab. "This goes with me."

Smacking his lips, Mr. Fogg whined. "You won't go and jam up my fun meter here, will you? An old man has to do something to get his rocks off."

"Your shit, not mine."

His lips puckered in lewd curiosity. "Say, did you ever star in blue movies?"

"My mama didn't raise a fool," I said.

He laughed, squeezing my arm in a way I didn't like. "Some fool. Six hundred dollars a session, more for the lady out yon. Down and dirty under the hot glow of studio lights, you'd be a natural for the gay scenes we shoot."

My fist clipped his bony chin. I didn't pull the punch either and felt his jowl fracture. He didn't swoon right off but by the time I got out the door, he fell under a table. Outside, a wrecker rumbled eastward as I lowered myself into the car. Sitting lotus-legged, Sheila turned down the radio's volume. The pain in my knuckles now screamed up to my armpits. Blood started to seep through the bandage.

Sheila coaxed the engine to deliver us from this homemade sin. "Who's on that tape?"

"The Phillips feuding," I replied.

"Does your arm hurt much?"

"No, but this script playing me as a thug, sure sucks. All right, the racecourse is straight ahead, then a left at Jefferson Street."

"We'll redress your wounds later, Rocko."

"It's only a nick," I said.

Admission to the Jetsam Races was free. We dodged a garbage truck beeping to back up to a dumpster. The grandstand—a palisade of yellow-red bricks—took money from all ethnicities. After parking between two RVs with Florida tags, we bumped through a turnstile to the concourse.

The noon sun toasted our shoulders. Race fans carried Igloo coolers and longneck beers. Sheila in a vantage visor and sleeveless top lent the place a degree of style. She was buffing her stripeless tan. Every male sidewise glance I pretended not to notice had an idea to buff her. Gate giveaways included a massage chair, a washer & dryer, and Frisbees. I gave our Frisbee to a kid.

For too long, horseracing has played the dinosaur and its extinction seems inevitable. I'd accepted that eventuality. Still, the general neglect here chapped my ass. Would a fresh coat of paint bankrupt the Jetsam Jockey Club? How about some sowing grass seed to patch up the infield turf? Couldn't some stoner making minimum wage push a broom to get up last season's ticket stubs and cigarette butts? Horseplayers had to be the most easygoing of people to please.

I bought us each a dog-on-a-stick never tasting any better. She had a Brownie and I drank an Orangeade. Live races, I read, kicked off at 7:15 PM. Whoopee, we had over seven hours to fritter away at a racetrack gone to seed.

For the better part of an hour, we goldbricked by the rail. I overheard trainers and jockeys fume about their prospects to win a blanket of roses and a bottle of champagne in the victory circle. Overweight electricians on scaffolds tested lights on the infield board. A stud groom carted a saddle by us to the tack room. Near several suits (I took them to be owners) I eavesdropped a little and heard about "a new encephalitis scare below Louisville." They detected my detecting and walked away from us. We next idled by a betting cage.

Fanning a Panama hat, a bookie in a seersucker jacket explained wagers to Sheila. "A 'win' means your hag has to cross the finish line first. 'Place' is your horse coming in first or second. Easiest is 'show'. If your favorite is first, second, or third, then you walk away a richer lady."

Sheila was stoked. "Let's do it! How much money have you got, Frank?"

"Let's wait a bit," I replied.

"An 'exacta' is when your nags come in first and second. It has to be in that exact order, though. Jockeys here race so fast they pick the bugs off their teeth." The bookie shoved a brochure at us through the wicket.

I smiled at him. "Your spiel is dynamite but we'll sock our bets a bit later. Track conditions, handicaps, and so forth need scouting out first."

"No rush. Take your time. I've got oodles of ways to win. Just ask for Bernie."

"No doubt you'll score us a long shot on the next Secretariat."

"You can bet your firstborn on it," Bernie said.

Strolling away, Sheila claimed my arm. "Was that a note of cynicism I heard back there?"

"A note."

"Cynicism. It must make your life a turd of misery."

"It does for a fact," I replied.

"Folks flock here for amusement," Sheila said. "That's all, Frank. For the sheer enjoyment of the racetrack experience."

My hand motioned in disgust. "It's just that the joint looks like a pig sty."

"They don't see it," she said. "You shouldn't either."

Below the grandstand, a casino guard winking at me carded Sheila. She was overjoyed. Old time nickel slots were a blur of lemons and cherries. The Wednesday afternoon crowd of Argyles and Quad Canes gambled away their social security checks at the video-lottery terminals. The racetrack had seen grander days and it now depressed me. Maybe we had come on the wrong day and for the wrong race. Sheila crept around me and tickled my ribs.

"Are you bored, Frank?"

I smiled, flimsy as it was. "Sorry. This case has me hamstrung. I'll perk up."

"You can start by replenishing me. I need rolls of quarters."

On my trip over to the cashier window, a jockey—a doubled-over quirt in his fist—tripped to stumble into me. He lisped an apology. I didn't fall for it. My hand at my hip pocket intercepted his and clamped down. His dark eyes burned to zap me with their death-rays. I only chuckled.

"Whoa. I'm broke is all. Inclement weather has nixed our races and we ain't drawing paychecks."

"We'd better hash this out in private," I said.

My arms wrenched him in a double Nelson and strong-armed him into the men's room. No Rent-A-Cop challenged us. I took his quirt and pushed him away.

"It's nothing personal." The jockey, a sawed off liar and petty thief, was also cocky. He dipped to the mirror and smoothed the part to his black hair. "You understand me?"

"It doesn't compute. Why would you frisk me in a near-empty arena?"

"Why? Hell man, money."

"Naw, you ran too much risk when you homed in on me."

"Not true. I deny it."

"Bullshit, you lame fuck. Who hired you?" I cut off his last chance to plunge for the doorway. The jockey backed into the wall. "I'm still waiting but not for long."

"Fine. No sweat off my balls," he said.

"Give it up then. Who hired you?"

"Ralph Phillips."

"Ralph Phillips? Yeah, I know him. What was the grift?"

The restroom door behind us swooshed. A geezer in Bermuda shorts and a Hawaii shirt showed extreme discomfort.

"I gotta pee," he said.

"We need a minute," I told him. The geezer disappeared from the door.

"The deal with Ralph," I pressed the jockey.

"Last Monday in the clubhouse Ralph accosted me. 'This loon,' he says, 'carries a wad on him.' He gave me your picture clipped out of some paper."

"So, Ralph Phillips knew I was coming here?" I asked.

"That was my impression. Anyway, I would do the pickpocket and we'd split the melon 50-50."

I lay a $20 on the jockey. "This joke is on Ralph. Make sure he hears the punch line."

We exchanged grins. "The jerk-off deserves it," said the jockey.

I left him wetting his comb to preen at the mirror. The geezer at seeing me come out raced through the door to find a urinal. Ralph's scheme to rip me off galled me. Ralph and Rachel were privy to Mrs. Taliaferro's affairs including how much she'd paid me. Only Ralph wanted some of it for himself. The jockey's screw up was by now back to him. So be it. I knew that Ralph wouldn't grow a yellow stripe and run off. He only had to deny his culpability.

Sheila unpeeled the rolls of quarters I'd brought over to her. She then hit all cherries and the slot machine spilled an avalanche of quarters. I ran more buckets over to her to catch them all. She spoke in a fervid whisper.

"Careful. I'm hot. This is a winning streak like I've never had before." Tomato red lipstick smeared her pearly whites. The girl was virtually panting in ecstasy.

"If you cool off, come pick me up in the bar," I said.

"Just don't fall off the water wagon," she warned me.

"And don't you loose your shirt" is how I countered. One cliché recycled as good as the next.

A neon board blazed above the far slot machines, "Brass Hippo Lounge." Happy hour started at 5 PM with no cover charge. The bar's interior was laid-back, cozy, and best of all, near deserted. The orangewood paneling was minimalist and the odd odor peppermint. A lesbian couple cuddled in the rearmost booth. At the Brass Hippo Lounge, no paper-and-toothpick umbrella came in your gin. Nothing but relieved, I also didn't spot a damn karaoke machine or a big screen TV with steroid sluggers hammering their homeruns.

"Are you serving?" I asked. The barkeep's ample stomach thrust in the cash register drawer.

"I am now. What will you have?" he replied.

I wrested a stool from atop the bar and set it on the parquet floor. After dropping his bar rag by the beer tap, he sidled down to me.

"You have Sharps or O'Douls in the bottle?"

His impassive features grew amused. "Hell no."

"A ginger ale, then please." Hiding my embarrassment, I mumbled. "A scoop of ice in a glass, too."

"No go on the sauce, huh?" He set the glasses of ginger ale and shaved ice on separate cocktail napkins.

"I saw too many MADD mothers on the Six O'clock News," I said.

That tragic image passed in the next moment. "Are you here just killing time?" he asked.

My "posie" appeared beside my glass of ginger ale, more than a blur under the mood lights. "Investigator. Freelancer. Over in Virginia."

"Yeah, I down with it, Easy," he said. "You angling to pick my brain?"

That was all the invitation I needed. "Have you seen him around?"

The bartender gazed down at Ralph's photo, then up at me. "Yep. They're fixtures here like the plumbing. I'm bad with names. Okay if I call him Asshole?"

"Fine by me." I put some ice into my mouth. "Does he give you grief?"

"Me? Shit no. If he does, I'll cut him an OJ."

"I can respect that. What's up with him?"

"Asshole is one of those barflies who hustles drinks. Either that or he's cooking up a con."

"Can you whip a for instance on me?" I asked.

"You know, sneaky, under-the-table shit."

"Filching wallets, rigging bets, shaking down some doper."

The bartender dealt me a thin grin. "Yeah man, you're pretty much on the mark."

The ginger ale, as usual, was flat. I curled a ten-spot on a five-dollar tab to stick in his tip jar. The bartender picked up the tip jar and swiped a towel under it. Our appreciation was mutual. My fore-arm was on fire. The hotness helped me dull a depressing thought that was I still stumped. What did I know? Ralph Phillips, a conniving lowlife for sure, didn't qualify as a killer twice over. I couldn't picture the big bastard slamming a bullet into Pierre's chest.

Behind a dolly on the docks, I ran across a First Aid station. I sorted out gauze and a roll of tape from the metal box. A tube of antibiotic ointment was under the surgical scissors. Doctoring the gash in a restroom, I went heavy on the antibiotic ointment that cooled the burn.

Following the din created by excited slot players, I made my way back to the casino floor. Sheila was a ball of fire. Any ninth-grade dropout realized betting against the house was a losing proposition but that didn't faze her. She would flush every cent, go out and scrape up a few bucks, and then be the first in line for tomorrow's start time.

On the quieter side of the cashier cages, I fed my quarter into a public pay phone and thumbed in Mrs. Taliaferro's private line. The rings were like a gnat hazing my ear.

"Halloo." Brandy for a liquid lunch lubricated Mrs. Taliaferro's slur.

"This is Johnson," I told her.

She snickered a little. "Johnson? Never heard of him. Does he work for me?"

"Unless your 200 grand was a big kiss off, yeah, that's my operat-ing assumption."

"Excellent," she said. "Now I've got a brand new task for you."

"My cup already runneth over."

She overlooked my comment. "Ralph has disappeared. We went for me to take my driver's test, came back home, and found his god damn belongings gone. Rachel is bawling her eyes out, too."

Chapter 9

Wednesday 5 PM, April 19th

After quelling Mrs. Taliaferro's abrasive whines, Sheila and I left Jetsam. I'd no problem prying her off the slots since she'd dropped every last quarter. I drove. She was big on small talk. That worked fine, so long as only a word or two response was expected from me. Grunts were even better.

I skipped bringing up Ralph who was dead meat in my book. At long last, I saw the Kaiser Welcome sign. It was a village of joiners: Lions, Rotary, Kiwanis, and Piedmont Hunt. Sheila bailed on me at Sally's Nails. Her palms framing my cheeks, she kissed until I broke it off subtle as possible.

"Phone me?"

"Uh, tomorrow. After breakfast? Sure."

"Is that a promise, grumpy?"

"I promise and swear on skin." Two fingers on my one hand tapped the wrist on my other.

"Slumber right, don't let the bedbugs fight." Pleased, she laughed sauntering over to the stairway leading to her mom's grungy walk-up. I wiped off my lips.

To drive through, Kaiser was hushed as the Vatican. I put in an appearance at the Boomerang Tavern, cased its bar, booths, and backroom. Happy Hour didn't include Ralph. Elbows pinned to bartop, brain buckets in clay-caked boots tossed back the half-priced beer. Tobacco smoke was thick as smog. Jerry Lee Lewis blistered a piano solo on "Touching Home." I looked past all the burgundy and gold Redskin jerseys. A bruised Adam spoke to a man in a wheelchair whose spade beard was shot with silver. Adam felt my stare, excused himself, and swaggered over to me.

"No fisticuffs." My warning was a weary snarl.

"Hey, you beat the living tar out me. Our fight was nothing but fair." Adam held up scarred palms. "I ain't about grudge matches, okay?"

Relieved, I asked him, "Who's your pal?"

"Old Man Shoemaker. Years ago he wedged a Triumph under a semi and awoke from a coma paralyzed from hips down. Ugly, huh?"

"Very. Only a Knievil walks away from that shit."

"After a plate in my head and a pin in my shinbone, I'd have to agree with you." Adam sucked on can of a malt liquor and smacked his lips.

"Ralph Phillips," I said. "Has he drifted by here?"

Adam's sleeve was a napkin. "I haven't put eyes on him since the weekend."

The temptation was to mess with Adam about his map I'd found to his pot patches in the pine woods. Instead, I asked, "Are your pals, the Kilby cousins, in tune with our fair fight?"

"Shit, they can go rot in hell." Adam broke for the door. "Later, Johnson. I gotta go fix my pickup's clutch."

I ordered two Coors, favored a seat with my best side at Shoemaker's table, and twisted off the caps. "These are on me," I said, setting both bottles in front of him.

"Mighty Christly of you," said Shoemaker. "What or who do we toast?"

"To bikers who survive plowing under big rigs."

"Yep and here's to hair on your balls, too." After a long belch, Shoemaker chugged the beer.

"Adam told me your biker saga," I said.

"Adam has a big mouth."

"He's a good kid."

"He's a schmuck." Palms pushing off the handles, Shoemaker raised himself up in the wheelchair to give his ass a chance to get some fresh air. "Some buddies ripped off his car parts. Next thing you know, he's in here crying me a river. Do I look like Mister Fixit? Hell, it's a major achievement for me to wipe my own butt."

Now that was ugly. "Maybe Adam can recover the car parts."

Shoemaker unhitched his chair's brake. "He has a bead on the culprits all right. If I know Adam, he'll bide his time, then get even with them."

"Have you seen Ralph Phillips?" I asked him.

Shoemaker replied after a bearish growl. "If I did, I'd shoot the bastard on sight."

"The law might object to that," I said.

Shoemaker snorted. "The law? Last week I was summoned for jury duty. Fine, okay. I'm a solid citizen and vote every November. At considerable personal effort, I show up at the jury pool. This wimp of a clerk assigns me a number. I sit on my thumbs. Well, my number finally comes up. I'm picked for a criminal case. Guess what the infraction was? The defendant had whipped out his schlong scaring the wits out of two old ladies. So, I wasted an afternoon listening all about peckers, masturbation, and perverts. The law. Leave it for TV."

I stood up, my face friendly. "Decent speaking to you, Shoemaker."

"You know where I party," he said. "Come any time, friend."

I signaled the barkeep to change a twenty. A candy jar by the cash register solicited cash donations for a local nine-year-old girl who needed a kidney operation. Her folks, like too many working Americans, had no medical insurance. Goddamn President, though, was bound and determined we'd rebuild Kuwait. My twenty fell amid the ones, fives, and loose silver. The jukebox put on Garth Brooks and fans began to tap their snakeskin boots in tempo. I exited the bar.

On Main Street at the store I gassed up and slurped in two quarts of their cheapest grade motor oil, a paraffin-based gunk. I tossed the empty cans. It was now pitch dark. One block over, grill-mounted emergency lights assaulting my rearview mirror were red. Sheriff's Department. Gliding over, I let my engine putter and scanned the mirrors. A lank figure loped up and rapped on my window. The blood pulsing in my ears.

"Evening, Mr. Johnson." Elevating my forehead off the steering wheel, I put a name with the familiar voice. He was the young fellow from the Dakota Farms guard house. He was also standing there attired in a new Deputy Sheriff's uniform. I could stand down.

"I thought that was your smelly ride," he said.

"Stinks, don't it? I'm in for tune up tomorrow. How does it feel to work for Pettigrew?"

"He hired me as part-timer. No insurance and no vacation." The kid hawked and a yellow gob of gunk tattooed my tire. "Night patrol is a drag. The biggest excitement is chasing off kids partying in a farmer's field. Scared of me, they now know better."

"Well, I wasted a perfectly good afternoon in Jetsam, West Virginia. My hot lead didn't pan out at all. That's the way it goes, I guess."

"You went out on a Code Brown, eh?"

"You said it—a shit run. Is Dakota Farms safe and sane?"

"The gate cameras run like a champ," he told me with pride in his voice. "We'll mount the others in the next day or so."

"Did the M.E. file Pierre's autopsy report?"

"By tomorrow is what Joyner told me," he said.

"Maybe you can lend me a hand."

"Nothing I'd like better." He had to shout to compete with the spring peepers raving in the swamps.

"Are you hip with using Luminol?"

He said, "It's pretty basic for detecting diluted blood."

"Applying it in the field, I hear, gets tedious."

"Naw. You can buy it in premixed kits now. The sheriff squirrels it in his footlocker." The kid produced a key.

I awarded him a thumb's up. "Who are you? Son of Felix the Cat?"

"I'm Thornbird, sir."

"Thornbird, the thing is the sheriff will oppose my idea."

"Not now. He went to the Sheriffs' Convention in Roanoke. For the next two days, I'm the lawman around here."

"Really," I said. Was it me or were the aligned planets ringing in sync? When I headed off, I appreciated the police reds shimmering in my mirrors.

I didn't run Kaiser's outermost traffic light. Waiting, I read a placard nailed to a gatepost, "Own a Computer? Put It to Work! $1500/week to Start!" I half-wished I'd gotten in on the ground floor with computers. Steady paycheck, health insurance, and regular hours. High tech was for the eggheads from the Class of `82. I was, it always seemed, shortchanging myself. As a private detective, I excelled better than most.

I wondered how long a middle-aged man could continue to work forty-eight hour stakeouts and pay off the bill collectors. It was doable as a kid, but I wasn't such a kid anymore. Suppose my prostate was a cancer grenade, its pin pulled next week? Suppose...

Green light. I dumped the clutch and drag-raced over the country roadbed. Velocity bucked up my mood. From out the windows came a frog orgy. Creedence Clearwater Revival's "Born on the Bayou" soaked me with its swamp rock. A row of sawhorses pulsing red appeared alongside a trench dug for underground cable. Too late, I swerved to miss it.

A tire, right front, blew out.

Have you ever tried to steer a ballistic missile? My car became one. It jitterbugged and seized a whim to slew hard right. Jerks. Bumps. An outcropping of rock came up. I stomped on the brakes. Big mistake. Spinning counterclockwise, I was a whirling dervish. Everything was a blur.

The car didn't flip or roll, God only knew why. I flowed out of the spin. Metal scraped sparks on the pavement. To cap off my acrobatics, I straddled the road's crown with the steering wheel high in my chest. The engine, running still, was a sputter. Burnt rubber stunk up the air.

I gasped with vertigo. I was still all in one piece and my worst complaint was dizziness. My heartbeat was beating fast. Wow, I thrilled. Simply, wow.

Catastrophe hadn't screwed the ass off me. I was intact. Shoulder harness and seat belts had functioned as advertised. My car was by and large undamaged, too. I couldn't have been any luckier.

Common sense spoke to me. Uh, hoss, you might want to move your vehicle out of the road. The ruined tire wobbled on its steel rim. I coaxed my car forward into the shallow ditch, a little better than half off the asphalt. My emergency four-way flashers pulsated. Why hadn't I replaced those road flares after my last accident? The spare and jack waited in the trunk. The problem was, I wasn't keen on some huckleberry in a pickup truck clipping me and end up like Shoemaker in a damn wheelchair.

John Fogerty rasped out the last radio lyrics. My accident, it shocked me to realize, occurred in a matter of a few seconds. I cut the engine and lights. My bones vibrated. My chest hurt like some ribs had sizzled apart. What came next? My fingers scrabbled under a floor mat. No tire iron. They slithered upward to the seat cover. I took up the iron wedged there, and clambered out. The fog mantling the ground felt warm.

I lurched to the trunk and threw up its lid. I removed a spare and bumper jack from the luggage compartment under an army wool blanket. The spare wasn't a fifth full-blown tire but a weenie wheel that came standard these days. Underfoot, the road's shoulder was firm and level. A chunk of stone served as a minimal chock. The tire iron broke the lug nuts' rusty seal. The bumper jack, me humping its handle, lifted up the car.

Ca-thunk!

The jack buckled, the metal hitch shearing off. It fell useless to the ground. My disbelief flared to rage. Screaming, I hurled the jack into a murky field where it splashed into an unseen pond. I sank to the road bank, hands at my sides, and started to sway back and forth. What now? Thirst. What I would have traded for a schooner of icy beer? No, on second thought, better cancel that idea. My final booze cure had come at too great a price...

My first night in the Psychiatric Treatment Unit (PTU), I'd glowed like a briquette. Glowed for alcohol. Some had it worse than me. Across the hallway, a diabetic wreckage of humanity was a blind man with all four limbs amputated. He hollered for a nurse. Mine was Ms. Beem. Was the bellowing amputee the "after" picture for hardcore alcoholics?

Ms. Beem brightened the amputee's doorway. "Here's your glass of Gatorade, sir." Her voice, and I'll never forget this, was soft and nice as April showers on the tulips.

"Gatorade!" the amputee said. "I screamed for a fifth of gin. What the fuzzy fuck good is Gatorade to me?"

Amazingly, Ms. Beem stayed polite but firm. "In here, it's Gatorade, sir, or it's nothing." I'm guessing the amputee drank nothing.

PTU was my hell-for-breakfast stand, my lifeline to reclaim sobriety. My goal was not to end up blind, legless, armless, and useless shrieking for a slug of booze. I was a briquette. I burned all over. Ms. Beem got me settled that first night. Four weeks bugged by. Four long weeks. Talk. Lots and lots of talk. One on one. Groups. The last evening they gave me a sobriety pin and I stalked out of there like a new man. That was five years ago. That zealous thirst for Johnnie Walker was what now powered my detective ambitions.

But here I sat now. My eyes drifted skyward. No North Star, no Venus, and no Mars. Far off to the west, a cautionary light blinked.

Behind it, Washington D.C.'s light pollution glowered. Better to be here than there. I debated about striking out on my own for help. A nearby cottage must have a telephone. They'd lend me a jack. Worst case, I'd march on to Dakota Farms, still an appreciable hike. I didn't cotton to abandoning my car so decided to give it a half-hour and see what happened.

All of a sudden, a racket flew up on me.

I whirled into a combat stance, the raised tire iron my club. Scared to the back of beyond, I first saw its nostrils. I didn't know what to think. I stood shivering. Had a local haint rushed in for my soul? Clippity-clop, clippity-clop. The noise's source blew into my sightline. A burly, black shadow raced parallel to the board fence. My laugh was a sardonic one.

Hellbent pulling a Houdini had escaped from Dakota Farms. He now romped back and forth behind the fence, his orange eyes riveted on me.

"Score one for you, you big nag," I said.

That fright had whittled five years off my life. Crazy as it seemed, never even having ridden muleback, I had an affection for Hellbent. If I reached Dakota Farms, I'd bounce that new trainer out of bed to bring the horse home. Goose bumps pimpled me. My armpits were sweat-drenched. I dug up a ratty sweatshirt from the trunk, and stretched into it.

Hellbent nickered. Something vexed him.

"Look, we just have to wait," I said. Again, the high-strung horse neighed. I retrieved the 9 mil and thumbed down the locks on both car doors. "What bothers you? All right. Quiet down. I'm leaving for help."

Hellbent followed me inside the board fence two or three hundred feet until he came to a woods too dense to penetrate. He neighed and I was sorry to forgo his company but pressed on.

The macadam under my soles guided my knock-kneed gait. I managed more or less to steer to the center of the road and moved in the direction of Dakota Farms. The road slanted up a gentle hill, then followed a long, lazy bend. Rising from a shallow dip, over my left shoulder I espied a glint of light. The gap appearing in the fencerow was a right-of-way for farm machinery to get in and out of the fields. Relieved, I left the road. It was 8:20 PM.

Here my footsteps sank in mushy contrast to the hard asphalt. I was walking on grass, winter wheat perhaps. My pace quickened. The peepers tooted shriller and off-key. Squash-squash. I traveled through darkness by touch and feel. Squash-squash. The smell of wild garlic pervaded the dampness. Squash-squash.

The mysterious glint drew me on. "Humph!" My boot had plunged into a groundhog hole, jerking me off-kilter. I groaned, but righted myself before heaving forward. Pain prickled my leg on both sides of my knee. I'd deal with the pain later, and have the fluid drained off. My progress slowed to a penguin waddle. What was the urgency? My damn car wasn't going anywhere.

Close enough now, by straining my eyes, I could discern two light sources, perhaps porch lamps on a tenant cottage. I prowled nearer. Fingering the sore spot, I pondered how I'd tow my car to a service station. Was the tire rubber too old, too dry-rotted to hold a plug or a patch? That had happened once before to me.

A woman shrieked!

I broke into a clumsy run without thinking, squinting at the lights where the second, more harrowing scream erupted. The lights were headlamps. Slantwise, they beamed through the fog and trees. My feet crashed on dry leaves, then splashed through a low-running creek.

Wading into a second smaller field, I saw jerky shadows blot the headlamps. She bellowed in sheer terror. I closed the short span to the pickup truck and dipped behind it. I peered over the tailgate. Deep within the pools of ragged light, I homed in on the imprints of three humans. Two men and a woman. She lay spraddle-legged on the ground. My breath stalled in my throat. I froze solid. Time crawled by. I felt outside myself, numb and paralyzed. Unable to react.

"Girls got to be made women." The standing scrote laughed his gleeful contempt. "Some fellow has to be the cherry picker. We're only too happy to be it."

"Yep. She lied to her mama," said the other man. "She insisted on running with the big dogs. Honey, you're about to meet the big dogs."

"Woof, woof. You can coin a phrase, cousin."

"Shit yeah. She'll like it with a couple tusk-hogs like us, now won't you, honey?"

"Oink, oink," the other said. Laughs. Catcalls.

I was still trying to believe my ears. She screamed.

"Shut up," one scrote hollered. "The damn rohypnol is wearing off. Quit that damn biting me, too."

"Here, gag the whiney slut."

The scrote standing over her gave an inhuman laugh. He muffled her screams all but a guttural squeak by now.

"Feels like more, don't it," the upright scrote grunted.

"Why sure," his partner replied. "Mm, mm-mm. Why sure, it feels like plenty more. Hurry it."

"I always end up with sloppy seconds," the upright man said. "Are you carrying crotch crickets? Or the clap?"

"Zip it" the other said. "We flipped and you lost. Be a man about it."

"Yeah, well speed it along, Casanova."

"I'm busy here like nobody's business," his partner said.

Flesh slapped against flesh. Naked flesh, it dawned on me. My fatigued brain at last spliced it together: RAPE. Nausea skewered my intestines. Was I waiting for my can of spinach to fall from the sky or something?

Trousers snaked down around his ankles, the standing scrote exposed a chalky paunch in the conical glare of the headlamps. The other scrote's pelvis pumped in and out, getting off on the violence.

"Your go, cousin."

"It's about damn time. Move it."

I'd slunk around the driver's side of the truck and emerged in the stronger light, moving up on them fast. My eyes adjusted before a gunshot cracked the night.

"What?"

I aimed the 9 mil at the bipedal scrote. His jaw sagged low. The rapist petrified in mid-stroke. Second nature to me, I put on my old MP command presence.

"You." My boot thwacked the rapist. "Off her. Now."

He complied, rolling like a possum on its belly. The second shifted to better his angle on me. The shifting 9 mil stilled him.

My gaze trained on her two attackers. "Lady, go assemble yourself. Inside the truck cab. Beat it. Be quick."

Sobbing in quiet heaves, the girl undid the gag, pulled down her dress hem from around her chin, and arose quaking and uncertain. I gritted my teeth. When she staggered by me, her face made plain in the bright headlamps was Carole Dawson's, the teller who'd helped me at the Kaiser bank. She stared ahead. The two men watched her go. The truck door latched shut.

"You assholes," I instructed, waving the 9 mil. "Get it together. Slow. No funny moves."

Keeping my back to the truck, I edged into its harshest beam. I knew them, too. Adam's pals introduced to me on Day One in the store's graveled lot. They were the Kilby cousins. Finished dressing, they slouched, artificial light boring into their red, predatory eyes. Gin breath was unmistakable.

"What's your play, mister?" the short one said. His drawl was sullen, calculating.

"Hands up," I said. "March to the rear of the truck."

They trudged zombie-like to the tailgate.

"You bind him. Make do with baling wire," I ordered, blooping the coil from the truck bed to land at their feet.

The tall one had to go and sneer. "Oh, yeah. Go eat shit and die."

I slashed forward; the 9 mil's muzzle whapped his head. He sank like lead ballast, to his knees and keeled over onto the ground. The short one swiveled to me. He launched a right-left combo at my head. Sparring off his assault, my uppercut clunked against his cranium an inch above the eyebrow. The 9 mil packed a wallop. He, too, caved. I concluded both were already half-out anyhow.

Rage.

I squinted at the two lifeless forms. Either could be dead, skull bashed in, their brains scrambled. I didn't care. I didn't. That recklessness taunted me to step over and slit open their jugulars.

Do it, damn it.

Leave the scrotes lying in this onion field, black hearts pumping them dry and dead. Instead, I patted the pair down. A .32 and the ever-popular commando knives I pulled off them flew into the brambles. I peeled out a swatch of 20s and 50s, from their unchained wallets. Wallets also went sailing into the weeds. Restitution, by God, had to begin somewhere.

From out the windshield, I felt Carole Dawson surveying my every action.

I scared up a pair of tin snips and Blue Mule leather work gloves. I banded both scrotes in baling wire about the feet, knees, and hands behind their backs. That wasn't secure enough so I clipped a couple strands of barbed wire from the nearby fence to tighten about their scrote chests and thighs. Satisfied, I dragged both up to the tailgate.

Flipping it down was a simple task. Loading each scrote into the bed was a different story. Their heads and feet kept tumbling off. The short one burbled. Lacking a sedative, I cracked the 9 mil across his crown. The thud of steel spanking bone was sickening. I did it again. Why, it did feel like more, just like the scrote had said.

I rested against the rear bumper, aware that Carole's eyes were affixed to me. I tucked the two scrotes to fit inside the bed, then slammed up the tailgate. I wasn't finished. After undoing the hood, I detached the jack from its mount and threw it in beside the scrotes.

Their keys conveniently waited in the ignition. The truck cab had a new car smell. The big engine cranked over to a well-tuned thrum. It was amazing what profits bought drug dealers. I cut a doughnut and knocked across the fields out to the blacktop. With its raised suspension and skid plates, the truck handled just beautiful. In contrast, our cargo in back rode mean and rough. I liked that.

Carole pulled up her torn dress to cover a shoulder. She shrank in her corner. Tensing, she drew both legs up under her. I threw on some heat. Fingers raked hair from her eyes sunken in bruised orbits. Her subdued crying gave way to congested sniffs. She was, I imagined, pretty bashed up. I taxed my brain except I was way too pissed to figure how to aid her. Once the truck revved into high gear, I spoke. "First, we'll run you to the Emergency Room."

"Oh Christ Jesus, no." Her dull voice stuttered. "J—j—just take me home. Can you, please?"

"Doctors and nurses will know what to do for you."

"Not a word of this breathed to my dad. Oh God. He'll kill me."

"Your dad? That's the least of your problems."

"What about them?" She may've smiled a little, too.

"They're going to jail for a long time if I don't kill them first." I removed something and held out my hand. "Here, this is for you."

"What?" wondered Carole.

"Go on," I said. "Take it."

"Why, it's money. A lot of money." Her voice modulated, shoulders quaked with new violence. I punched the truck's gas pedal just as Carole Dawson fell into shock and blacked out on me.

By God, restitution had to begin somewhere.

Chapter 10

Thursday 1 AM, April 20th

Puffing on a cigarillo in his '98 Oldsmobile, Thornbird sat minding his business parked out in front of the sheriff's office. He looked plenty bored, but I was about to shake all that up. I glided alongside him and droned down the power window. He followed my example.

"Hey there Frank," said Thornbird. "Did you go and buy a new truck?"

"Nope. I brought you two prisoners." My thumb jerked behind me. "Hog-tied in the bed."

Thornbird's outburst was a high-pitched laugh. "Man, you could make a living off of busting my balls." We locked stares, only mine outlasted his. My thumb indicated again.

"Hog-tied," I said. "For your custody, Deputy Sheriff. Two prisoners."

"You can't be serious. Can't be." Thornbird flicked away the cigarette butt and sparks caromed off the truck's pinstripe.

"Be my guest and have a look. I grabbed up both in the act."

"The act? The act of what?"

"Rape. The Dawson girl was the victim. I already dropped her at the ER."

"Naw." Shaking his head while grumbling, Thornbird climbed out to the street, then leaned in to squint. He jumped catlike.

"Relax. They're restrained. Is your male lockup empty?"

"My male lockup?" Thornbird stared over at me, flustered.

"It'll be your collar."

Breathing heavy, Thornbird gnawed a callus on his thumb. "Whoa, here. I'm freaking. First off, how about some proof, Frank? We need evidence that this rape took place. Or is it just a case of 'he said, she said'?"

"I was the eyewitness. The ER is doing up the rape kit. What else do you need?"

Thornbird splashed his flashlight into the truck bed. "The Kilby cousins. How come I'm not surprised? What's this? Blood?"

"They resisted arrest."

Thornbird contorted his baby face. A fretful kid, it occurred to me. He lowered his tone and glared over at me. "Now what the hell happens, Frank?"

A stricken groan issued from below us, then a lowbred moan.

"It's straightforward enough," I said.

"Ouch! Shit!" Thornbird sucked on his thumb.

"Kilby's DNA is slathered over the Dawson girl," I said. "That alone will convict both."

"Barbed wire? What the shit? You tied them up in barbed wire? Help me twist it off them."

I handed him the pair of tin snips. "These might work better."

A groan was followed by a moan.

While Thornbird worked the snips, he asked, "How did you catch them?"

My reply was honest. "Dumb, blind luck."

Forty minutes later, I slumped into Thornbird's cruiser and we left Kaiser. The truck jack went with us, too. Hopefully, the Kilbys would wake up in a couple hours behind bars with only migraines and cuts and a few bumps. Their truck was impounded. As we rambled by, my car didn't look vandalized. Thornbird concentrated not to exceed the posted speed limit, 45 miles per hour. I hadn't told him yet about Ralph Phillip's apparent flight. Thornbird activated the Dakota Farms crossbar by a remote control. Stanley Pettigrew, head under hat, snoozed inside the stone hut.

"Holy Mother. What a slacker." Driving through, Thornbird blasted his horn but Stanley didn't budge.

Thornbird halted on Mount Olympus, but before I could roll out, he grabbed my sleeve. "Mr. Johnson, we're not in too much hot water are we?" he asked.

I smiled. "Cops do dirty work, too."

"What if the Kilbys sue me for false arrest, unlawful detainment, police misconduct, or civil rights violation? Remember Rodney King and the L.A. riots?"

"False arrest? What jury would buy that? It doesn't ring true," I said. "Just do the Miranda bit once they regain consciousness."

"I know their relatives," Thornbird went on. "The Kilbys are so spiteful Hell won't have them."

Fatigue vapor-locked behind my eyes. "Man, I'm ninety-nine percent gone. Are we done here?"

"I'll let you go," said Thornbird. "Good night, Mr. Johnson."

"Night, Thornbird."

After getting up late the next morning, I didn't relax showering in the scalding water. Toweled off lobster red, my nerve endings were on fire. Screw the shave. My chin stayed gray and grizzled. After plucking clean clothes off a closet shelf, I dressed with alacrity. With the 9 mil wedged against my back, I tromped downstairs to the chef's kitchen.

The spread included eggs, jam, toast, bacon, and croissants. My bile was still pretty consumed with digesting last night's events. No Mrs. Taliaferro or anyone else for that matter was about. Rachel, I suspected, had perked the Columbian coffee. Two cups, hot and black, steamed down the hatch while I planned out my morning. Ralph was a quandary that could wait.

For now, I'd roust out the new trainer, James Martin. Hellbent without fences spelled disaster. Also, Martin might spin me a theory or two about Ralph's whereabouts. On the patio, I greeted a blustery and overcast morning, my first in Kaiser. A north wind lofted the Martha Stewart umbrellas into the air. A few cold raindrops pelted my cheeks. The bracing air portended snowfall as I hiked down to the stables.

Again, the stable floors gleamed. Out a side window, I saw skewbald horses clustered in a nearby field. I then spotted the new trainer, a tall and lean man, hitching a blue tarp over a hay roll behind the breeding shed. The stiffening wind made his job almost impossible. I would've volunteered to pitch in except that I'd fallen behind on my paperwork. I retreated to a warm utility room and screwed in a socket bulb over a wickerwork chair to sit down and read.

This case's highlight reel had been clanking in my subconscious since the small, wee hours. Clanking, I grimaced, was the operative word. Every detective is hired to flex his acute powers of observation. Rock, mineral, vegetable—everything over which his camera lens for eyes panned was recorded for later use. Ninety-eight percent was superfluous, footage destined for the cutting room floor. Select scenes, however, interested me. Something I'd noticed here in the stable before interested me. What...what was it? I saw the inner screen go blank on me.

I unfolded Emily Taliaferro's autopsy report, taken from beneath my shirt, and absorbed it word for word.

KAISER COUNTY AUTOPSY REPORT—SUMMARY ONLY
OFFICE OF MEDICAL EXAMINER
NAME: EMILY MAYFLOWER TALIAFERRO
Case No: 4F-2000
Address: 666 Dakota Farms Road, Kaiser, Virginia 23819-0014
Age: 15 (DOB: 4/30/84)
Height: 5'4"
Weight: 104 lbs.
Gender: F

I hereby certify that on the fourteenth day of April 2000 an autopsy on the body of Emily Mayflower Taliaferro was performed at the Kaiser County Medical Examiner's Office in Kaiser, Virginia and upon investigation of the essential facts concerning the circumstances of the death, I am of the opinion that the cause of death was as follows.

Estimate Death Date: 4/13/00 between 7:30 AM & 8:30 AM (No later than 9:00 AM)

Detailed reports are on file in M.E.'s Office. (NOTE to Sheriff: Reports are archived on microfiche three months after the autopsy.)

EXTERNAL EXAMINATION - SUMMARY:

Sheriff Pettigrew presented the unembalmed body in a zippered blue plastic bag. At the time of my examination, the body was entirely clothed in a red nylon blouse, ecru jodhpurs, and black leather riding boots.

Jodhpurs were ruined, 2-3" horizontal tears in both knees. The lady's undergarments included bra and panties, both white and cotton 100% cloth.

The contents of her pockets pulled inside out had been vouchered by the Sheriff's Department, thus nothing was inventoried. No purse or other personal effects accompanied the body, as well.

I next determined the body was that of a normally developed, well-nourished, well-hydrated Caucasian female at the stated age of 15. (NOTE: Only seventeen days shy of her 16th birthday!) I also observed a fixed lividity in her face, neck, and chest regions.

The scalp had lank (9-11 inches) blonde hair secured in place by a black velvet scrunchie. The body hair was female, shaved under the armpits and over both legs to mid-thigh as I would expect. I detected a body talc powder and a feminine deodorant. No analysis was run to ascertain brand names. I also detected minor abrasions on the palm heels of both hands and cuts on both kneecaps. These type markings on hands and knees are consistent with those caused by a violent fall. Soil matching samples collected where the body was discovered was also identified on the hands and knees.

Fingernails were natural and intact, without polish.

I reported these preliminary findings to Sheriff Pettigrew (8:35 AM) via telecon. I was advised by him to proceed with normal protocol.

I found the skull symmetrical and trounced on the right side to the extent summarized below. The eyes were closed; irides were blue and pupils even.

Two prescription contact lenses were removed. Both upper and lower teeth were natural. They showed four cavities recently filled (within last 12 months?).

Dental records will verify further identification of victim, if so ordered.

(NOTE: This office recommends such action.)

The 36" breasts were young female and displayed no lesions.

Abdomen appeared flat; pelvis was intact. External genitalia were female. The hymen was not intact. No trauma, internal or external, was discovered at the anal area, over the thighs, or over the buttocks.

Size of uterus was as expected. Spine was healthy with slight right scoliosis in lumbar region. Recent back X-rays at Kaiser Hospital further detail this condition.

I detected no body piercings, tattoos, birthmarks, blemishes, moles, or other remarkable markings. No amputations or deformities were present.

A 10K gold adjustable toe ring was seen on the right foot, no other jewelry encountered.

DESCRIPTION OF INJURIES - SUMMARY:

There was one serious injury to the body, in addition to minor injuries already cited. Over the right hemisphere of the head, a preponderance of cranium was crushed evidencing extensive bone splintering and fragmentation. A grayish brain matter was also external to the injury.

INTERNAL EXAMINATION - SUMMARY:

I uncovered no evidence of a struggle, forced or consensual. There was, however, evidence of recent intercourse.

Stage of rigor mortis coupled with body temperature recorded at site of discovery indicated the time of death to be on 4/13/00 between 7:30 AM and 8:30 AM

TOXICOLOGICAL STUDIES:

My toxicological studies detected no presence of drugs (legal or illegal) or alcohol. Traces of nicotine were analyzed from both lungs.

CAUSE OF DEATH:

I ruled the cause of death as craniocerebral trauma inflicted by a blunt instrument to the right half of the head. This trauma was consistent with that inflicted by a shod horse hoof with which this Coroner's Office has had previous experience observing in equestrian-related fatalities.

Final findings of this autopsy were communicated via telecon to Sheriff Pettigrew on 4/14/00 @ 9:30 AM to expedite his investigation.

/s/ Dr. P. Windwood, M.D., MEDICAL EXAMINER
April 14, 2000 Date
Kaiser County, Virginia

Some interesting items came to light. Case in point was "a blunt instrument," an overrated phrase Medical Examiners were fond of sprinkling in reports. Simply put, the M.E. couldn't put his finger on what the actual murder weapon was. A horse couldn't premeditate murder. Did the M.E., then, deem Emily's death as an Act of God? A sour smile pricked the corners of my mouth. The sheriff had been correct. A horse was an irrational beast but so were many people. Far too damn many.

While stuffing the report in my pocket, my gaze alighted on the columnar ashtray stand. Alarm bells went off in me. The blunt instrument! Grunting, I went over to it. My pair of hay gloves preserved any prints as I lifted the stand. A sand ballast welded inside its black body added heft—ten or twelve pounds, in total. Its three-quarter inch lips top and bottom were spotless—no dried blood, flesh, or hair. I chunked it as an impromptu battering ram. Yep.

How to test my theory? I remembered asking Thornbird about using Luminol. Sure. That's where his help came in. Specks of Emily's blood would prove the ashtray stand had been used to dash out her brains.

"Cool antique."

The tall, spare man doffed the mesh cap and exposed a windburn, long face. He could vouch for white even with his skin hued like a pecan shell. His hangdog smile was benign. From the get-go, I liked him, a rarity for me.

"Martin." His right hand sought mine. "James Martin." It wasn't until then that I noticed his left coat sleeve hung slack and empty.

"Johnson, Frank. I'm doing a side job for Mrs. Taliaferro. Just a temporary gig."

"The private snoop," he said. "Ralph told me to expect you."

"You and Ralph are friends?" I phrased it as a question.

"Not exactly," said Martin. "We were in FFA, that is Future Farmers of America, together."

"Can you explain Ralph's going off into the wild blue yesterday?"

Martin stuffed on the mesh cap. "To get away from his wife, probably. Rachel's bossy, finicky, and bitchy—all her good qualities. You want the bad ones?"

I changed gears. "You're still learning the ropes here?"

"Some. With this killer gallivanting about, I've had damn little peace of mind."

"You know that Hellbent crashed his corral."

Martin spat. "Yes, I know about it. I've been running my legs ragged since before dawn, looking for him."

"Get out of here, man. I spotted the horse last night," I said.

"You spotted him? Where?"

"A fair piece up Kaiser Road." We made toward the door. "You'll have to drive because my car is on the rag."

"Lemme gas up my Jeep," Martin pointed. "I'll meet you by the garage."

~

Having returned in my car on its dinky spare, I'd an inkling Mrs. Taliaferro was waiting for my report. I didn't want to give it to her. Martin and I had had no success. Hellbent was a figment. Fresh hoof prints were visible in the field where I'd wrecked. We hunted both sides of the road but with no luck. Martin's fury had invented a new art of cursing. I loitered in my car watching him now hobble off to the stables, the armless sleeve whipping in the wind like a kite's ragtag tail.

A soft light shone in her bedroom window. My engine was idling and the heat trickled out. Gusts rocked the car. My client waited inside my least favorite mansion. Gloom presided there. Let her wait. The heater blower switch was jammed to its maximum setting. Still cold, I hoisted myself out of the car.

A frigid blast slapped me across the face. A buffalo romp propelled me to the patio. Twin doors rolled away and I surged through. Mrs. Taliaferro was setting out a centerpiece bowel of ornamental wax fruit.

"Johnson, quick." She motioned. "Come and sit by the fire."

This morning put her in ash-colored slacks and a matching turtleneck sweater. They accentuated aspects a fortyish woman such as herself might pronounce as a mature beauty. I'd have to concur. The den had a flower garden pleasance. Potpourri, I believe, was the correct term for what I smelled. The wallpaper was a jaundiced yellow, reminding me, a history buff, of Walter Reed, Cuba, and mosquitoes.

Oil portraits of Taliaferro champion horses stood under the track lighting. With the wrought iron poker, Mrs. Taliaferro rearranged snow-white birch logs sheeting sparks up the flue. Satisfied, she added the fire screen and we subsided to our respective recliner and hassock. Her head dropped back and her eyes scoped the ceiling.

"What do you have for me?" she asked at length. Her hands choked the chair's armrests as if anticipating the worst.

Our last chat when I'd badmouthed her daughter had ended rocky and I relied on my tact to make this round go smoother. The room's warmth, however, goaded my restlessness. After rising to the mantle, I braced my hands to lean over and contemplate the flames before saying: "After busting my tail for twenty-four hours, the most I can tell you is that Ralph's a crook."

Mrs. Taliaferro didn't act peeved. "How so?"

"He tipped off a pickpocket in Jetsam to fleece me but I spoiled it."

"Perhaps Ralph fears your reprisal. Maybe that explains his erratic behavior to run away."

I shrugged even if hearing her say it made me also wonder. "Does Rachel know anything? Can I go up and talk to her?

"Oh no, you don't," said Mrs. Taliaferro. "She's asleep. I gave her several tranquilizers. Nembutal. Have you any thing more?"

"Just to show you Emily's autopsy report."

Mrs. Taliaferro clawed the pages from my grasp. "Where did you obtain this? This is the first I've seen of it."

"My source isn't important. Two items jump out. Item One, the M.E. isn't one hundred percent sold on what clobbered Emily. Item Two, your daughter"—at this point, I hesitated but couldn't soft-pedal it—"was not a virgin."

Mrs. Taliaferro's mild reaction wasn't expected. Her look was clear-eyed, her cadence sure. "My daughter, I concede, was a popular if not vivacious girl. Until I've had a quiet juncture to evaluate this"—her coral-lacquered fingernail tapped the autopsy report—"we'll leave Item Two where it lies, Mr. Johnson."

Mrs. Taliaferro slunk over the yellow carpet to a cocktail cabinet. She lit up an extra long, slim filterless, plucked from the cigarette tray. "I'm intrigued. Fill me in about Item One."

"I saw an ashtray stand at the stables. Black top and a silver body, it's made of steel."

"What of it?" Mrs. Taliaferro snicking off ash missed the saucer held in her other hand to land on the carpet. Smoke irritated my nostrils. Give me a 3-pound lump hammer and I'd smashed out the windows. A truism says reformed smokers are the most militant anti-smokers.

"Has it always been here?" I asked her.

Her cloudy eyes, trending off to gray-green, leveled on me. "You still haven't told me why it interests you."

"Solid and heavy, it was ideal for faking Emily's murder to look like a horse's hoof had mauled her."

After another drag, she expelled greasy smoke. Her eyes boiled. "Yes indeed," she said. "It's just as I said all along. Now, can you substantiate it and catch the murderer?"

"Possibly as soon as tonight with Thornbird's expertise."

"The sheriff has no qualms with you using his deputy Thornbird?"

"The sheriff is away at a convention in Roanoke."

Mrs. Taliaferro buried her gaze in the fire's blue coals for a lengthy pause. I had a strong sense she was relieved and elated at hearing about my gainful headway. The next moment, however, she peered up with an air of abject weariness. "Martin said Emily's stallion blew through his fence."

I nodded. "We've put out the word to the other farms to be on the lookout."

"Emily gave that horse too much love," said Mrs. Taliaferro.

"Why did you let her ride him?" I ventured to ask her.

"Emily was my wild child." Mrs. Taliaferro smiled, the wistful sadness too painful to see. "Without a father, she was a handful. Who was I to stifle her sportive nature?"

Mrs. Taliaferro's responses seemed contradictory. My solving this case, however, didn't hinge on following her convoluted logic. To me, Emily wasn't overly complicated. She was another spoiled rich tomboy. Running balls out on a bangtail racehorse was just another thrill raring to go. How many thrills had this girl experienced before turning sixteen? Probably more than I would in three lifetimes.

"The bottom line is my daughter got a raw deal." Clucking her tongue, Mrs. Taliaferro crushed out her half-smoked cigarette. Her next question blooped from out of left field. "Johnson, doesn't our state have a death penalty for capital murder cases? You should know something like that off the top of your head."

"Capital punishment in Virginia was reinstated in '76," I said. "Executions resumed in August of '82."

"Is the electric chair the institutional method of execution?"

"No ma'am."

"Then how is it done?"

"Lethal injection strapped down in an eight-point restraint on a gurney."

"The day Emily's killer is executed will bring me great comfort."

"I truly doubt it, ma'am."

"What? My high-priced attorneys say I can attend should I choose. I will be there, too. You will accompany me."

"Do what you have to do, but I won't be there."

"I extra goddamn will...where are you headed now, Johnson?"

"To buy a set of new tires," I said, not trusting myself to speak any further to her. I retrieved Emily's autopsy report on my way out of the cheerless room.

Crossing the yard, I saw Ralph's rototiller in a half-tilled plot. I walked away riled. You couldn't talk to Mrs. Taliaferro without argument. Bandying words with her was tiresome.

What did she know? The specter of potassium cyanide mainlined into a death row inmate's veins had never placated my clients.

Jarrett, Virginia. Both pale pink dawns I had arrived there at the insistent pleas of the victims' families. Both trips set a chill at my bone down to the marrow. Kroger's in town supplied me headache pills. Doped up, I shot through a daisy chain of death punishment protestors holding a candlelight vigil. They loomed up like George Romero's zombies, yelling and banging on my car.

The facility reeked of a coppery disinfectant. Pine-Sol, I believe. I can't whiff it today without reliving the next few terrible minutes. Once we were seated in the witness stall, the starchy red curtains fell away. Through wire-reinforced glass, our peepshow unfolded. Dirty light bathed the gurney, guards, and doomed inmate.

At the last second, both killers had peered over, arched a perverse eyebrow, and winked at us. My skin crawled as the needle pricked them. Specialists worked the plungers to release the lethal cocktail. The countdown was ticked off. Smiling devil-may-care, both killers slumped asleep in a smattering of seconds. Death was that quick.

"At long last, some peace of mind," a distraught father rasped. I wasn't convinced.

An old lady grabbing my arm supported herself. "For Christ's sweet sake, it's done," she said.

I shook her off, saying, "Your cross to bear, not mine."

Her eyes crackled with hate. "You're such a judgmental bastard."

Twice I kept my eyes open at the vigil but the others shut their eyes. After life force was cancelled, the slack inmate drooled as a rosy-butted infant. From a PI's standpoint, the two executions did bring closure. Killer exterminated, report typed, and invoice posted. Last check payment was received, endorsed, and banked. Wham, bam, and thank you ma'am.

Now at the bottom of Mrs. Taliaferro's hill, the gate yielded. I crept through and poked along at a tortoise pace toward Kaiser. The blown out tire laying in my trunk had worn down to show its bias belts. Two of the other three tires looked in the same condition. I had to break down and buy new replacements.

The father-and-son auto shop in Kaiser was an erstwhile Howard Johnson motel gutted to create three bays with mechanical lifts. A free potholder came with each 10-gallon fill up. A chalk signboard advertised fireworks, propane tanks, and those silly whistling devices that went on bumpers to repel deer. A play-in-progress Parchisi board lay on a card table.

The old man, a black cigar stub unlit between stubby, brown dentures, got up and scribbled me a ticket. He tacked on a bogus towing fee. His high, narrow shoulders jacked up and down while speaking. "That way you can chisel your insurance company for a few extra bucks," he said in a sly growl.

"Those greedy sons of bitches," I said. "Do you take personal checks?"

"If it's from a local bank and doesn't bounce, sure."

"Check the oil, too. I'm low. Now, is the hospital in walking distance?"

The old man wheezed, "You'll burn some shoe leather. Go six blocks down Main, one over on Forrest. The yellow brick building crops up on your right. Why don't you pay me now?"

I laughed. "My health is fine. I'll be back in a couple hours."

The green shards of shattered Muscatel bottles littered the sidewalks. They crunched under my boots. Gazing globes reflected thatch brown lawns. A pair of towhead girls in bright coats and scarves jumped rope in a shingly driveway. They ignored me. I kept throwing glances over my shoulder. No devils chased me. Lo and behold, the old man was right. A no-frills, yellow building did care for Kaiser's infirm on its two floors. A knot of smokers in surgical greens guarded the emergency exit. A parked ambulance having a flat tire earned my askance look.

The lack of a metal detector didn't challenge my wearing a gun inside. A Candy Striper maneuvered a cart brimming with magazines, crossword puzzles, and rock candy. Ammonia fumes destroyed germs. Visiting hours weren't until 2 PM, but I came to scratch up information. A glass divider had a muskrat hole through which to speak. The injured clerk wearing an immobilizing halo on her head looked how Herman Munster did recharging his neck electrodes.

"Johnson. Detective for the State Police." My PI license pressed to the glass didn't wow her half as much as the 9 mil's black stock I let flash.

"Yes sir?"

"Our dispatcher logged a report of a rape victim brought in late last night."

With robotic grace, the clerk half-pivoted to her computer and plinked her fingertips on rows of keys. "I had a Jet-Ski accident, in case you're wondering, detective. Okay now, what's here? Oh yes, our victim's name is Carole Dawson?"

"Dawson. Yep, that's it. What's her latest condition?"

A firm hand settled on my right shoulder. "Stable," replied a young man.

The clerk beetled her brows. "Yes, her prognosis is excellent, I see. Poor baby."

"Obliged, ma'am," I said. "And thank you, Deputy Sheriff Thornbird."

"Mr. Johnson, we've got a problem," said Thornbird. His pupils were broad with icy fright.

"Not in here," I said. "Take it outside."

We scurried over the sidewalk, his cruiser coming into eyeshot. Thornbird's mussed uniform looked as if he'd worn it mud wrestling. His nervousness was jazzing up my own jitters.

"Those Kilbys are making noises." Thornbird gestured like a college basketball coach. "I'm at my rope's end with them."

"Like what kind of noises?"

"Lawyer talk about illegal arrest and violation of their civil rights."

"Have they gotten in bed with an attorney?"

"They sure as Hell demand one."

I swallowed. The confidence in so abundant force the night before was fast deserting me. "But they were facedown drunk."

"Last night isn't a complete blank," said Thornbird. "Their memory is lucid, especially the part about you blackjacking them to see stars."

"Let me go rap with them," I said.

Thornbird sighed. "Is that such a smart idea?"

"Are any of your ideas better?"

"What ideas?"

"Right."

We hopped into his cruiser and made for the sheriff's office. Inside, the Kilby cousins lounged on monkish bunks in adjoining cells. Black scabs had crusted over their knobby cuts. Used breakfast trays lay on medieval sinks. Commodes were holes punched in the concrete floor like I'd last seen on a case while in Turkey. A foulness dredged my sinuses. Their glares were forks in my eyes. The outer steel door banging to a close echoed.

I smiled. "So, you hamsters want a lawyer, huh?"

"We want to exercise our constitutional rights," said the tall Kilby.

The short one smacked his food tray sent crashing to the floor. "Some-damn-body ripped off our wallets and money, too."

My sudden step crunched a roach. "Could be you lost them in transit."

The tall Kilby levered up the middle finger. "Perch and rotate," he said, exhibiting subpar people skills.

"I see things like this." My words were muttered in the event Thornbird's ear was planted to the outer steel door. "You nut bags did a big crime and will do a big time."

"What? Hard time at the super-max?" said the short Kilby. "Contact our attorney, Elmer Peabody in Middleburg."

"Super-max? You never mentioned that, cousin."

I continued. "If you trash the Deputy Sheriff or me, I'll advise my friend, a federal narc, about your marijuana farms."

The threat cracked up the tall Kilby. "What marijuana farms?"

"The pot patches in the piney woods north of Middleburg." It was an out-and-out bluff but one that scored big. "Your shitheel pal Adam led me to them. Feast your eyes. Does this map jog your memories?"

The Kilbys focused on the piece of paper in my hand that I'd found in the woods. Alarm wilted their smirks.

"That money spigot will plug up and run dry." I snapped my fingers. "Quick as that."

The runty one blessed with medium brains bristled. "But nobody benefits that way."

I took it one step further. "Yep. Plus a narcotics rap will fatten your prison stretch. Those needle tracks I see on your forearms will be the Government's Exhibit A."

The tall Kilby rubbed the scabs. "You gave us these. Something sharp stuck us. What was it?"

The runt wised up. "Okay. The arrest went down like Thornbird writes it if you forget what's on that damn map. A quid pro quo."

"Don't fall for it," said his cousin.

"Aw, quit your whining." The short Kilby's glance withered the tall one into sitting on his bunk.

"We've brokered us a jailhouse deal," I said before shouting, "Ho, Thornbird. On the gate. I'm coming out!"

Chapter 11

Thursday 8 AM, April 20th

Searching for something, Thornbird picked up the Yellow Pages, then dropped it on the noisy space heater. "Where's a lousy dictionary when you need one?"

"What are you endeavoring to spell, Faulkner?" I asked.

"Incarcerate," he said.

"Type it as 'jailed'," I told him. "J-A-I-L-E-D."

I switched on the desk's gooseneck lamp and directed its rays on Emily's autopsy report. I yawned into my fist and pondered it. I wasn't thrilled by what I pondered. The M.E. Windwood had detected no signs of sexual assault. That hosed my bid to pin her murder on the Kilbys.

"How did you get that damn report?" asked Thornbird.

"Your boss promised it to me," was my half-truth. "Is this Windwood in town?"

Thornbird spooled out the typed page. "No, he's in Saint Pete fishing. Joyner handled Pierre's autopsy."

"Yeah but Windwood did Emily's," I said. "Is he competent?"

Thornbird's voice changed. "Should be. He's retired from the LAPD before hitching on here."

"That's a ringing endorsement," I replied as the telephone squawked. Listening to the receiver, Thornbird's baby face grew grimmer.

"I owe you one, Susie." He cradled the receiver. "That was the lab. Carole Dawson's rape kit came back inconclusive."

"Can't be. Didn't they test her clothing?"

"They just started on that part. If anything positive develops, Susie will give me a holler," said Thornbird. "To close the loop, she's requesting the Kilbys' DNA."

"A lab technician can cut open a vein," I said. "They've already agreed to it."

"How did you talk the Kilbys into that?"

"Never mind," I said. "My détente with them in the pokey is a fiction, too."

"Right, it never happened. Here. Give this a once over." Thornbird slid their arrest report over to me. The brunt of it was gospel except that I'd morphed into Thornbird. While out on a routine patrol, Thornbird had bagged the Kilbys red-handed at the local party hang-out.

"It's your magnum opus," I said. "After the vampire leaves, the Kilbys can contact their lawyer, a Peabody from Middleburg."

"Without a positive on the semen, we're dead in the water." Thornbird's dejection was heartbreaking to hear.

"You have Carole Dawson. She'll leave any jury crying. She's your ace in the hole."

"What was she even doing there?"

"Carole dated the runty Kilby. Too young, she didn't know any better."

"Date rape," he said reflexively.

The heat of rage hardened my words. "Hardly. Gangbang. It was going down like the Stephanie Roper case." Thornbird was too young to remember, but Stephanie Roper had been a co-ed stranded with car trouble on a hick road in rural Maryland. This was in April 1982. Wrong place at the wrong time. A couple of good ole boys, stoned out of their minds, gave her a ride. A ride from Hell. Later discovered raped, tortured, and murdered, she gave serious impetus to the victims' rights movement. Every year I kicked in a few dollars to the Stephanie Roper Foundation. Restitution, by God, had to begin somewhere.

"Okay, I stand corrected." Thornbird reshuffled his notes. "I spoke to Carole's grandma downstate in Narrows. Her parents are divorced. She lives with her dad and sisters. He's on travel, a plumbing supplies sales route."

"Good sleuthing. This morning go interview Carole. Speak to her attending nurse and doctors. Keep in mind that you're building an airtight case. Be thorough. Document out the wazoo. Establish a chain of custody for any evidence from the hospital to the forensics lab. This bust has to stick."

"Where can I reach you?" His query verged on panic.

"Try the auto shop or Joyner at the morgue." I stood to leave. "But with or without me, you're doing fine here, Thornbird."

"The Shelton homicide and now this gangbang," said Thornbird. "When will it end?"

"When the crow shits," I told him over my shoulder.

Sunshine had broken through the morning gray sky—it augured for bright, shiny days that deep down I didn't believe. For one thing, this spring was a tease. Warm one minute, cold the next. This sweatshirt in these cold temperatures felt threadbare. Sheila then jostled my thoughts. Sally's Nails had been taking morning appointments for a few hours. Later just maybe I'd manufacture enough guilt to drive over and see her.

My crate at the auto shop, stripped to scarred rims, teetered up on a lift. The old man had his weekday gopher hustling to an auto parts warehouse in old Chantilly. My foreign model, always the anomaly, required a special order. Mechanics had described my car as a mutant Yugo or Vega, built and designed best for a .44 Mag bullet planted in its engine crankcase. Its odometer had frozen on 32,986, but whether that was on the two hundred or three hundred thousand cycle, I'd no way of telling.

Kaiser's morgue—a squat, square cinderblock building under a corrugated tin roof—was a chip shot behind the hospital. Under a carport, a cavernous, black hearse shiny as patent leather doted on the dead. I obeyed the sign: Ring Chimes For Admittance. A man, lips parched and hairline in a widow's peak, slid the steel door wide. A welter of salty, refrigerated air whooshed over me. The bray of an air compressor chugged within. He bade me to enter.

His Hush Puppies flounced over a checked linoleum floor to unplug the compressor. My ears still rang in the new quiet. Sensing my discomfort, he shuttled me into a side office. Suspended on piano wire from the ceiling was a model Fokker triplane. I sneezed at the salt-cured ham odor mingled with his aftershave and formaldehyde. He cranked up the dimmer switch.

"You must be Joyner," I said to his partial nod. "And I'm Johnson."

"I know who you are. The renegade PI. You came for Pierre's autopsy report."

"Should I hop on your desk and bark—oof, oof—like a walrus for it?"

"Why did my headache just migrate lower?"

"Hey, an oral status will do, doc. For openers, was the murder weapon a .25?"

"Yes, Pierre was killed by a .25. At close range no further than you are to me now."

"That's it?" I regarded him. "Your evidence is pretty skimpy."

"It happens. One trivial matter puzzles me." Joyner withdrew an envelope from a cubbyhole. Photos of Pierre's murder scene scattered across his desktop.

I picked up the top one. Their vivid colors emphasized the startling clarity like viewing an afternoon soap opera.

"Check out Pierre's death mask. It expresses horror and shock. Okay, I'd expect that. Yet there's something more. Very subtle, but it's there nonetheless."

"You've lost me. What?"

"My trained eye sees the expression of betrayal. Grin, go ahead. Seldom am I wrong, though."

"You propose that Pierre knew his killer," I said. "And could've cursed him in the last minutes that he circled the drain?"

Joyner licked his lips. "Some true blue pal, huh?"

"Did the .25 slug you pulled out identify the gun's make or model?"

"Nothing exotic. A Raven semi-automatic."

"A single shot through the heart," I said. "An expert's aim."

"Or a beginner's luck," said Joyner. "Interesting wound. It jammed up a coronary valve. Got a minute? The cadaver is here on a slab, its skull sawed apart." He pointed a scalpel with an inviting smile to the door.

"No, your word is good as gold," I replied. "When's the funeral?"

"Mrs. Taliaferro said the late Mr. Shelton preferred a cremation. Memorial is here Saturday 9 AM"

"Be thorough, then. We can't autopsy ashes. Now, about that report, when?"

Joyner popped his knuckles one at a time before wiggling his fingers. "As soon as my hunt-and-peck job on the typewriter is done. I've lobbied my superiors for a PC. To date, no cigar."

"I'm looking for Ralph Phillips."

"Phillips? Try Dakota Farms," said Joyner. "He's their Handy Andy."

"Except Ralph yesterday took off for parts unknown.

"Then check the inside rail at the Jetsam Racetrack."

"My search there also came up empty," I replied.

Head shaking, Joyner's eyes lifted to a wall clock. "You got me, then. Oops. My instruments are ready to come out the autoclave. Excuse me, please."

"I'll stay in touch."

The mid-morning dark clouds had bagged the earlier sunshine. My stride quickened. Angry strides, too.This case still had a throttlehold on me. Hellbent rushed pell-mell through fields like theories pinballed inside my head. I stepped on the cracks in the sidewalk. Impulsive, brooding, brawny Ralph pulled at my thoughts. I recalled that Pierre's wallet was never recovered.

Desperate gamblers killed for money to pay off loan sharks. Rachel could shed further light on him. The .25 handgun. Couldn't my Richmond friend Darl Adkins compile a record from the database of local gun owners? All the good citizens here would volunteer their .25s for ballistics testing. One bright spot encouraged me. Sheriff Pettigrew was out of my hair for the foreseeable future.

"Excuse me, squire."

A derelict emerged from behind a soft drink machine, holding a straightened coat hangar in one hand. He'd been chinking it in the coin slots to dislodge any loose coins. He outstretched a scabby hand. Laceless golf shoes encased his skinny ankles while a pepper-and-salt saddle blanket sagged off his shoulders. Damn if he didn't reek like a nag put out to pasture, too. I drew out what money papered my billfold—a few tens, one five, and perhaps a dozen ones. Déjà vu stopped me—I'd dealt with his kind too many times before so I put back my wallet. "I'm going to try something else instead."

"Huh?" Crooked fingers twitching, his outstretched hand still waited.

"You'd better come with me," I said.

The derelict's eyebrows bristled in bewilderment but he did as told. The heels to his golf shoes, his toes exposed, shuffled over the cinder-packed path through a vacant lot. His knee-length overcoat lacked buttons. He gloried in being a bum. A shave and shower might make restore his dignity. We paraded in single file to the sidewalk and crossed the street to the general store. Bystanders gave us a few askance stares.

"You make like the Sphinx and sit on these steps." My command was stern.

"Why should I?" he wanted to know.

"Because my charity won't be guzzled away on Mad Dog 20-20," I said.

"Taint so," he said. "I've never even been inside a liquor store."

"Just sit tight anyway."

Perched on a wood stool, the old storekeeper was sorting spark-plugs at the end of a cluttered aisle. "Johnson, it's good to see you. What's going on?"

"Just taking care of business," I said.

I threw a pair of jeans, a long-sleeved shirt, a bindle of socks and underwear into a shopping cart. For footwear, the black Dingo boots proved serviceable. I grabbed sundry men's toiletries from their bins.

"Bag 'em and ring me up," I said.

"Aren't you going to the wall for that bum?" asked the old store-keeper.

I ignored his comment. "What's the total?"

"With tax, $198.43."

"He loves clove cigarettes," the old storekeeper said. "At least that's what he used to shoplift in here."

"This will do us fine," I said.

I toted the grocery bag out the store door and the derelict fell in step behind me. We proceeded to the Kaiser Motel where the derelict again sat on a bench. The day-old newspaper I handed him may as well have been written in Mandarin Chinese. "Look at the pictures," I said.

Inside, I rang for the proprietress. "Single, one night for my guest."

"What guest?" I pointed. She appraised him through the window glass and snapped her licorice gum. "It'll set you back a few dollars. Still interested?"

"I'll cough up a hundred plus your going rate. That includes your making Clem Kadiddle-Hopper presentable in public."

She dickered. "Plus fifty for your messy room."

"Fine. Half now, the balance later." I nopped. "Toss some gainful employment his way, too. He needs the work."

"Damn tooting," said the proprietress. "Just because you've got a crack in your ass, it doesn't make you a cripple. My gutters could stand rehanging with 8-inch screws."

I dashed out a check for her. The last sight I had was her marching the befuddled derelict to his doom. He could've hailed from one of a hundred villages in Virginia, mine included. Only then did I wonder what his name was and if he would've given me an alias, one of a half-dozen he'd likely concocted.

Back at the auto shop, I saw that my car still sat atop the mechanical lift. Four new tires were stacked by a long-handled broom. The old man and his pit crew were at the front fender to a 1970 demolition red Camaro sporting a spoiler, hood scoop, and mag wheels. Its customized 427-cubic inch engine gave them hard ons.

"If it's not too much hassle, can you mount my tires?" I asked the old man.

"Hey, chill. I'm on top of it, bud," he replied. "Grab some bench in the customer lounge. Pour yourself a hot cup of java. It's on me. Check out the flick on TNT. I'll be in right behind you."

The offer of coffee turned out to be one of creosote. A Nellie Chaise action film was airing. I stomached watching it through long yawns. Who was she kidding with that lived in smile? All looks and no talent, she'd fit right in starring on sitcoms. Rocking back in my chair, I saw through the glass door a kid busy bubble balancing my new tires. That was a shade better than no progress. A few minutes later, the old man ambled in, passing me a limp-wrist wave.

"Mister, I apologize for that delay," he said. "Your stock arrived ten minutes ago."

"The mechanic just brought my car around."

"Settle up then and you're off."

I stopped before leaving the parking lot, and stole a peek under my hood. Sure enough, the oil cap needed tightening but the hoses and cables were all attached. My radiator was topped off with green antifreeze. Brake fluid level was adequate. I prowled around to each new wheel, knelt down, and fingered the lug nuts before pulling a tire pressure check. Two lug nuts on each of three tires were loose as a goose. I opened the trunk and snugged down the spare tire and the Kilby's truck jack now mine. Good service anymore was a thing of the past.

When I scooted over to the sheriff's office, Thornbird's Olds was in its customary berth. I went inside and saw Thornbird sitting behind his desk scribbling furiously on a legal tablet.

"Did you chase down the Dawson girl's story?" I asked.

"I'm writing it up now. You nailed it right. Carole was out on a date with the runt," said Thornbird. "They stopped at a service station over in Delaplane for his cigarettes and hooked up with the other Kilby. Marooned, he said he needed a lift home. Being sweet and naïve, naturally Carole didn't object. They'd cooked it all up in advance, no doubt."

"Next the family fun revved up," I said to complete the sordid tale. "Until I came along and jammed their spokes."

"Carole was awful edgy and upset," said Thornbird.

"The genuine shock has yet to touch home."

"A prison sentence is too good for the Kilbys," said Thornbird. "They should be drawn and quartered."

"Justice sometimes has a screwy way of working out. Did they autograph their confession you typed?"

"Oh yeah. They gave up their blood, too. Their lawyer still hasn't showed his face."

"Evidently they're not the fullest deck of cards."

"Is your car back on the beam?"

"Yep. Ralph Phillips had bolted for the border, in case you didn't know it."

"I already got of an earful. Mrs. Taliaferro called here. Hysterical, too."

"Can you drive out tonight with the Luminol," I asked.

"Sure. Have you hit on something solid?" asked Thornbird.

"Maybe yes, maybe no," I said. "See you later."

I couldn't rationalize why I drove there, but when I did, Sally's Nails was a beehive. Rapping a knuckle on the plate glass, I signed for Sheila. Seeing me, she kissed her fingertip and blew it to me. She situated a blue-haired lady to roast underneath a hair dyer, and helped Sally to pick up an air-conditioner to fit into a window bracket. She hurried out and joined me. Bent from waist, she checked the wall clock inside by looking below "SALLY'S NAILS" lettered on the glass.

"Franklin Johnson, it's past ten o'clock already."

"Out late last night, I hit a patch of mean road."

Distress tensed her voice. "What happened?"

"Just my usual carnival. First, a flat tire. Second, a runaway horse. Third, a brutal rape."

"A rape?...who in the world?...is she hurt?"

"Carole Dawson. She's coping. In the hospital."

"Does her dad know?...is he out of town?"

"Yeah but Thornbird is handling that side of things," I said.

"Jeez. A rape." Her initial horror centered to anger which radiated in her eyes. "Who did it?"

"The Kilby cousins. They've been arrested. But that isn't all. Ralph Phillips has left his wife and the county it would seem."

"He's a railbird in Jetsam."

"Maybe. Rachel is being awful closed mouth about it."

"Look, my shift here ends at noon," she said. "For now, go interrogate Rachel. Shoo."

Within the next few minutes, new tires had me rolling out of Kaiser. My car no longer listed left while the traction felt smooth and natural. If I billed my client by the mile for all this travel, I'd be worth what's in Fort Knox. She was good for it.

The scratch field where I'd extricated Carole Dawson flew by. Rising bile soured my throat. Inebriated or not, both Kilbys had crossed the line. I wished I'd poured it to them. Was a gunshot in the kneecaps cruel, unusual punishment? It didn't strike me that way.

That triggered another thought about rape which struck closer to home. My kid sister, a flirtatious but somewhat naïve sophomore, had been tending bar in downtown Richmond, Virginia. The bar was eight blocks from Old Dominion University. In the nascent hours one April morning, she thumbed a ride to her garden apartment.

She'd mopped the kitchen floor, fed the canary, and watched a little TV in bed. She dozed off. Apparently all along hiding in the shower, the rapist unsheathed a stag-handled hunting knife. He was an animal. Later I played a minor role in his capture. She picked his snarling lisp out of a police lineup. The rapist went on to serve serious slammer time.

I decided that I needed to take a breather from the violence crashing around me. Maybe by the time I stepped back on the down escalator to Hell, Mrs. Taliaferro and such nut jobs as Ralph Phillips would have bumped each other off. No gladiators would be left standing in the Coliseum. Everybody could go home.

I shook out my new Shakespeare fishing rod and reel. No fishing license was required, I told myself. All I needed was a shady hideyhole along a clean trout stream. Or a farmer's lazy pond made mellow by swooping dragonflies and drinking icy cold Rolling Rock straight out of the green bottle.

A ramshackle country store that I'd passed before rolled up. I stopped and went inside its musty, drafty space. Ceiling fans whirred. A vague smell of vinegar permeated all. Not discouraged, I went out back to the dandelion-studded lawn. A geezer sat on a small cable spool whittling. A taxidermist chainsaw lay underneath his dangling feet. He sucked on a putrid panatela between coughs. He gave me the once-over, smiled a little, crooked grin.

"You look lost," he said. "Is that so?"

A wry humor tinged my reaction. "Just the opposite, pops. I know only too well where I've been. Now I want to try and lose myself."

Lips caved in, his toothless gums were tar black. "How are you fixing to pull off that stunt?" A tongue licked twice. Cough, cough.

My eyes cut back to the gravel lot. "With my fishing hardware still in its shrink wrap."

"A virgin rod, huh?"

The joke wasn't lost on me. "Is it too early in the spring for bass?" I asked.

"Depends. Are you shorebound, casting plastic worms and whatnot?"

"Unless you sell me live minnows or a carton of night crawlers."

"Can't. I did once. No money in it these days. You're more than welcome to use this hoe." His palsy hand showed a sharp angle off from us. "Dig under cow pies. Any earthworms under them are yours free for the taking."

"Obliged, but I better stick with artificial bait."

"Bait casting is best. Experiment some with fake blood worms that are bottom-fished. Where are you headed?"

"Where's the hottest spot?"

He rubbed a wrist across his forehead. "The back eddies of big rocks is where they congregate. The white water is too cold and fast. Plunk in your line there."

"Any catties?"

"Suckerfish, too."

"I don't go in for suckers."

"I didn't reckon you did."

"The eating is no good."

"Yep. Niggers now, they flock to the river for suckers. Up before the crack of dawn, they go in their junkers. Yep. Only the Micks are any dumber. Um, are you Irish by chance?"

"Black Irish," I said.

"They'd be okay in my book."

"That's a relief to hear." I looked but the bigoted bastard didn't react to the barb.

"What's your line?" he asked me.

"PI, private investigator."

"PI? The hell. You work for the high and mighty Mrs. Taliaferro? How much is she paying you?"

"Yes and not near enough. About her daughter, what was the girl's name? Edna? Emelda?"

"Emily." He smirked while correcting me. "She was a real barn burner. Mature for her age, she made the sap rise in this old root. But I shouldn't speak ill of the dead."

"No you shouldn't," I said. "What killed her?"

"Emily was hurled off a stallion, clucked her head, and died."

I spat in mock disgust. "Damn thoroughbreds, wild as jackrabbits."

"No. Wilder. Now the river shallows are chocked with largemouth bass spawning. Some of them top five pounds. You just gut out their roe before frying 'em up."

"Any crappie?" I asked him.

"Indeed, so. They lurk by logs and stumps and overhangs. Bridge pilings are a great fishing place. They're skittish, almost bony as a jack fish. Maybe, maybe not worth your while. I'm not partial to picking out all of their bones."

"Jack fish, eh?"

"Yeah, jack fish, you know. Yay big. Some know them as pickerel. Their saw teeth, sharper than a razor, will rip the skin right off your fingers. Where you from, sonny?"

"South, more toward Central Virginia. Small town is called Pelham."

"Pelham? Named after that sawed off Rebel major?"

"One and the same. He died at Kelly's Ford on the Rappahannock River."

"Any decent fishing there?"

"Best bass hole in the state."

The geezer kneaded gums with his tongue for a small while. "I'll level with you. Your lady boss is probably right. Emily was murdered by somebody clever with horses and rigged it to look like a riding accident."

"She's convinced as much."

"I expect that's now for you to ferret out, ain't it?" The geezer's high-pitched laugh chopped into raspy coughs.

Later, after led on a goose chase by the geezer's inaccurate map, I lay loafing under a railroad track bridge on a riverside. The late afternoon sun having broken through the cloud cover toasted the sandbar under me. It felt good. The rod and reel lay unused beside me. My shoes and socks were off; my pants cuffs rolled up. A fantasy had me stretched out on a tractor inner tube drifting downriver. The lattice of sycamore branches overhead formed a cathedral ceiling. My eyelids shut with the sunlight beating through them created a bloody red scene. That stirred a small fright in me.

The geezer at the country store had said one thing right. Mrs. Taliaferro did fly high and folks indulged her. Then my irritation picked on Lawyer Gatlin, my sometimes employer. Yeah, he was the fool who'd dragooned me into taking on this damn case. Man, oh man, but did my professional attitude ever stink. I stood up and kicked the sand. Duty, no matter how drab and dirty it seemed, compelled me to screw my head back on straight.

My latest logic tracked like this: Emily loved horseback riding. People considered her an accomplished rider, but her horse Hellbent had spooked. The mystery was what or who had thrown that much a scare into the horse? The only way to answer that question was to return to Dakota Farms, the direction I started walking in back to my car.

Chapter 12

Thursday 10 AM, April 20th

Dark clouds bunched up and released torrential rains to thrash my car parked by the garage at Dakota Farms. Could I wait it out? My patience had worn thin enough to see through. As I jumped out of my car, my boot sank in a puddle. I shot through the yard's gate, entered the twin doors, and stomped my boots on the jute-coir mat. Water flew every each way. Thumps echoed off the plaster walls and tile floor.

Click, click, click. Switched on lamps, chandelier, and wall sconces blazed into my eyes. Mrs. Taliaferro listed into my field of vision. Raven hair tamed by a ponytail knocked ten years off her age, but a smidgen of rouge also made her into a sophisticate. Her lips, always grim and tight, were glossed with Vaseline, a fashion model's beauty tip. Shivering in my wet clothes, the discomfort didn't dampen my hyper-vigilance of her.

"Where is Rachel?" I asked her.

"Upstairs asleep," said Mrs. Taliaferro.

"She's the key to finding Ralph."

"Oh, Ralph is off on another binge."

"What? Another binge?"

"Ralph and Rachel always blow a bundle at the racetrack and they're at loggerheads. Every so often, he disappears on a binge. Who knows where? I wish he'd start up his therapy again. But enough about Ralph. Tell me your progress on Emily." Before I could have out a word, she interrupted. "Wait. The log fire in the den will warm and dry you."

Mrs. Taliaferro heeled to stride by me in her sleeveless, look-at-me turtle-necked dress. She couldn't be wearing a damn stitch under it. Her breasts jostled and nipples snapped against the knit fabric. There was, I detected, a lot of woman under it. On Sheriff Pettigrew's visit, she'd crossed that sun-splashed patio for the same cheap erotic effect. She may as well have announced, "You can gawk, but you can't touch." Blatant sexuality, never her most subtle form of manipulation gave her the upper hand among willing men.

"Follow me," she said.

Once more we wandered into her yellow den and settled opposite each other. Despite a log fire crackling on andirons, I saw her quick breaths. The *Middleburg High Life* she lay on the coffee table was open to a steeplechase photo-spread. Fine horses bred on Dakota Farms were her consuming passion. My client re-crossed her knees, smoothed down the knit fabric clinging to her thighs. I didn't miss a stitch.

At length, she sighed. "If Emily were alive, oh, I'd hug her till my poor arms dropped off.

"For one person, you've been through a lot."

"I was a good mother and Emily was a good daughter. Her killer will pay a heavy price, too." Her eyes drilled their icy black intensity at me. You had to believe her. "That's what obsesses, what drives me night and day."

"That's understandable."

"Oh yes."

"You've my sympathy and support."

"Thank you. That means a lot coming from you."

In the next second, breaking down in sobs, Mrs. Taliaferro stumbled over to perch on my chair arm. She dangled both arms around my neck and nested her head on my chest. I didn't mind too awful much her up close and personal. The next moment, however, stripped away the fleeting lust and excitement. Her breath made bitter by gin and rancid by tobacco mugged me. What a turn off. Chin raised, she spoke:

"Your service is inestimable."

"It's also a compliment you hold me in high esteem."

That was her first invitation to smile. "You're also a big, handsome man."

That utterance sounded as corny as it did trite. Except her body heat grilling me was genuine. Except she flirted as if expecting to enjoy every result from it. Except sick with grief, she didn't know what she was saying. Or doing. In a sober frame of mind, she wouldn't go out with me for a bucket of chicken. She evoked my pity, why I sought to restrain her.

"Mm-hmm," said Mrs. Taliaferro. "Here, register my pulse, Johnson." She indicated her heart. A swelling breast filled my grasp.

I reclaimed my hand. "Mrs. Taliaferro..."

"No, it's Mary. Please. Call me Mary."

Mary's head slanted near my chin, and her hair smelled enticing. Sandalwood. My hands held off her sinewy shoulders. Her tilted mouth went unrequited though her roving curiosity found my center of gravity. I had to shift in the armchair.

Near her emerald earring, I said, "Mrs. Taliaferro. Sorry...Mary, I mean. This wouldn't be a smart move for either one of us. We'd revile it later. Take my word."

She recoiled in indignation. "Just says who?"

I unbridled her collapsing arms and pushed her with a little too much force. "Just says me."

Falling, she reacted. "Johnson, you by God work for me."

I stood up, my words low and severe. "But I ain't your gigolo."

Her pointy toe launched for my groin, what my hands intercepted. "Too much booze makes you like hurting men, huh?"

She retrenched by doing what she did best—issuing orders. "Get out! Go help Martin. Get!"

I left her huddled in the yellow room heartened by a cheerless fire. Outdoors I could breathe again. The drench hammered me into an old man's stoop but I plunged on to the stable. Slouched against a shadowy post under the overhang, James Martin was firing up a hand-rolled cigarette. Breathless, I flopped down beside him on an upturned 5-gallon bucket. The temperature hovered right at the freezing mark. Piercing cold had my teeth chattering behind blue lips. The lean trainer studied the end of his orange, glowing-cigarette. He flicked away casual embers and took another drag.

"Johnson, you better rustle in before you catch the death of cold." Martin ground out the butt under a heel. His vapory breath mixed with the smoke.

"I wondered if you'd ever invite me in."

Martin scooped up a bundle of cedar wood from a jumble he'd busted up with an axe. Inside, he chucked the fuel inside a potbellied stove. I fronted my rump to within inches of its dry heat. My shaking dwindled. We heard sleet tick against the windowpanes.

Martin speaking from a swivel chair read my mind. "That rich bitch makes me crazy, expecting us to go fetch her precious stallion in this piss cutter of a storm."

"You said a mouthful," I said.

"I for one aim to stay put. How do you like my digs? I rigged me up this here woodstove. Ordered a cord of firewood." His gaunt hand panned around us. "Got a fart sack. Revamped a Zenith radio I found in the tack room. Stole a griddle from the kitchen for making me flapjacks. I'll squeak by just fine. By the way, pour yourself a cup of coffee."

"Thanks, no. I'm fine now. Why your move out here from The Big House?"

"Cause life in there was weirding me out."

"Too much craziness?" I asked.

"And that was the least of it, too."

"Lighten up, Martin. The poor lady has been hauled backward through a knothole."

"Boo-hoo, boo-hoo." Martin's slow eyes fixed on me. "Good thing this job is only to tide me over. Cigarette?"

"Thanks no," I said. "Which reminds me, the sheriff has earmarked that ashtray stand as evidence."

"Smoking all my weeds outside, I never touch it."

I shoveled a hand up under my sweatshirt. The 9 mil was wet. Rust was a danger. Its magazine I ejected and put by the gun on a wood stool near the stove.

"Holy crap!" Martin pointed. "What are you packing?"

"A nine millimeter," I said.

"You any good at handling it?"

My shrug was noncommittal. "I make it pull its weight."

"Magnificent. Go grease that damn stallion."

"Feels good to get that off your chest, huh?"

"For a dollar, I'd ship that runaway to Purina Chow for dog food."

"Otherwise I assume all is well."

He nodded it was. "My phantom arm entrances you, I see."

"Only as an idle curiosity, Martin."

"It speaks a rich history. Just turned fourteen, I was mowing hay for thirty cents below minimum wage. Anyway, my hand slipped and wedged in the machine cogs. The baler mangled me to just above the elbow. I sued. Besides covering my medical bills, the skinflint farmer will write me a check for $1.03 every month for the rest of his born days."

"Prosthesis?" I asked.

"I never got measured for one." He flourished the stump like waving a baton. "This makes for a bang-up dildo. Anyway, are you up for a little music?"

"I'd just as soon skip it."

Ignoring me, Martin fiddled with the Zenith's radio dials and telescopic antennae. CCR's "Fortunate Son" blew out our ears before he moderated the volume.

"Those Fogerty brothers," he said, "didn't have it in them to stay together. Any chance they'll reunite?"

"The oldest, Tom, died in 1990. He was a young 48."

Martin's head inclined. I should've known—he was a musicologist. "You're wrong about Tom Fogerty."

"Sorry. I confused him with that lounge lizard in the fake leather coat. You're right." I retained a poker face.

Martin's cowboy boots scraped on the floor tiles. "Easy mistake to make. Wood in the stove needs topping off."

"Mind if I use your phone?"

"No skin off my nuts. The rich bitch is paying for it." Martin slipped outdoors. I heard him going at it with the axe.

I dialed Chet Peyton long distance.

"Is that static on your end or mine?" Chet's shout sounded far-off.

"Have you strangled my tomcat yet?" I yelled back.

"Get this. Now he'll eat only swordfish."

"Swordfish? Fat chance that will continue when I get home."

"Is your case shaking out okay? You need my help? I can round up Gerald and be there in no time flat."

During the pause, I debated it before saying, "I'm winding up things. Should be home in a few days." The land line fizzled out. "Hello...hello?" No response. I racked the receiver. I smoothed out the list of suspects on my knee, vexed how every alibi had remained unshakeable.

Ralph Phillips W/wife Rachel at racetrack in West Va.

Sh'riff Pettigrew W/me part of afternoon

Stanley PettigrewWorked at guard shack

Mrs. T Was in mansion, found corpse at stable

My stream of spit sizzled on the hot stove iron. As the bard said, I concentrated my mind wonderfully and zeroed in on big, bad Ralph for both murders. He was on the lam. He'd detested Pierre, reason enough to kill. He'd had opportunity and means. His mercurial temper and impulsive nature fit the profile of a killer, if ever anything did. Fitting him with Emily's murder was less clear, but the gravel in my guts guaranteed me that both murders were somehow linked.

Martin clumped to the stove and dumped his load in the wood box. "The damn rain has changed over to all sleet. You sticking around until it lets up?"

I reloaded the 9 mil's magazine, eased myself up. "I'm fixing to chase down Ralph but he could be in Rangoon sailing in a red balloon for all I know."

With a calculating glint in his eye, Martin grinned knowingly. "Check out the slaughterhouse. That's one of his havens to escape from Rachel."

"That rundown shambles by the hospital?" I asked. "The rusted sign calls it 'Meats Merci'?"

"You're right on the money. Mrs. Taliaferro bought it to spruce up for an art museum. She was going gangbusters at one time. It cooled off. The lady has a lot of grandiose ideas that are never seen through."

"Thanks for the tip."

"Sorry to hold out on you before," he replied. "You seem straightup enough, though."

"Later, Martin."

Back at my car, I cranked the key, and once through the gate, the new all-weather radials skated me over roadway clear to Kaiser. My car docked in an illegal street space by a mailbox. Sleet peened my hatless scalp. Bent over, I coughed. The slaughterhouse was constructed of brick, a pinkish medium rare in color. Cretins had stoned out its glass panes. Oval windows were accessible only by an extension ladder. Posted "NO TRESPASSING" signs didn't apply to me. More bad coughs.

At first sight, the slaughterhouse struck me as a clever lair. Six rear doors, however, were braced from inside. Between hiding from taxi cabs and four-wheelers exiting the hospital, I also couldn't ram open the three front doors. I ducked behind a propane tank, and watched a slowing Toyota with daytime running lights. The lady driver hurled out a cell phone from the open window to smash on the pavement and she fishtailed down a side street.

Had Martin fed me baloney?

Sizing up the chute, I knew cattle brutalized into beef shanks shambled in through their own private gate. I scooted ass-first down the icy chute and toed open the steel door. I sidled inside. My eyes acclimated to the dim. A retch of hydraulic oil, grease, and feces infested this ex-kill shed.

I coughed up a handful of phlegm. Probing the murkier shadows, I disentangled the 9 mil from my beltline. Sleet slashed through apertures above me letting in my only sources of light. My guts clenched thinking about the beasts sent to their slaughter in here.

A steel spiral staircase led to a catwalk circling a cauldron-like vat. I saw where Mrs. Taliaferro's dream had wrecked. The drywall sheets piled by a concrete pillar under a painter's drop cloth rotted. What Art, I wondered, did the lady hope to create inside an old packinghouse?

Welcome boys and girls to Dr. Fu Manchu's fabled torture chambers. Indulge all five of your senses. Feel the treble meat hooks. Hear the pneumatic nail guns. Taste the sawdust and offal. Smell hell's lowest sinkhole. See my teeth gnashed to trap the blue curses behind them. I made out pails, drums, and squeegees. Rubber boots and aprons, chest pads, and hockey masks had been doffed by the last butchers at the last quitting time.

Behind drooping steel cables appeared a ventilation shaft, my auxiliary escape hatchway. I trudged onto the main floor. The strongest window light had diminished. A fat lot of good the flashlight in my glove compartment did me now. My outstretched fingers grazed glass, then descended to a doorknob which turned in my grasp.

I reached around the door corner, and toggled on a light switch. The space illumed by four caged bulbs was twelve by fifteen. Maybe it had once been an office. Joss sticks smoldering inside pop bottles surprised me. Dented malt liquor cans strewn about a battered executive chair were new. I saw paper bags and plates, napkins, bamboo chopsticks, and a row of half-full demijohns on an ice chest. What left me to wonder was an old gravity-flow gasoline pump leaning in one corner. On a credenza under whiskey bottles also drained dry, I riffled through horseracing tip sheets and Burpee Seed catalogs.

I'd tracked down Ralph's crib but no Ralph. In essence, I had nothing.

The soundtrack must've cut to cellos, syrupy and heavy-handed, only I failed to detect it. Blackjacked across the head, I staggered. If I recalled anything, it was the advice given to epileptics to fall with a shoulder roll.

Back again, I spat out the sudsy nastiness in which my mouth had landed. A ginger touch determined the blow had almost hacked my scalp in half. I wasn't bound and gagged. The lump gouging my thigh was the 9 mil. Propped on elbows, surveying beyond my boot tips I recognized the oblong of light from the office doorway. I hadn't been moved either.

I knitted together enough wits to draw up to my knees. Firecrackers crackled behind my nose. I gave my brain the necessary time and space to unscramble. Moving to arise, though, an intense nausea lay me out flat again. After zoning in and out, I floated on the hard concrete, every nerve ending snapping in raw, red pain. My eventual aim was to stand upright. For now, I was okay with just feeling alive.

I surmised Ralph had overheard me breaking into the place. He'd slipped out of the office, lurked along the outer glass wall, and then attacked me from behind. Given a few minutes, he could make good on his getaway. I'd erred. Ralph was clever, resourceful, and violent.

I took charge of my legs. My nerves commanded them to unfold and levitate. Wobbling, I listed forward and drooped against the doorjamb. A bustling disturbed me. A brown rat sniffed up at me, squeaking. One bleary eye squinting and one shaky hand pointing, I capped the scrawny booger.

The gun report left my ears ringing. Cute, Johnson. One dead rat. Better him than me. Sprawled in the executive chair, I took closer measure of the office's shabbiness.

That 1920s bubble-headed gas pump entranced me. Ralph had towed it in here from the old loading docks. Eight feet tall, it extended through the drop ceiling tiles. A bar owner I knew had acquired a scaled down replica of one for $650. I herded the chair over, hiked up, and scooped away ceiling tiles. I noted the bubble head atop the pump was beveled glass. I got down and towed the chair closer. Inside the glass receptacle, was what object? I strained my eyes to see better. Yep, it was a handgun.

It took three tremendous heaves to uproot the gas pump. Like a chainsawed tree, it slid down scraping the wall. The glass receptacle shattered upon striking the concrete. The fall's noise reverberated past me into the vaster space. My ears were already deaf. The handgun, what I'd sought, skittered under the credenza. The din died away. Using my boot, I cleared a path through the glass slivers. With a hand on the credenza, I hunched down. That did my monster headache little good.

I found a .25 Raven semi-automatic, a "Saturday Night Special." Its engraved logo was a crude raven. I ejected its magazine packing a five-cartridge load and slapped out the chamber round. The .25 bullet pried out of Pierre's chest could be matched to this popgun.

After pocketing the racing tip sheets, I backtracked. Scuttling and clawing, I conquered the ice-clad chute, spraining my wrist on one of several spills. I wobbled over to my car. Falling sleet continued building up the silver patina but failed to endow the neighborhood's dreariness a clean sheen. I went to the morgue. Joyner answered my knock. His dismay at seeing me again was distinct.

"Johnson, you look like Hell. Now what?"

"Do you still have that bullet pulled out of Pierre?" I asked him.

"Absolutely. Why?"

"A .25 I uncovered just might match it.

"My lab is in Middleburg," he said. "Thornbird can process whatever you have."

I unwrapped my handkerchief to show him the .25.

"You recovered that handgun where?" he asked.

My head shook. "That's not relevant here. Fast-tracking its ballistics is."

"Okay just leave the piece with me," he said. "I'll phone Thornbird before lunch."

Another headshake. "His office is right on my way."

Joyner set down a beaker he held. "Johnson, you thumb your nose at the most basic police procedure. Why?"

"Two cadavers stink up your bone shop, their killer unknown. I bring in a possible murder weapon and you want to quibble with me about police protocol. Why?"

Grumbling oaths, Joyner crouched beside an evidence safe and twirled its combination lock dial. "A sharpie defense lawyer will screw the prosecution. His client, the killer, will go scot-free. That will fall on your shoulders, not mine."

"They're big enough," I lied through my teeth.

He deposited the small envelope sealed with the .25 death slug in my hand. I left him to his fun. Bundled in my car, I hated the blasting defroster for its lukewarm air. I rooted out a broken scraper and chiseled at the windshield. Ice-caked limbs to cedars and hemlocks sagged and bowed. Telephone lines lagged in stiff submission. An April sleet storm in Virginia was freaky but not out of the question. I crawled in second gear, staring out the porthole carved in my icy windshield. I braked to a sliding stop at the sheriff's office, and stood up on the street. Opening the door for me, Thornbird busted a gut laughing when I wiped out falling on my tailbone. Man, it hurt, too.

"The weather has gotten worse." He was grinning still.

I limped inside over to the desk where I flipped on the gooseneck lamp. "Come take a look at this find."

Thornbird shook out the .25 slug that had been tweezed from Pierre's heart muscles. Its tip was mushroomed. Next he tapped the .25 Raven. "Whose snub nose is this?" he asked.

I explained how I'd come by it and what I wanted to do now.

"The roads to Middleburg are treacherous," he said.

"This cold won't persist. Getting this handgun to the lab will give us a leg up in the investigation."

Thornbird nodded, his smooth forehead fluted with lines of new anxiety. "The Kilbys claim that this storm negates your jailhouse deal. What damn jailhouse deal is what I want to know?"

"Walloped on the head, they're a shade confused," I told him. "Let me take care of it."

"Just for a few minutes," said Thornbird, wary. "No more."

I stepped into the cellblock and pulled the outer steel door shut. Both jailbirds were flaked out on their bunks, ankles crossed, hands and clasped behind their heads. The bunks I saw were concrete slabs padded with gymnast mats.

The brainy, short one smirked up at me. "Look at this lousy weather. Boy, I'm all sick inside, Johnson. Your evidence is all destroyed now, as in what pot patches?"

The tall one said, "We gonna sue you. You pissed in the soup and you're gonna slurp it down."

The short Kilby stretched out nearest to me gloated. He couldn't let it go at that. Oh hell no. Canting his head on the pillow, he dared to wink at me. He winked like those condemned bastards did on their death gurneys. Lowlifes were having barrels of laughs at my expense. My hands lashed through the cellfront bars and grappled an ankle. A vicious tug dragged the short Kilby toward me. He jerked up, cussing.

"Hey, what's the big idea?" said the tall Kilby.

Snaring a shock of scraggly hair, I next conked the short Kilby's head against the steel bars. His teeth clacked together. He did his best to buck away from me and nearly shook free. I clutched more hair in my other hand to whack his skull again. In a thuggish way, this was fun.

"Ouch, ouch," he said. "Ouch, shit, ouch."

The tall Kilby hurtled off his bunk and lunged but his cage was a safe enough distance away. He doubled both hands into fists. "Thornbird!" he hollered from the bottom of his lungs.

The steel outer steel door to the cellblock creaked behind us. The tall Kilby's voice grew shrill and vehement. "Thornbird, he's psycho." He pointed at me.

The short Kilby could only agree. "T-t-tell him to unhand me."

"Your lawyer phoned me," said Thornbird. "He's coming in on a tow truck. He plowed into the ditch driving over from Middleburg." His boots scraped close. I could smell his tense sweat. He swatted a baton in his palm twice.

The short Kilby rolled his eyes at Thornbird. "Tell Johnson he's making things worse for you both."

"Mr. Johnson," said Thornbird. "They're correct. Turn the prisoner loose."

I flung away my captive. "Only at your say-so."

Thornbird sidled around me. From a ring unclipped off his belt, he handed me the cell keys.

Wary, the short Kilby blinked at us. "What are you doing, Deputy?"

Thornbird's smile tightened into a gash. "About to have my pleasure watching Mr. Johnson tear you from limb to limb."

The short Kilby shivered. "All right, It all went down like we said before."

Chapter 13

Thursday noon, April 20th

Thornbird hung up the phone receiver. "That was the forensics lab in Middleburg."

I slumped down in the seat by his desk. "And?"

"Carole Dawson's clothes yielded semen traces."

"And?"

"The DNA testing will take a few more days."

"Don't worry. It'll match the Kilbys," I said. "Now, is your Luminol ready?"

"Yep." Folding his arms on his chest, Thornbird leaned back in his chair. "Once the weather is on the mend, I'll get these to the lab, too." The .25 I'd found in Ralph's lair and the slug envelope disappeared into a drawer.

"The sleet will soon slack off," I said. "Then we'll see a fast spring melt."

"Assuming that does happen, the Kilbys will face arraignment tomorrow. I talked to the Commonwealth Attorney about it."

I nodded as he fielded a quick phone call. Afterward, Thornbird zipped up his parka. "Kilbys' lawyer is at the auto shop. Can I trust you to hold down the fort and not maul the prisoners?"

"You'd better shake a leg," I said.

After hearing Thornbird's Oldsmobile fire to life and bolt off, I punched "5" on the phone to get a long distance line. Eleven annoying buzzes later, Darl Adkins, my forensics expert in Richmond, picked up. I asked her to compile a list of any Kaiser residents who owned a .25 caliber handgun.

"But Frank, that gun ownership database is on a secured Unix system. I don't know if I can get access to it."

"Please just try," I said. "If you get any hits, leave the information at this number with Deputy Sheriff Thornbird. He's a good cop."

"To put up with the likes of you," Darl said, "he must be."

As I hung up, I wondered if Darl's telephone conversations were monitored by Big Brother. Aw, screw Big Brother. I nudged back my cuff and saw it was a few minutes to noon. Sheila was livid about now. Aw, screw Sheila. I had one more phone call to place. Directory Assistance connected me to the Excelsior Hotel in Roanoke, Virginia, where I knew all the big conventions were held. I requested to speak to a party by name.

"Hello, Sheriff Donovan here."

"This is Johnson."

"Johnson? Mike Shayne Johnson, the PI fellow? Is that you? How are the drumsticks baking back home, boy?"

"Can't say, sheriff. I'm up in Kaiser working on something."

"Kaiser, huh? Is Sheriff Pettigrew putting the screws to you?"

"How's that? I heard tell he's with you party animals."

Donovan chuckled. "Not this year, he isn't. Pettigrew was a no show."

"Well then, where the hell is he?"

"Beats me. Look, I'd love to stay and chew the fat with you Johnson, but you're standing between me and free chow downstairs."

"Ciao, sheriff."

So, Sheriff Pettigrew not where he claimed to be was a liar. It was noon. I also had to mush. The prospect of battling the sleet on a trip to Middleburg didn't thrill me. Then again, the Kilbys' attorney seeing me hanging around here didn't either. The jailbirds roosted quietly. I left Thornbird a note, dialed up Sheila, and next drove over to the hospital.

In its lobby, I flumped down into a Naugahyde chair to wait. Eye-popping pain also blew up my head to double in size. An orderly pushing an empty wheelchair nodded at me. I wondered if I was supposed to be wheeled off in it. The PA system crackled like blowing lint off of a phonograph needle. A droll accent paged a Doctor Warbucks, or a name pronounced like Doctor Warbucks.

Sheila hurrying inside wore a knee-length taupe overcoat unbuttoned over her blue beautician's smock and pants. Blonde hair piled off her neck contained ice fragments also on her overcoat. Under these yellow lights, the ice chips glistened sequin-like.

"Sorry to take so long," she said, "but the streets are a mess."

The same lady clerk as before minimized a game of Computer Solitaire. The halo brace turning with her head, she smiled her cat-who-ate-the-canary guile. "Yes, Detective Johnson?"

"Detective Johnson, eh?" Sheila said in a low, sardonic tone.

I ignored her. "Has Carole Dawson been assigned a room?"

The lady's fingers danced over her keyboard. She studied the monitor. A green-haired troll doll and piglet Chia Pet perched on it stared back at her. "Carole Dawson was moved into Room 146. Directly down this hall, it's midway on your right."

As we hiked by rooms filled elderly patients, my stomach went a bit queasy. I muttered out the side of my mouth, "This place gives me the willies."

"We can do without sarcasm," Sheila said.

Prints of hounds and horses dotted the walls to impart an artificial cheer. A twenty-something, clean-cut doctor whisked out of Room 146. His laser blue eyes suspended in rimless gold glasses disliked seeing us. Twirling a stethoscope, he conversed in an insistent whisper. "If you've come to see Miss Dawson, I can't allow it, I'm afraid."

"And you are?" I asked.

His manicured forefinger tapped a nameplate. "Dr. Randolph, Miss Dawson's family physician," he said. "I permitted her dad and sisters only five minutes a little while earlier. Miss Dawson is too exhausted to see more visitors."

"We understand," said Sheila.

With a snippy disdain, Dr. Randolph asked me, "And you are?"

My jaw jutted an inch. "We're..."

Sheila cut into my sentence. "Friends of the family. We wondered how Carole was doing."

"Miss Dawson has been under sedation," Dr. Randolph said. His chest puffed out. "I've diagnosed her with Rape-Related Post Traumatic Stress Disorder."

"How did you figure all that out?" I asked. "I happen to know she went through hell."

Dr. Randolph smiled. "Really? Did you witness her unholy horror?"

"You arrogant little fu..."

Again, Sheila broke in, her hand pressing on my forearm. "Mr. Johnson had hoped to see Carole, if only for a second."

"Absolutely impossible, Johnson."

My impatience seethed. "Maybe I'll stick you down a laundry chute and visit her anyhow."

Sheila interposed herself between the door and me. "You can't muscle your way inside. Not this time, Frank. I won't let you."

I glared at Dr. Randolph.

"Escort him off my hospital wing. Immediately. I've my rounds to complete." Dr. Randolph removed his stethoscope. A nubile but pigeon-toed nurse whisked over and they huddled to confer.

"Reel in your horns," said Sheila.

"Let's hit the fat man's deli," I said. "My treat."

"That's a sweetheart deal I accept," said Sheila.

❧

At a window booth, we talked and ate our hoagies. Sheila sipped a beer. Lucky duck. I told her what all had transpired since our return from Jetsam. The sleet quit falling. A spring sunburst cut through the overcast skies. The mercury spiked upward. The ice melt gathered in puddles and runnels trickled to the storm grates. Only in Virginia, I thought peering out the window.

"Ralph likes his liquor alone," Sheila was saying. "But you crashed his scene and got clobbered for your trouble."

I'd omitted telling Sheila about the .25 I'd scratched up in Ralph's crib. A successful ballistics analysis linking it to the slug pulled from Pierre could bring this case to a head. If the clue didn't pan out, though, I didn't care to publicize it. "What about Sheriff Pettigrew?" I asked. "He lied by never showing at the Roanoke convention."

"With two unsolved murders hanging over his department," said Sheila, "him skipping off, no matter where, is weird behavior."

"Thornbird calls the convention a big blowout," I said.

Sheila crunched on an ice cube. "Sure, it's Tailhook wearing a five-pointed star. Boys being boys. That never changes."

Wiping off mayonnaise on a napkin, I screwed on a wry face. "Stanley Pettigrew might know what his sheriff brother is up to."

"Didn't you say that you saw the Phillips bickering in that motel cabin?" asked Sheila. "You left that videotape at our place. We've got a VCR to watch it on."

"Good idea," I said.

We strolled over to Sheila's walk-up. Coats folded over our arms weighed heavy and seemed a burden with the now gorgeous weather. Wet streets and buildings erupted in Easter egg colors. My eyes weren't deceived. Along this slant of sidewalk, I also saw snuff tins, cigar butts, and chicken bones. Dirty condoms and hypodermic syringes discarded inside a blind alley repulsed me. A mail van smacked in and out of a chuckhole dousing our calves with muddy water.

That's when I knew that Kaiser was a dirty little town. Do the right thing, I thought. Be a professional. Finish what you agreed to do. I wanted to gas up and hit the highway. I jingled the car keys in my pocket. Oh yeah, Kaiser was definitely a dirty little town. I was kidding myself to think otherwise. Sheila stirred by my pensive sulk hooked my free arm in hers. Did she sense my ambivalence? We walked two abreast.

"Do you regret getting into the private cop biz?" she asked me. "In the interests of honesty, I realize that I goaded you into taking it. You just needed something better to do at the time."

"Most days, no, I don't."

"This then is a bad day?" she asked. "Sure, today is a bad day." Her question-and-answer combo confused me.

"Look, I'm treading water okay. Let's leave it at that."

"What if I'll lend you a hand?" Sheila asked. "We worked as a team once."

My head wagged an emphatic no. "You've done too much already."

She persisted. "The past, I speak of our past relationship, ended on unpleasant terms. There's never a day I don't regret that."

"You don't own a monopoly on blame. My head wasn't exactly

screwed on straight." I steadied my eyes on a blue jay in a tulipwood tree but didn't smile to dismiss her deepening frown.

"You've established quite a name for yourself."

"Man, I'm needing some boots over here."

"No, I mean it. I've clipped out a couple wonderful write-ups about you."

"The paper ran a human interest piece. Or so I heard. I didn't read it."

"Did you date the reporter?" Her inflection turned icy and coy.

"Only friends. It was also to drum up business."

"Did it bring you any?" was her next logical question.

"One client," I said. "Her husband was a retired diplomat. He vanished in central Turkey."

"A diplomat...did you find him?"

"Sort of. It turned out that she'd killed the poor bastard. Only I wasn't supposed to topple her apple cart."

"Why? To get his life insurance?"

"I've yet to figure that one out. At our last showdown, she came within a gunshot of whacking me." I shuddered. Did the breeze chill me?

"What became of this vicious lady?"

"Like any snake, I crushed her under a rock." I grinned at her.

Sheila pulled up just short of her door. "Oh, what bullshit," she said. "That entire tale was a fabrication of lies."

"Do you see it now?" I asked. "Why we'd still drive each other nuts?"

Sally's Nails was taking a siesta. Sheila poked me upstairs. Stench de jour? Burnt bacon. Mrs. Dompkowski didn't sing out at us. At the door she slotted in a key but had a little trouble. I took a crack at it and we were inside. A wand of sunlight lay across the wicker hamper, a perfect nook my tomcat would claim for a snooze.

I saw dishes drying in the rubber rack on the drainboard before the duct tape fixing a window crack. A bottle of multivitamins by the toaster made Sheila the Bionic Woman and me the Incredible Hulk. In our heyday, we'd seemed that invincible, but this was now.

Sheila gasping a vulgarity, darted ahead to slam shut her bedroom door. The entire walk-up was messy. "That squalor even turns my stomach," she said. She fired up the VCR and fast forwarded the videotape I'd confiscated from the Chewink Motel. At the frame where Ralph schlepped into Cabin Seven carrying luggage, Sheila flicked on normal speed.

"It's practically worthless without audio," she said.

"True. I can't read lips from overhead," I said. " Rachel looks plenty pissed."

"Arguing over gambling debts?"

"Well, she's his partner in crime playing the ponies."

"Ralph has to feed his addiction." Sheila seemed to be on the right track. "Rachel just tags along and serves as a brake on him."

"Brakes don't slow down men like Ralph," I said. I saw from a wall clock, it was 1:30 PM. "Thornbird asked me to come by his office. I better scoot along."

Sheila tilted a plucked eyebrow at me. "What, is Thornbird your sidekick now?"

"The Kilbys' lawyer had a meeting with them. Lawyers, especially the Middleburg strain, make Thornbird skittish. He's green as grass but learning fast."

"Oh hell, get along then. Mom's due to call here in a few minutes. She's raring to come home."

"Later," I said, the word out before Sheila could nick me for a favor. That daily bus ran just fine between Kaiser and Paw-Paw. Hitting the sunny street felt like sweet freedom to me. I detoured to make the Kaiser Motel. A pickup outfitted with a camper shell hung a right, bumped over the curbstone, and parked. With Adam's ambush a vivid memory, I scurried into the crosswalk. An old man took his time unfolding out of the truck. I laughed, not at him but at me.

The motel proprietress, armed with a crossword puzzle and dog-eared dictionary, sat on a milkmaid stool by the window to take advantage of the afternoon sunlight.

"Mr. Johnson," she said. "Your reclamation project cleaned up real nice. Real nice, yes sir."

"Did you put him to work?" I asked.

"I stuffed a tin bucket of soapy, hot water and a mop into his hands. Then I explained it like I would to a child. 'You swab out this here john and I'll pay you ten bucks.'"

"Did he do a presentable job?" My tone was hopeful.

"A presentable job! Man, that's rich, the last I looked, that no-account rascal had lit out over the train tracks. Naturally he has a flop over in guppy town."

I scribbled a check to cover the second half I'd promised her. "Guppy town?"

"Guppy town." She pointed. "Shanty town over there."

"Thornbird can route him back here."

"Don't make me no never mind," she said.

"The down-on-his-luck guy just needed another shot at redemption."

The proprietress folded my check lengthwise to stow in a ratty purse. "Look, he's eaten up with sorry. I wouldn't let it rattle my bones. Write him off. Once a bum, always a bum."

Licking my lips, I shrugged a shoulder except disillusionment saddened me. She came over and patted my arm, assuring me the moon would rise again tonight. I thanked her, and struck a course to the sheriff's office. My mood didn't lighten up.

Some men signed away their lives to a barstool. Hank Williams signed on such a dotted line. Jailed weeks before his death for drunk and disorderly in Toronto, Ole Hank moseyed out of his cell saying "cheese" mugging for the camera. Shirtless, he looked like a sad sack of bones. You could count all of his ribs—an accursed thirteen.

Thornbird met me at the office door. Any idiot could decipher his baby face. A crisis was stewing.

"The Kilbys are pleading not guilty," he said. "When they post bail tomorrow, Mr. Johnson, don't you fly off the handle. I'm confident our evidence against them will win us a grand jury indictment."

"Where's their damn lawyer?"

"He paid through the nose to catch a cab back to Middleburg."

"Can we make Middleburg?" I asked him.

Getting with my plan, Thornbird jangled a key ring. "I'll go notify the lab we'll be bringing in the Kilbys' pickup. You go round up the tow truck. But first, wait a second." Thornbird strode over to the desk. "That bulge in your britches looks obscene. Here, wear this." A leather holster whiffed through the air. The 9 mil was a perfect fit hefted on my belt.

The old man at the auto shop balked at putting his tow truck in Thornbird's hands. I wooed him with a fat check. Brandishing it before him to snap like paper money, the old man munched the cold White Owl. "That digital camera is as good as mine. Sweet." As an afterthought, he asked, "Did Thornbird keep his CDL valid?"

"He must have," I said, banking on what a tight-ass Thornbird was.

Thornbird bustling into the auto shop exchanged a perfunctory nod with the old man.

"You got the .25 and slug?" I asked.

"All safe right here." As we exited, he patted the Tupperware canister held under an elbow.

We hitched up on the tow truck's running boards, and got into the cab. I met my age as a twinge of sciatica zapped through my thigh. Concentrating, Thornbird directed me on how to fine-tune the angles to the mirrors. We sat a country mile off the road. The deep-throated engine got us over to the dumpster in their impoundment yard.

"You hook up the Kilbys' pickup truck," I said. "I'll be inside the cell-block for a few minutes."

"Huh? What for?" Thornbird asked. A second elapsed. "No, you'd better scratch that. I'd rather not know. I'm in enough hot water as it is."

"Just hang loose if I'm not right out."

Six overhead lights inside the sheriff's office flared on and I paced to the rear to open the outer steel door. Both Kilbys prone on their mats ogled the centerfolds in stag magazines, reading material smuggled in by their sleazy lawyer. The short Kilby did the first fearful double take at me.

"Johnson. Why are you back in here?" His throat made coffin lid squeaks.

"Just piddling around, boys."

"Where are you towing our pickup?" said the tall Kilby.

"Why? Do you have hotel reservations in Atlantic City?"

The short Kilby's alert eyes glared as if to pick up my intentions. "Clarify piddling around," he said.

"Naw, that's too hard." I removed a key I'd lifted off Thornbird. "What we have here, I believe, is a dire need for a more face time."

The short Kilby darted to the far wall, and chopped his shoe like a club in white-knuckled fear. "This cell is off-limits to you."

I scowled. "Coming from you, is that a threat or a warning?"

"You shit-kicking ridge-runner." The tall Kilby glared at me. "Move on. We don't want any further police brutality with you."

'Police brutality' was a term only lawyers would use. It'd sound dramatic when played back in a courtroom. Seizing his cell bars, I leaned in with a savage leer. "Either you cough up that wire on you or I come in to appropriate it."

The tall Kilby unbuttoned his shirt and clawed away the tape attaching a wireless transmitter to his torso. "Take it and scram."

"Now you, hot stuff," I ordered the runt. Both transmitters got stomped under my boots. "On his next visit to the station house," I said, "your lawyer gets strip searched."

Their enlarged eyes afforded me a clear glimpse at soul-curdling hate. I'd seen it and ignored it too many times before. Without another word, I left them.

Chapter 14

Thursday 3:30 PM, April 20th

By the time Deputy Sheriff Thornbird and I struck out along the hilly, twisty road to Middleburg, it was late afternoon. At my last minute suggestion, Thornbird tucked his Luminol kit behind the seat. The tow truck, a 1994 GMC Topkick, had clocked better than 300,000 miles, but its rebuilt CAT diesel engine was a dynamo. In fact, the Kilby pickup truck trailing behind us created minimal, if any, drag.

Thornbird raved. "This CD player and heated seats are for candy-asses. But this 7-shift transmission? Man-o-man, it's awesome."

"Sho-nuff," I said. "Give me a turn at driving it?"

Thornbird hesitated. "Maybe, Frank. We'll have to see."

At a lickety-split 30 miles per hour, we took a curve. The pickup's rear-end grated over blacktop. I saw it'd left some of its skin. The noise grew deafening. I reassured Thornbird not to sweat it but he did anyway. We powered on to reach the forensics lab in Middleburg before the drawbridge was raised at the 5 PM quitting time. Our talented contact, Susie, had agreed to wait for us. Even so, we didn't want to crowd our luck with her.

Thornbird shouted over the diesel's engine din, "My dad was a cop."

"Yeah? Which contingent?" I asked.

"Virginia State trooper. A seventeen-year vet."

"He didn't stick around for twenty and out?"

"No. A sawed-off twelve-gauge cancelled that option. Off-duty, he walked in on a holdup."

"Liquor store or a cash-and-carry?"

"Neither. A bank. He made the big mistake of going inside still wearing his cop uniform. That painted a bull's eye on him. He never got off a shot."

"The guilty scumsucker, was he ever arrested?" I asked.

Thornbird's fair features toughened. "Nothing much to go on. They wore Halloween masks and got away clean."

"There's no statue of limitations on murder," I said as a reminder.

In a pensive voice, he asked, "Would you take on such a case?"

"To help manhunt a cop killer? Absolutely, I would. It'd be an honor."

Sawing the steering wheel into a turn, Thornbird braced his arms on it. "Mr. Johnson...did you ever...cut down a man?"

"That, like my loves and politics, I won't discuss."

A hurt embarrassment flushed his cheeks. "It bugs me."

"Don't let it. Cops can go their entire careers without once firing their piece." I very nearly added "but not in my law enforcement experience" but then this was a pep talk.

His features flushing livid purple, Thornbird's neck muscles corded and jaws knotted. "The damn streets are so anti-cop, see? Every punk growls at them. We've become a land without laws except laws of the jungle."

"I disagree."

"Why? Are you all-fired certain of that?"

"I've seen things like two convicted killers executed in Jarrett. A front seat, too."

"How long did their appeals drag on?" asked Thornbird.

"One had twenty-six months. Out of boredom, he learned to crochet baby clothes."

"Okay, you nailed two blood-crazed greaseballs. That's something we can both be proud of."

I deflected the praise. "Once anything concrete developed on the cases, the sheriff took over. No gonzo PI, I respect such boundaries."

"How did both of these bad ass killers die?" Thornbird's question, banal, matched my response.

"Desperate and alone. But I didn't see fear enter their eyes. They were cold blooded right until the bitter end."

Thornbird's curt nod gestured to a fence gap on our immediate right. "Is that field where you caught the Kilbys?"

"Yeah, but more back toward the treeline in the second field. Don't forget to make a pit stop at Dakota Farms."

"You bet. We can ask Stanley why I was left here holding the bag while his brother is off who knows where."

We rolled along, each stewing in our own juices. Gazing out, I pictured Hellbent cantering through lush, green fields. Horse barons kept their shit tight. No real estate developers dared to invade their bucolic playgrounds where Old Money pursued horse polo and fox hounds. A brief while later, Thornbird braked the tow truck at the Dakota Farms pull-off. Stanley Pettigrew as viewed through the guard shack's big window propped his boots on the desk.

Thornbird nudged me. "Get a load of this."

We trooped into the shack and I let its door shut hard. Thornbird swatted Stanley's boot heel. "Look alive, road pizza."

Fumbling to right himself, the dumfounded Stanley started up with the excuses. "On the flip side of a double shift, I was resting my eyes..."

"This must be taxing work."

"Who let you in here, Johnson?"

"Johnson is with me," said Thornbird. "Where's the god damn sheriff?"

Hanging his head between his knees, Stanley scanned beneath the desk, then peeped into the wastebasket. "Hoo, boy. I've misplaced his leash again."

"Ha-ha. That's hilarious."

Clinking coins and keys, Stanley shot himself a neat round of pocket pool. "Your boss is at the Sheriffs Convention in Roanoke at the Excelsior Hotel."

"That dog don't hunt," I said. "Try again." Thornbird also glared at him.

"He is. The sheriff told me so himself."

"Uh-huh," Thornbird and I grunted in unison. "Except his reservation went unclaimed," I said.

Stanley's eyebrows veed a nervous tic. "Good Lord. Did you call the hospitals along I-81?"

"Any such report would've broadcast over the police band."

"I'm stumped then," Stanley said. "This is a first. He's never before missed that big blowout. Lots of broads and booze."

"The very second he contacts you, notify me," said Thornbird. As we walked out to the gate, I spotted a Willys Overlander just dodging around the final oak-shaded bend. My damn eyes liked to play pranks on me, too. My optometrist swore wearing corrective lenses would take such spontaneous fun out of my life. I was still too young.

Pointing, Stanley Pettigrew's face lit up. "That's the Kilbys' truck, isn't it?"

"Be grateful it isn't yours. Now butt out." My words to Thornbird, "I'll drive this time."

"No can do, Mr. Johnson. You don't hold a CDL. Like it or not, we good guys in the white hats have to stay law-abiding."

We hoisted up on the tow truck's running boards and buckled up in the cab. Thornbird cranked the dirty, noisy diesel to chew up some roadway. Our ride soon grew into a bone-jarring torture. Thornbird had to put the pedal to the metal just to muster 20 miles per hour.

I hollered over at him, "What gives with the engine?"

Pumping the accelerator, Thornbird downshifted. "It's bogging down. Water in the fuel line? Maybe dirt clogs up the carburetor."

I scoped the various gauges studding the instrument panel. The overburdened motor hesitated. Lurched about, we clamped fingers to our seats to stay planted.

"Gas, oil, temperature," my eyes rechecked each gauge, "are okay."

A hand whapped the two-way radio. "This is on the fritz," said

Thornbird.

"A cell phone would come in handy," I said, regretting how I lacked one when my car had crapped out.

"Not here. We're in a dead zone."

Again for a measured beat, the tow truck's motor spluttered before droning on but more sluggish. Bit by bit, we conceded speed. The pickup truck behind us was like dragging around an anchor.

"Smell that? Hot metal," I said. "The pistons and rings are overheating."

Thornbird's lips pressed against his teeth. "Unbelievable. Why?"

I recalled the fleeting image of the turquoise-white Willys Overlander. "Some smart aleck at the arm gate sabotaged us. I caught a quick glimpse of them leaving in a jeep."

"Stopping wasn't such a hot idea," Thornbird said.

We doddered around a hairpin curve, crawled up a gradual hill, and limped down into a slash pine hummock. Pine-needle shade, cool and clammy, enshrouded us. The stench of dead, decaying flesh filled the truck cab.

"Jeez," I said. "What stinks?"

"Local farmers haul their dead livestock to chuck into this sump," said Thornbird. We clunked in and out of a pothole. The pickup deposited bumper chrome on the crumbling macadam. "Wet all the year long, it promotes a fast rot."

"Not near fast enough."

Thornbird's baleful laugh ran a chilled down my spine.

Tangy slash pines parted in a fire-scorched clearing to unveil a patch of blue sky. Off to our right, I spied a dead sycamore tree. High up, amid its stark branches, creatures flexed their oily dark wingspans to catch the bright, toasty sunrays. Ten, baker's dozen or maybe as many as twenty.

"That's a vulture tree," Thornbird told me.

"Far out. I've never been this close up on one."

"Count that as a positive thing."

I studied their heads, raw and red like amputations discarded from a field hospital tent. Their yellow eyes were fierce. Their misshapen beaks formed deft utensils to pick apart carrion. A horrific shiver tingled to my molars as they mesmerized us until sinking from view.

Thornbird rubbernecked for a parting look. "They're ugly enough to gag a maggot."

Pow!

Was that noise cherry bombs set off under a coffee can? That was my initial reaction. No, the tow truck had backfired. A second and third clarifying blast told me we were drawing gunfire. A lead round nicked the hood to carve a bare metal scar.

"What the hell?"

"Rifle fire!" I told Thornbird.

Making a dash to outrun our ambush was foolish. Thornbird stomped on the brakes, throttled the engine to drift a few yards. A crisper staccato punched spiderwebbed holes in the rear window. We balled under the dash, our hands raised to shield glass cascading down on us.

Thornbird dropped his voice to a hoarse whisper. "They're not strays from gobbler hunters."

"Wanna bet? Only we're their turkeys." My punch line was weak.

The next volley erupted. One round pounded through the cab's door and lodged in the seat batting. Fear? Well, I didn't soil my britches. My tailhole was too tight for that.

"Armor-piercing bullets will shred us to ribbons lumped inside here. Did you see from which side the shots came?" My shaky hand fisted the 9 mil.

"Both," he said. Thornbird's big .44 Magnum roved into sight. It could've defended the Alamo single-handed.

"A crossfire?" I said, incredulous.

"Kilbys. Told you their folks would come gunning for us." Thornbird pulled the latch to the driver side door and nudged its crack to a couple inches.

"Don't try it. Their rifle scopes are fixed on both our flanks," I said. A new shot smashed out a side mirror to underscore my point.

"Position the mirrors for a wider view to the pines," he said. "Sucker in their fire. Look sharp for a muzzle flash. Better yet, see if the shooters move in closer."

Doubt twisted my mind. "That's all you got?" I said. "We need automatic rifles, not bullshit smoke and mirrors."

"Mr. Johnson, feel free to correct me. I'll gladly acquiesce to your vaster experience."

"We'd better go with what you say."

Three bullets mangled jagged runs in the cab ceiling with can opener precision. I extended a tire iron to prod the side mirrors outward. Next hooking the tire iron in its curved part, Thornbird wigwagged his door. The ruse worked the charm. A rifle round zinged to our right and chipped door paint. The mirrors didn't lie. I saw a blur shrink behind a pine trunk. No underbrush obscured my sightline either. A cheer welled up in my throat.

"Numb Nuts, right side, ten yards behind us," I told Thornbird.

"Now, wave your door." Thornbird was whiter than a ghost if that was possible. "I'll spot."

After undoing the latch, I bumped out my door. No shots barked. The tire iron edged the door out wider. Still, no marksman chomped at the bait. All the way out now, my door attracted no rounds.

"So, we'll assume just the one Numb Nuts thirty yards in our rear." Thornbird's voice sparked with youthful hope but it wasn't contagious.

"We'll wiggle from out from my side, lure in Numb Nuts—"

"—then pop the cocksucker," Thornbird horned in.

"Great minds think alike."

Exiting my side, we lowered from the running board to the graveled shoulder. If Numb Nuts was canny, he'd be scoping the truck's undercarriage. I gave him too much credit. We duckwalked to the oversized double-tires and together prairie dogged over the bed to have a look. A forest of trees greeted us. Thornbird's younger eyes detected a silhouette melding into its patchy recesses.

"Numb Nuts! See him, Frank?" Thornbird reeled off three expert rounds—pop-pop-pop—in the same sector. An anguished yell stormed through the woods. "Numb Nuts has to do his penance." Smiling in a grimace, Thornbird stooped down again. We rested our backs propped against the truck tires to breathe normal. Hollers filling the pine woods had grown into wails.

"Help. Help me. Please!"

"Numb Nuts is playacting to sucker us in," I said.

Thornbird tapped out the .44's spent cartridges and replenished them. "I only winged Numb Nuts on my first shot."

Thornbird's color was heating to red, the same as mine. Our collective relief hardened into collective rage. We elevated to our feet. Bursitis bit through my knees. Were this job's physical rigors outpacing me? The next yells for "help" were dramatized with horror and pain. Straining my eyes, I couldn't make out where he'd fallen.

"Thornbird, you drilled him," I said. "He's your responsibility, not mine."

Louder: "Help! Help me! I need a doctor."

Doing a walk-around inspection, Thornbird said, "Well, I'm not about to go track him in the black lagoon."

Chuckling, I hefted myself into the tow truck cab. "Then come on. Let's roll."

"Help me. Please!"

Thornbird slid beneath the steering wheel, rotored down the window, and shouted out between cupped hands. "Hey! Hey you, Kilby! This last laugh is on you!"

"You sound like me now," I said.

"That's a scary thought." Somehow Thornbird coaxed mobility from the engine. "Once in Middleburg, I'll summon him an ambulance. Maybe."

"I knew you had a heart."

The tow truck, its temperature gauge dipping into hot red, barely finished our demolition derby into Middleburg. The diesel, in the throes of death, surrendered compression. The hot grease and steel commingled to singe our nose hairs. We banged into a paved lot across from a funeral home.

"The State Police give us access to their forensics lab," said Thornbird. "Their impoundment lot is through that gate."

I checked. "Ten minutes after five."

Thornbird nodded to show me. "That's red Mazda is Susie's. I knew she'd come through for us."

The state police barracks, a concrete monolithic structure really a bunker, had all of three small windows. A toothpick of a girl in a white lab coat over chino culottes emerged from the one steel door. Walking at a giddy pace, she hurtled the chain link gate out of our way. The impoundment area contained few vehicles and a couple paddy wagons.

"The watch commander will let us ditch the wrecker here," said Thornbird.

Waving, Susie caught up to us. "Is this the pickup?" Her cadence held that, resonant twang of Piedmont natives.

"A local high school girl was sexually assaulted inside it. Mr. Johns—, er, I busted them with their pants down," said Thornbird.

"I see," said Susie. "Why is it all bullet torn?"

"Hunting accident," said Thornbird. "Susie, this here is Mr. Johnson."

Dishing me the once-over, the smiling Susie liked what she took in. "So, you're the infamous Johnson?"

"Correct." I threw a hard glance at Thornbird who gave me a little, sheepish shrug.

He handed Susie the Tupperware container. "Can you run the ballistics on this .25 caliber handgun and a slug? The smart money here says they're a match."

"Expect a call first thing tomorrow morning," she said. "I have class tonight."

"Super. Tell Captain Waxman I'm parking the tow truck here. Is the car rental on Euclid Street still open?"

"They close at six," said Susie. "Mr. Johnson, let me take down your cell phone number. The need to call on my own private detective just might arise sometime soon."

"Sorry, I never carry a cell phone on me anymore. I had a bad experience with one."

"You better get over that," she said. "An office number is fine."

Frowning, I gave it out to her while Thornbird smiled.

The night air smelled of briny seaweed. With Thornbird driving the rental VW, we rambled through the gate and up the hill to Dakota Farms. Asleep at his post, Stanley Pettigrew dreamt of boundless whiskey springs. An upstairs light, Mrs. Taliaferro's room, glimmered inside the ruined mansion. She was done for the day. It was still early, too. Only quarter after eight.

Thornbird wrested the bowling bag from behind his seat. The bag contained his Luminol field kit. After resting it on the VW roof, he clipped on his flashlight.

"Somebody is at home," he said.

I stretched out my legs. "Mrs. Taliaferro likes to hit the rack early."

The spring peepers were raising a ruckus throughout their marshy kingdom. I itched to knock out the Luminol test and be off.

"The trainer bunks at the stable," I said. "His name is Martin. Come on."

Thornbird nodded. "James Martin and I go back a ways. He's okay."

We trudged through darkness, guided by the outside flood lights Martin had left burning. Talking fast, Thornbird prepared me for what awaited us.

"Luminol, of course, isn't a panacea," he said. "It's used as a last resort and only looks sexy on TV. That slicky stuff you see on CSI is bullshit, too."

He was the authority. "Is it admissible in court?" I asked.

"Hell no," said Thornbird. "Unscientific and unreliable, Luminol falls in the same category as the polygraph."

I didn't like the sound of that.

"Once applied, Luminol's window is also short." Odds any reaction is a false positive also run pretty high. Like I said, you have to work fast and sure with it. We'll be okay with it. I'm that good."

"So, no reaction, no blood stains?" I asked.

"I can always fall back on using benzidine and phenolphthalein tests. But we'll know soon enough if blood stains really exist."

The stable's rankness came on strong. Cigarette smoke vined up from Martin slouching at his customary hanging post. His cigarette butt sailed in a sparkling arc and hissed upon impact with the sodden turf.

"Johnson," he said. "Hi there. Who's your shadow?...oh...hey, Thornbird."

"Thornbird brought along his medicine bag," I said. "Show us that ashtray stand."

"We're seeking any presence of bloodstains," said Thornbird.

"Gruesome," said Martin. "Come warm your bones first at my stove."

Martin had decorated his walls with crying-clown art held by stud nails over an unmade cot. A ratty pair of moccasins and an apple core lay under the cot. Charred remnants of minute steak in a frying pan waited in the sink. I heard a rockabilly tune playing low on his radio. From under a pillow, Martin resurrected a near full bourbon bottle, Jim Beam vintage. "A toddy, gentleman?" he asked swishing the amber nectar.

"I still have a long night ahead of me," I said, begging off. Martin's raised arms shrugged before he sloshed three fingers into a dirty thermos cup.

Thornbird, nettled by the offer, also rejected it. "Not right this minute, Martin. Can't you see that I'm still on duty? Once I'm done here, then you can hit me."

Martin swigged. "Whoowee. What's that stuff you're mixing up?"

"Luminol," Thornbird replied.

Again Martin drained his thermos cup. With a captive audience and loose tongue, he had to wax philosophic for the occasion. "Guys, I never aspire to go before my appointed time. Some do. A longshoreman I knew in Norfolk pummeled his old lady. Bruises and welts covered her body. Broken noses, missing teeth, cracked ribs, the whole shebang. Well, see this fellow came to regret his rough ways with his wife. He had to square his accounts with the Good Lord. So he'd beat his chest, cry into his beer, wear a briar shirt..."

"Does this story end soon?" asked Thornbird. "It's boring the shit out of me."

Martin was unruffled. "One night after a hellacious drinking spree, he staggered behind a tattoo parlor. Hoodlums bushwhacked him. A skinning knife slit the old boy's throat from ear to ear. The big, ugly gash was a way for him to whistle for ice water in Hell."

My comment: "That's some trick."

"Did you ever," Martin asked me next, "lay hands on Ralph?"

"Afraid not. It was more like he laid hands on me." I touched the tender spot on my head.

"Ralph is an asshole," said Martin.

"When we get done here tonight," I said, "he'll be a wanted man."

"Okay. The Luminol is primed." Thornbird swirled a clear liquid inside a plastic misting bottle. He'd donned latex rubber gloves. The goggles and organic vapor mask perched on his head.

"Why all the hazmat get-up?" asked Martin.

"Because I'm allergic to Luminol," Thornbird said.

Martin couldn't suppress a snicker. He was in no shape to help us.

"Let's rock-and-roll," I said to Thornbird.

We exited Martin's pad and strode by the stable stalls occupied by champion thoroughbreds whose manure did truly stink to the high heavens. Pierre's chalk outline was still visible on the floor.

"According to Hoyle, we should photograph the grid and compose a crime scene sketch," Thornbird told me.

"Only this isn't a crime scene," I said. "We're inspecting a potential murder weapon."

"Okay, you're calling the shots," he said.

The ashtray stand, like before, propped open the tack room door. Thornbird scooted the stand into the walkway to tip over onto its side. I flipped off the overhead lights, then directed the flashlight to focus on the object of our attention.

Now wearing the vapor mask and goggles, Thornbird pumped the hand sprayer to atomize a dew settling on the ashtray stand. I extinguished the flashlight, he put on the black light, and we waited. In a little, a bluish-green corona glowed along the ashtray stand's bottom crimp. The Luminol had reacted with something evil.

"Congratulations." Thornbird clapped me on the back. "You may have yourself a winner, Mr. Johnson."

My heart did handsprings in my throat, and the overhead lights blazed back on. "Bag it and tag it," I said. "Our trusty forensics lab can do the confirmation."

Thornbird was also ebullient. "This moment has been a long time in coming."

"We're not home free yet," I said. "Like you said, false positives are all too common."

"But this one is a winner. I can feel it." Thornbird hoisted the ashtray stand now wrapped in a clean trashcan liner to his shoulder. "Martin's Jim Beam will be great to toast our success."

"Amen to that," I said.

I dove into the strong spirits again. After my first lucky break in my toughest case, I celebrated. My backslide was a backward five year one. Parked on Martin's cot, I was sipping bourbon out of a mayo jar, singing "Arnie's Goat" between lush swallows. I cherished the shrapnel shattering to tear apart my guts. We had a riotous laugh when I muffed shuffling a deck of playing cards for a game of poker.

"Joker is the wild card," I said. "Where's that frigging joker? Thornbird, are you hiding it up your sleeve? Lemme see, boy. Cough it up."

More than a little disgusted, Thornbird put on a frown. "Damn if bourbon doesn't juice you up," he said. "I guess that's why I'm the designated driver."

After Thornbird refused him, Martin glugged more fortification into my mayo jar. "A joke is ten times better than a joker," he said. "You're up, Mr. Johnson. Regale us. A joke, please."

"Just give me a moment to clear away the cobwebs and slip down into the old joke vault. Um, okay, here's a dandy. Once there was this Romeo boinking another man's old lady in their bed."

"This is rich," said Martin. "I love it already."

"Yeah well, the old lady's husband drove up and naked Romeo had just time enough to grab up two cigarette packs and shimmy down the gutter spout."

"Oh for gracious sake," Martin said, snorting.

Thornbird shook his head. "I already heard this one."

Martin interrupted. "Well I haven't. Let me top you off, Johnson. Go ahead, sir."

"Nope, we're done here," said Thornbird. Always the classiest drunk in any crowd, I could hold my liquor. I couldn't understand why Thornbird collected my mayo jar and tossed its contents into the sink. "You've outdone my one drink by five," he said. I couldn't dispute him. "Not to mention that's the lamest excuse for a joke."

"Aw, Mother of Christ, Thornbird. Let the detective enjoy himself," said Martin. "It's my booze. Don't be such a square. Here go, you need more yourself. It'll loosen up your tight-ass disposition."

"Shut up," said Thornbird.

"Thornbird is right," I said. "Shut up, Martin."

"Can you wobble out to the VW?" Thornbird asked me.

"You lead and I'll follow." My head swirled. Or the room did.

Martin in the doorframe lowered a shoulder. "Lean on me, Johnson. Come on, buddy. You ain't too heavy."

Thornbird spun Martin around by the belt to end up flat on his cot. He cracked the seal on a new Jim Beam and told Martin, "Take this and marinate your liver."

Leaving, I tramped behind whistling Thornbird weaving to and fro. Our rental VW vibrated before my eyes. Thornbird laid the ashtray stand in the rear seat.

"Mr. Johnson, you'd better tighten up. And PDQ, too," he said.

Bumping my head against the window of the moving car, I gurgled a few words. Kaiser soon came up. It had rolled up the sidewalks. We parked. Slamming the rental VW's door shut brought the girl down the street on a run to meet us. It was Sheila. Her shoes scuffing pavement was bad news, too. Thornbird was attuned to it before I was.

"This is where you and I part company," he said. "Tell Sheila you haven't touched a drop and she's liable to knock off your block." He pulled out the ashtray stand.

"I was with you." That was a whine even to my ears.

"No, Mr. Johnson," he said. "My story? Simple. We hooked up a few minutes ago when I saw you stumbling out of the bar."

"Thornbird, don't be a jerk. Don't you let me catch her flak alone."

Striding toward the sheriff's office, Thornbird chuckled. "Sheila will sober you up. It'll be good for you."

"Thornbird," I said. "God damn your hillbilly ass."

"I gotta go. Shannon is overdue for relief," said Thornbird. "Ciao. And good luck."

"Frank!" Sheila hollered it again. Now at arm's length, she first caught a whiff of my breath. "What have you done?"

"Me? Nothing. Maybe guillotined by rear-ending a tractor-trailer." My whiskey-logged wit didn't charm her. I grabbed a memory too late on how it never had in our past.

"Maybe I ought to guillotine you," she replied. "The brains in your present skull are defective and stupid."

"All right," I said. "A few nips. So?"

"But why? Have you taken up drinking again?"

"Last time. Never again, I swear to you on my skin."

"Save it, Frank. I've heard that pathetic homily too many times before. Carole Dawson was asking after you. I can't see why. We can go tonight if you don't make complete fools out of us."

"Why sakes alive, I'd love to visit Carole. Lead on," I said.

Chapter 15

Thursday 10 PM, April 20th

Our brisk trek to Kaiser Hospital didn't dispel my mental haze. The anxiety ripping me in half was new and scary. Was the true Mick in me shining through? Was I yet again a falling, facedown drunk? I sought solace by recalling Ephesians 5:18: "Don't destroy yourself by getting drunk...but let the spirit fill your life." That Scripture oft-quoted at my AA meetings sounded ass-backward, didn't it? The real spirits filling our lives was 86-proof.

"Hi, I'm Frank and I'm an alcoholic. I've been sober for..." All I ever saw in the AA legions were sympathetic eyes. They were now disappointed eyes gazing on me. I scoffed. Beating myself up like this was knuckleheaded. I'd had a relapse, a slight one at that. Knocked back one baby step. Big fucking deal. Whip me. No here, shoot me. It was a far cry from a total meltdown, from my staying five years stone sober flushed down the toilet. I was strong. I was a man.

Grasping the hospital door's handle reading PUSH, I pulled. Was I so helpless? Intervening, Sheila held the door. I invaded the lobby deserted except for a Portuguese cleaning lady standing in front of her broom closet knitting her puppy a red sweater. In the gift shop window, I saw a bobble-headed Elvis doll wishing a speedy recovery and a dog-eared copy of *The Complete Bolivian Diaries of Che Guevara*.

It was after hours, well past sick folks' bedtime. Sheila dialed the information desk telephone and talked in guarded murmurs. Perched on a brick wall, I waited. The potted bamboo jungle—Made In Singapore—that covered us was cellophane and silk. How fake.

"Pardon me, Miss. Has the Tiki Lounge stopped serving for the evening?" I asked Sheila now back with me. Bad joke. Her eyes and lips slitted, she stared off. Ah, now I remembered. The cold shoulder. With not a hair out of place, she was so perfect. Her frosty inner bitch was on queenly display. I shivered.

A bureaucrat, baldheaded and dour-faced, arrived from stage right. He led us down a rat maze of low-lit corridors. Doctors orders were taped to patients' doors. "Draw Mr. Boyer's blood @ midnite, 2 AM &

4 AM." Sweet dreams, Mr. Boyer, you pin cushion among men.

My boot soles besmirched the bureaucrat's lily-white floor tiles. I liked that. The foxhunting prints on the beige walls screamed tacky and I'd exceeded my quota for tacky.

"Tallyho," I sang out.

Turning, Sheila and the bureaucrat together went, "Shhh!"

The bureaucrat first nuzzled inside the door. He muttered a few words, then shoehorned us into the matchbox, what HMOs designated "a semi-private room." A TV was strapped on the bed railing. My Hollywood brethren, *Magnum PI*, in scuba diving gear was fending off mechanical sharks. Magnum, a stud muffin, left me looking like a lard bucket. So it went.

The first bed held a wizened old lady, her pipe cleaner leg held in traction. Her bed tag read "Mrs. Boyer." Carole Dawson lay in the second bed. She bunched sheets up over her chin stitches. Her puffy eyes were recessed and I saw cuts and bruises dominated her cheeks. She cowered as if shriveled by the light. Two IV drips were going. Chrysanthemums from well wishers crowded the windowsill where I parked my rump.

The bureaucrat cupped a hand to his prissy mouth. "Pssst. Mr. Johnson. Regulations do not permit alcoholic beverages on these premises. Just a reminder."

What? Did I smuggle gin inside a peg leg? Saying "but they do permit pansies, huh?" would reflect badly on me, so I only nodded. "You have three minutes." He wiggled three doughy digits.

Carole's swollen lips moved slow, thick. "Thanks for seeing me."

"How are you, dear?" asked Sheila.

"Better. The doctors say I might go home tomorrow. I hope so."

"Terrific. Frank. Quick. Say hi to Carole."

I nodded while she said, "Hi, Mr. Johnson...I can't thank you enough."

"You just get better and better." Right then, the scene jerked me into a judge's sobriety.

"Might we get you anything?" asked Sheila.

Shock clouded Carole's mangled expression. Sniffs punctuated her speech. "I-have-bad-dreams-they-are-still-over-me."

"Never again," I said. "You just get better and better."

Sheila whispered behind a hand at my ear. "Never again? How can you say that to her? How can you guarantee it?"

Because I just could.

Shuddering, Carole's eyes teared up.

A soft rap signaled at the door. The bureaucrat fussed, "You must leave at once."

I saw Carole one last time. "Thanks," she repeated.

The bureaucrat clucked at me. "Mr. Johnson, didn't you understand? You must go. Right this instance. I insist."

Outside Carole's room, I lost what little restraint I had. "Do you carry a stopwatch in your navel?"

"Frank," said Sheila. "Zip it and follow me."

"Sir, that last remark was rude and inappropriate."

"You've insulted enough people for one night," said Sheila.

"Sheila, next time it's normal visiting hours," the bureaucrat said. "No more favors for you."

Sheila snared my forearm. "It's fine for him to have the last word."

"Like hell it is." I jabbed a finger in the bureaucrat's chest. "You can kiss the freckles on my hairy Irish ass."

As we left, Sheila spoke from the corner of her mouth. "Careful Frank or you might get what you ask for."

In the warmer night the spring peepers were a colossal chorus. We returned to the sheriff's office where Thornbird stood at a filing cabinet stuffing in folders. He heard us come in.

"Looks like you found your land legs," said Thornbird. "That's an improvement."

I scowled. "You were a real buddy. Thanks."

"The evidence bullet we supplied Susie didn't turn the crank," he said.

My scowl furrowed into deep lines of disbelief. "That .25 didn't fit the slug shaken out of Pierre?"

"No. She couldn't swear to any degree of accuracy whether or not it was fired by that .25."

"Oh for balls sake," I said, my grand murder theory now aflame in a tailspin. "Was it even a .25-caliber bullet?"

"Definitely. It was a .25," said Thornbird. "But it could've been discharged from any one of thousands of Ravens ever made and sold."

"What .25?" asked Sheila.

"I uncovered a .25 that belonged to Ralph," I replied. "Except now I'm hacked to learn that it didn't kill Pierre."

"A list of locals owning .25s could be culled from the state database," said Sheila.

Although my idea too, Sheila's saying it crystallized a new insight. "The trouble is citizens carrying Saturday Night Specials don't register them. Just the same, I'm having that record generated."

"Richmond called earlier," said Thornbird. "Your lady friend, I think her name is Ms. Adkins, is still conducting her search. Her network is sluggish."

"She won't leave us hanging," I said.

Thornbird smiled, "How do you charm these ladies?"

"Why Frank is a certified lady killer. Aren't you, Frank?" said Sheila.

"Darl is compiling the database records," I said. "It's nothing more than that."

My belly growled. Thornbird dug out three Almond Joys from his coat pocket. We each unwrapped one. When coupled with adrenaline, the candy bar wasn't that shabby for dinner.

"Tomorrow I'll run the ashtray stand to Susie in Middleburg. Weather permitting." Thornbird's knuckles knocked on the wood.

"Ashtray stand?" Again, Sheila was confused.

"The one from the stable. Mrs. Taliaferro claims it's been there forever," I said. "We believe it was used to bludgeon Emily to death."

"Luminol showed positive on it," said Thornbird.

"To incriminate the poor horse," Sheila said. "Slick."

Just then the fax machine near Thornbird's elbow whirred. Sheets of paper curled into a wire basket.

"Three .25s are registered in Kaiser." Thornbird was reading from the fax. "Only high end stuff, though. Two Berettas and a Browning. No junk guns, no Ravens. Big bummer."

"Frank, don't look so disappointed," Sheila said. "Your Richmond sweetie did her best."

Thornbird wheeled in his chair. "After squaring away a few chores here guys, I'm calling it a night. I'm nothing but bushed."

"These latest dead ends will thrill Mrs. T, " I said.

"Bring her up to speed only if she asks."

My eyebrows raised. "Thanks, Thornbird. But I prefer everything kept aboveboard."

"Good night, all." He called out from the door.

I signaled to him as we took our leave. The ignition key's edge felt notched. Sheila's whole frame tensed. My impression was she'd had to wet nurse this lush one too many nights. I didn't fault her. My three sheets to the wind was sadistic as it was sad.

"Mom's home from Paw-Paw," she said. "I better get back."

"That's right in my direction. It's no hassle to drop you."

"No...I suppose not. The exercise will help me clear my mind."

"No bother, Sheila. What say?"

"Frank." She sighed and hitched up her purse's shoulder strap. "Franklin, you disappoint me. Bitterly. I—I—I can't cope. You and whiskey are a volatile mix." Her words whipped me with stinging chastisement.

"Get this. Do you see me thrashing in the gutter with the DTs? No blue devils have attacked me, either. Drinking a little liquor doesn't ring the death knell for me."

"But I think that it does," she said. "At least for the two of us."

"Shit happens, Sheila. Life goes on. I go on. We can go on, too."

Lengthening her faster strides, Sheila spoke over a shoulder, "I'm going home now. I suggest you do likewise. Be good to yourself, Frank. Please. Good bye."

That blow-off sent me reeling as if Sheila had beaned me with a 2x4. I gaped as her fluid tread cut the street corner. An electrical impulse to sprint after her, to hoot out her name to the stars, to vow I couldn't exist without her fell flat. It was useless. The self-sorrow in my Irish ancestry set off the damn brooding again. An inner voice told me, "Kaiser is a dirty little town."

I piled into my car. Spinning out, I did my damnedest to whip NASCAR speed in that broke-dick foreign jobber. Gearing through a four-speed transmission was salsa for the soul. Praise be, brother, pour it on. My 70 miles per hour pierced Mach One.

I reached Dakota Farms gate without a smashup, and toed the brakes to slow to a crawl. Roadside flares split the night. My beams fell on a pedestrian. Arms winging up and down, Stanley Pettigrew blocked the roadway. Pants cuffs were stuffed into his boot tops and his shirt hung open unbuttoned. His penguinlike walk drew up beside my car window.

"Um, Johnson?" he said. I discerned he was more trashed than I'd been. "Oh, it is you."

"Power outage?" I asked.

He nodded dumbly. "Yep. Electricity has been intermittent since the ice storm."

"Can't you sober up?"

"Does my present state worry you?" Truculent fists banged on my car roof.

"Sure. About as much as sloughing off dead skin does."

I dumped the clutch and breached the hill in second gear. A orange moon outlined the mansion in its profile. The ruins were dark. Didn't Mrs. Taliaferro stock candles or Coleman lanterns for such emergencies? The car's clacky pistons stopped as its lamps dissolved. I waited. The Navaho Indians had a tradition of lingering just outside an abode until their host showed to bade them welcome. I liked that tradition.

The spring peepers screaming their shrill whistles put me on edge. I listened to a different noise.

Jerking to gaze up into the skies, I trembled. A hedge-hopping military chopper breaking over the horizon whooshed-whooshed over me. Its red lights swirled. Reverberations bowled and bounced over the Piedmont's hills. I got it together. The U.S. Marines at nearby Quantico were playing war games.

Heat lightning sheeted behind the mansion like paparazzi flashbulbs. Its bulk was big and ugly. A black and white picture developed in my mind, more black than white. Murder painted it black. Black as original sin, black as the fallen angels falling into the black pit.

Something clicked at the base of my skull to put Mrs. Taliaferro in that picture.

My gaze transferred to those trashcans by the garage overhang. I went over. Prying off the lid to the first can, I became a bum scrounging in rich folks' detritus but for good reason. I clenched the flashlight in my teeth, untied each white plastic bag, and spilled its contents out on the ground. Insofar as garbage went, it was above par. Take, for instance, the long-stemmed yellow roses brought out from a Kaiser florist. Mrs. Taliaferro's foyer table demanded fresh ones daily.

In the final trashcan inside the last plastic bag, my tenacity won a gold star. A prescription bottle was nested inside a Maxwell House coffee can. Its label submitted that "Mrs. Mary Taliaferro" was ingesting 500 milligrams of lithium, AM and PM. 1000 mills a day was industrial strength and explained tomes about my client. In short, she was a fucking nut. I picked out two strips of sliced inner tube like those used to make a slingshot.

Squatting there with this evidence, I noodled that around in head, then homed in on the morning when Mrs. Taliaferro went to Middleburg with Rachel driving the BMW. On how she'd brought back potted flower plants and wasn't afraid to get her hands dirty. Or to get commercial plant fertilizer on them. Up until this juncture, I'd never related to her in those earthy terms. Sure, but that was it. Mrs. Taliaferro did her own dirty work and played me for the sucker that I'd become. Shame on dirty Mrs. Taliaferro in the dirty, little town of Kaiser. Shame on me.

Flashlight in hand, I marched toward the brick patio. Not a brisk march but a careful gait like threading through a Cambodian minefield decades after the war machine had moved on to rage in different lands. The twin front door, unlocked, admitted me.

I went into the vaulted foyer, and placed my house key on the gateleg table amid the Taliaferro photo gallery. The curtain had closed, my third act here pretty much finished. My flashlight drifted across evidence of a once apparently happy, healthy family. Here a pose at the beach, there an outing in the mountains. Dad, mom, and sis made three. Home sweet home. But dad and sis were gone. Home bitter home.

My light stabbed up the stairway. A new fright seized me. Why? I was at a loss to know. I took off my boots. Carpet underfoot further muffled my advance up to my client, my foe. The flashlight beam probed three hallways branching off at the stairhead. A hidebound silence swaddled me. At this late hour, I expected a drugged Mrs. Taliaferro was off chasing white bunnies with Alice down black holes. That put Rachel in her room unless Ralph had returned. How likely was that?

"Damn!" I muttered half aloud. Guess where the 9 mil was? Right, still out in my car.

My flashlight cut a bright shaft down the center corridor. Ralph had told me my first day here Pierre's room was the last one. After picking that lock, I ran my light over a narrow iron bed, a nightstand, a chair, and a footlocker. Inside the footlocker among male toiletries were an electric razor, a shaving cream can, and a straight razor. Odd. A man would have one shaving preference – either electric or razor blade. Not both. The bottom of the shaving cream can screwed off (an old MP hiding place). Grinning, I untucked an Aigner glove, the right hand.

Back down the hallway, I stood in the sewing room where Mrs. Taliaferro and I conversed on that first morning. My flashlight showed the doorknob was missing. An antique Singer Sewing Machine set against the wainscoting was powered by a foot treadle. Sewing filled rich ladies' days like crocheting baby clothes did for Death Row inmates. The left hand Aigner glove lay on the Singer where I'd seen it that same first morning.

Pierre had recovered its mate at Emily's murder scene, knew who it belonged to, and then added it up the same way as I did now.

I entered a walk-in closet, and moved my light over the cramped shelves. Riffling through hangers, I touched sundresses in petite sizes. It crossed my mind that Emily with a similar physical build could wear her mother's clothes. Or vice versa. On a high rack I found foxhunt livery—red coats with split tails and white riding breeches of a tweedy fabric. Unlike the new summer wardrobe, the coats and breeches showed recent wear. I searched on.

Imelda Marcos never had these many damn shoeboxes. The first two I sampled contained new sandals wrapped in white tissue paper. I offloaded the top stratum. The flashlight upended at my feet threw a yellow oval on the ceiling. Pawing through a lady's closet was like going on an Easter egg hunt.

A music box surfaced amid the second layer of shoeboxes. Its wood was a hard brown grain—walnut or mahogany? Shaking it revealed items inside. Chapping with the sole of a wood clog, I forced open the lock, then flattened the switch that tripped the device to play a lullaby as the lid sprang up.

At this point in the game, its contents weren't all that shocking to me.

Nude photos documented a somewhat younger, trimmer Mrs. Taliaferro. They lacked the profound grief now harrowing her eyes. She smiled at the click of the shutterbug, her impish body relaxed, sensuous, and potent. I appreciated a sense of humor. In one print, she sat at the breakfast table reading The New Yorker decked out in an Annie Hall outfit. In its companion, she reprised the same pose but in total buff. In one raunchy shot Mrs. T sat astride Pierre's face notched between feather pillows. That cleared up any confusion I had about their "friendship." The thought how that could be me in the photo left me with no regrets.

Oh, what was this? A second batch of photos.

These weren't of Mrs. Taliaferro but her late daughter, Emily. Lady Godiva was the theme—the film captured a naked Emily on or near Hellbent. They didn't strike me as dirty or pornographic, only about as pathetic as the others. I assumed Pierre had operated the camera. Flipping through them, I could attest with assurance that the nubile Emily rivaled her mother's once seductive charms.

Poking deeper, I grunted. In the bottom of the music box was Pierre's billfold containing Emily's autographed headshot. Snick. Electric power was restored. Hands shielded my eyes from the lucent force of the overhead light.

"Mr. Johnson." A meow greeting clawed at my back. "Hello."

I met Mary. Taliaferro's cynical regard for me head-on. She, however, had the upper hand. In her fist was a .25, a nasty little model with pink handgrips, a Saturday Night Special that Raven customized for American madwomen. The black dimple for its muzzle was lined on my nose short inches away. Its fresh cordite smelled dangerous, too.

"Mr. Johnson," she said. "You've grown into such a yawn." Her eyes, grim as the slaughterhouse, hit me.

"Boy, was I ever off base," I said. "Ralph was only a red herring."

"Red herring. My favorite of the fish group." Her deep-socket eyes glittered. "You're doing fine. Please go on."

"Pierre was diddling you."

"Pierre was also in my employ, yes."

Her terse statement by implication lumped me into the same category. The checkbook I tore out of my hip pocket landed at her feet. "Our deal is in the past, lady."

"I'll fire you the same way I fired Pierre when he dared to contradict my wishes. But please go ahead and spin your silly yarn. Amuse me, court jester."

"You murdered Emily in a jealous rage. Why? I can only guess. Maybe she was too much competition. You staged it to look like a horse riding accident. The dawn before Emily's ride, you skulked down to the stable, snatched up the ashtray stand, went out to the woods, and hid near that big holly tree by the bridle path."

Mrs. Taliaferro's hideous leer encouraged me.

"Once Emily was dead, you knew that the stallion would return to the stable. Upset, Pierre also predictably charged off into the woods. With ease, you evaded him and returned to replace the ashtray stand. You stood there conveniently available to phone for help when he tore out of the forest yelling.

"Except Pierre learned you'd killed Emily. Stupid, little glitches jam the best planned murders. You dropped a glove. I was with Pierre the morning he discovered it. Now I have a line on why he got so angry at me when we were heading back to the stable. He knew you were Emily's killer."

"Pierre was all mine," she said.

"Except Pierre didn't go along, did he? What then, did he threaten to expose you to your high society friends? Did he squeeze you for blackmail money?"

"What's the difference?" asked Mrs. Taliaferro. "I was done with the son of a bitch."

"How could Pierre resist test driving the younger model of you? The newer Jaguar, if you will."

"My daughter became a little slut." Her oath was soaked in venom.

"You killed Emily and framed Pierre. I was then hired to finger him." My lower back muscles wrenched in resentful spasms. "The slingshot you lost was the other big tip off."

"With one jagged little pebble, that giddy stallion shied and spilled off the little slut." Her colorless eyes grew distant, inhuman. "In a frenzy, I dropped things. I went back later and looked in vain. I figured some kids had made off with the slingshot and glove. Not my stupid detective."

Mrs. Taliaferro transferred her weight to one hip. Her wan face was bleached of any emotion. A marble mask became an evil gargoyle. Killing Emily was a necessity. With one murder under her belt, the next murder, Pierre's, had to be a piece of cake. It was just taking care of business.

A knot tightening my throat, I stammered on my oath. "C—c—christ, lady, how could you dash in your own daughter's skull?"

"I have complicated reasons you'd never understand, Johnson."

"No shit," I replied "But they made it easy for you, huh?"

"Be quiet," she said. The .25 quivered. It was a small caliber gun but could also inflict irreversible damage.

Just seconds from hanging as the third scalp from her belt, I had to go for broke. She was unstable, unpredictable. I edged one pace nearer. She flexed, catlike, into a semi-crouch.

"Don't stir a whisker" was her commandment.

My next advance drew fire. Knifing sidewise, I narrowed her target.

Blam!

I knew I took a hit. Her bullet winged my side, a searing slit along the gristle.

Blam!

Her subsequent round drilled the cedar planks high up between my legs.

The first bullet hole bled. Burn, baby, burn, my nerves chanted to my ringing ears. I reacted. Adrenaline coiled the springs in my legs. My fist slugged her gun hand away. My other hand grabbed her wrist and twisted it down hard. She yelped.

The .25 fell out of her fingers and clunked to the carpet.

Chapter 16

Thursday midnight, April 20th

Mary Taliaferro, a screaming ocelot, assaulted me. Her glued-on nails strafed my cheeks. Backtracking, my reflex threw up both hands to parry her blows. She only lashed out that much faster and harder.

"Hold it!" I said. "Hold on!"

"I'll fight," she said. "Or die trying."

I was pinned like inside of a sarcophagus, and had no room to maneuver. She cracked me across the nose. Cartilage tore. Pain radiated. My hand jerking down managed to blunt her pointy toe assailing my nuts. Seeing how I was a target of violence, I retaliated in kind.

The heel of my palm cuffed her bony temple. She squealed as if astounded at my show of physical force. My hands fumbled south, grappled her blouse front. Buttons pinged off and fabric tore down the seams. She wore, of course, no bra.

"You scumsucker," she said.

Her bared breasts, malevolent and mocking, whipped out. That distracted me, but only for the tiniest moment. Pumping her legs, with new reserves of strength tapped, she thrashed free of my clinch. She next came at me, her fists hammering away.

My sense was the .25 lay closeby to our rear. Her backhanded slug across my mouth split my lower lip against my teeth. While I touched my bleeding, she scored a direct hit. A whap sent up a starburst behind my eyes. I growled deep in my chest, and hawked out red-thick salvia.

Mary Taliaferro had been trained in self-defense. Only now did that salient fact dawn on me. As if she could read my shock, she snickered. Fear unsettled me inside. My mind raced to hit on any advantage to use in my favor. I outweighed her. That was about the only option left to me before she mopped the floor with my ass. Toro, toro, Johnson. Lowering my head, I charged straight on, an incensed bull tackling her about the waist.

She screamed.

Fists thwacked my shoulders as I propelled her backward through the threshold and out into the room. Shrieking, she toppled down to the floor. Crawling, I then sat astraddle her, my weight anchored across her hips rocking to buck me off. Spitting blood, I staked her one hand, then the second.

"You can say uncle any time." My rushed words were suggestive.

"No way," she said. "Roll off me."

"Not in a million years." My answer came in breathless gasps.

The .25 gleamed some six inches away. I pounced to scoop it up. Her released hand chopped, but I snared it again. Her struggles weakened. I put the .25's muzzle in the tab between those wild eyes, their fury hard and shiny.

"Hike off me," she said. "You bastard!"

"Shut up." I was in charge now. Some time elapsed for us to collect our breath and wits. "Where's Rachel?" I asked her.

"Screw you," she said.

"Rachel is in her room, isn't she?" Impatient, I reamed the muzzle to enlarge her nostrils. "Am I right, lady? You doped, then imprisoned Rachel?"

"Yeah," she said. "Are you satisfied?"

"I'm going to tie you up. Don't sass me. I ain't having any more of you."

"No sass," she said. "Just facts. I phoned up Sheila Hamilton."

"Why?"

"I told her about our eye-popping sex," she said. "In the foyer. Remember, lover?" She laughed with bitter humor.

"Not true. Sheila knows you're a conniving liar."

"On the contrary. Sheila was enthralled. So much so she asked me to repeat every juicy detail of it."

"You're a liar," I said. "On top of being a ice-blooded killer."

"Possessive, jealous, vengeful—that's your Sheila. M'm. She's a lot like me."

"Shut up," I said before gagging her.

I'd truss Mrs. Taliaferro mummy-fashion if need be until Deputy Sheriff Thornbird came to haul her off to jail. Pantyhose plucked from a lowboy drawer went tied around her sinewy wrists, then ankles. Before knotting her ripped blouse at the midriff, curious, I had to rub her breasts. They were, as expected, cold and hard as stalagmites. She squirmed, her topaz snake eyes pinpoints of furious hate. Laughing, I rounded up the incriminating music box and her .25.

Rachel's bedroom door was locked. My raps didn't rouse her. I dipped a shoulder to bash down the door. Three tries and aches did it. The wood jamb splintered ripping free from the brass hardware and screws. On her bed, Rachel stirred and rolled toward me.

Through a yawn, she asked, "Who is it?"

"Johnson. My guess is you were drugged."

Rachel's elbows propped her into a sitting position. "Was I? Feeling sleepy, I came in a while ago to lie down. I must've dozed off."

"Where is Ralph?" I asked.

"Vanished. But he'll be back. In his usual good time. The silly man I love and married always has for the past thirty-one years."

Rachel's simple faith in her husband's return went a long ways to persuading me that she wasn't in cahoots with Mrs. Taliaferro. She only laundered the multi-millionaire lady's clothes and scrubbed her toilets and cooked her meals. She served, as I had, at Mrs. Taliaferro's pleasure.

"Mrs. Taliaferro, bound and gagged, is in the sewing room," I said.

"Why is she tied up?" asked Rachel.

"For the murders of Emily and Pierre."

Adjusting her glasses, Rachel accepted that news as if she'd anticipated its eventuality all along. "I knew she was spiteful but never so bloody and vindictive."

"How is that?" I asked.

Rachel shuddered. "Of course, I'd never gossip. That's not how I was raised."

"Duly noted. This is different. Murder. Quick. What did you overhear?"

"Mrs. Taliaferro and Pierre at all hours of the day screwing their brains out."

Time was short as was my tact. "Except Pierre moved on to bone Emily and her mother flipped out."

Rachel swung around her legs and steadied standing on her feet. She projected all the serenity of a Carmelite nun. "Insane raving jealousy, I'd say, is what goaded Mrs. Taliaferro to destroy them both."

"Take this and go stand guard," I said. "Don't talk to her."

"Why would I? We've nothing left to discuss," said Rachel.

She accepted the handgun with squeamish care. I followed her but hurried into my room, packed up my duffel in a spare pillowcase, and beat it downstairs. I threw the luggage inside my car and seized the 9 mil. Oh hell. Up the hill probed a pair of headlights. My heart began to bang at my temples. As I waited for the intruder, the 9 mil rested on my car roof. As his vehicle prowled into the lone streetlight's circle of illumination, I recognized the truck model with the distinctive orange camper shell on the rear. It was Adam.

I grunted. My thumb stretched to cock the hammer. Dark humors oozed inside me. If the young turk yearned for more fight, then this old man would dish it out. And with pleasure. The beams raked over me as the truck tromped around to a halt. The engine quit, both doors flapped outward. Beams remained on me.

"Johnson!" Stanley Pettigrew's loud entreaty surprised me. They stalked around the truck into its bright beams. "Is that you standing there? It's Stanley and Adam. We come as friends. Don't pop off on us."

"What's up?" I asked.

"We know something that might interest you," Adam said. "The Kilbys did a jailbreak."

"How?"

"Somebody broke into the jail and sprang them."

"But Sheriff Pettigrew radioed us," Stanley said. "He's en route."

"That makes me feel warm and fuzzy," I said. "Does Thornbird know about it?"

"I woke him," Adam said. My casual aiming the 9 mil at Adam hyped him to explain faster. "Look. I drove by and noticed the office door was ajar. I parked and poked inside. The Kilbys were gone. That's it. Exactly, from start to end."

"You setting me up?" The 9 mil fastened on Adam's head. "Are you sore at the Kilbys and playing me for a fool? I know about the car parts they stole from you."

With vigor, Adam denied it. "Not at all. I'm arrow straight with you."

"He's right," said Stanley.

"I can vouch for him." The declaration belonged to Rachel Phillips. She drew up beside me. "I believe him. Adam speaks the truth."

"Pot farmers aren't credible sources," I said. "Neither are their family assistants." The last statement was for Rachel's benefit but she didn't react.

Stanley Pettigrew horned in. "The Kilbys vowed to kill you. Do with our news as you see fit, Johnson. We don't care. At least I know I don't."

"Really?"

"Really. Why should we give a damn?"

"Can you find them, Frank?" asked Rachel. "Where would they run?"

"Some bloody place you wouldn't suspect. Like a warehouse or a church. Like that damn Catholic church." Before darting into my car, I looked over at Rachel. "Contact Thornbird to come and arrest our killer. Tell him to voucher that damn .25, too. This one will be a match. He'll know what you mean."

A red, shiny crucifix glowed atop the Charismatic Catholic church's single spire. I doused my low beams and prowled dark and silent another quarter block to reach it. I got out of my car. Spring peepers drubbing my eardrums were the soundtrack to a slasher flick. I had never felt so edgy, so savage as I did now. Running in a crouch, I darted over the parking lot, crossed the sidewalk, and knelt behind a leafy bush.

Emptiness confronted me. Sodium vapor lights illuminated no cars. Stay calm, I coached myself. The gory slow-motion footage of me mowed down by a chokebore shotgun dizzied my control. Stay calm. In the ER with my washboard chest racked apart, high-risk surgery was performed by insectlike surgeons. My eyes drifted to the red, shiny steeple. Stay calm. I tried to reel off a prayer but was fresh out.

At a dead run, I came on ten, twenty, thirty strides to end at the bottom of the church steps. No volleys leveled on me. The luck of the Black Irish, that's all. I crouched, breathing hard and heavy. A large moth flittered against the porch's globe lamp. With faith, the moth had survived the winter. Survival was good. Dark was good. Have a little faith, you moth-man. Survive and do some good.

Squatting by a hydrangea bush, I got a better hold on the 9 mil's grips. My adrenal glands pumped wild out. Stay calm. My mouth puckered, gums ached, and chest constricted. I peeled a wary eye for the Kilbys. If they lurked here at all.

The pit of my gut told me they'd raced to the church, only because it was the weirdest of hideouts. Moreover, they'd gamble right that I'd tap into their warped logic and put it together. Sooner or later, I'd show up here looking for them.

My boots scuffed up the concrete steps. I planted my ear against the wide oak doors. Inside was the quiet befitting a place of worship. The knob rotated and the chink in the door broadened. Sucking in my gut, I sidled into the dingy vestibule but left one door cracked, my escape valve.

A dirt-brown oak crucifix gleamed behind the altar. Ashes to ashes, dirt to dirt, bullet to bullet. Twice I swallowed, got no spit on either try. I defogged my brain while removing my boots. What did I see? Rows of pews flanked the center aisle. Stained glass windows gleamed. From the kneeling rail, pyramid steps, carpeted in red, built up to a simple altar. A gold chalice, a red gem in its stem, beckoned. A phalanx of votive candles flickered at the feet of the Virgin Mary and Saint Joseph both cast in clay.

Through my socks, I discerned the floor was well-worn wood, rife with squeaks and groans. Both Kilbys packed heavy ordnance—12-gauge Mossberg shotguns filched from the sheriff's gun racks I'd seen in his office. My 9 mil, by comparison, was a flit gun.

I nudged against the baptismal, then had an idea. The glass container the size of a catcher's mitt inside the baptismal became a weapon. Any of those pews could harbor Kilbys lusting to blast off my head. My arches ached like walking on rebar. My fright sweat was rancid. Head scrunched down, and knees bent, I crept up the center aisle, stopping before each row to clear it out. I strained to catch the slightest disturbance.

The gas furnace kicking on sent me up the beanstalk. The fire whistle next screeched a long-winded wail. I listened. No fire trucks sounded. It was a false alarm. Rather than expose myself for a turkey shoot, I played a ruse by heaving the glass container as a shot put. It shattered inches from the kneeling rail.

The resounding crash brought up the Kilbys hiding behind the front row. I could spot their outlines, arms throwing up pump shotguns against shoulders. Tongues of fire came not from the Holy Ghost but muzzle flashes before exploding thunder. The shots threshed a hole in the floorboards. My ears left bleeding heard their shouts.

"Did you nail the turd?"

The other hesitated. "Not sure."

"Could be he's saying his prayers."

"He'd better be saying his amen."

"You never said that truer."

Now or never, it was my turn. I jacked upright, the 9 mil an extension of my arm. I rolled right, my natural side. Kilby was at the pew's end, three rows off to my front. The backlit stained glass windows imprinted his lank profile. It was a sweet shot. And I took it. My finger jerked the trigger.

The 9 mil pulsed one-two-three, crackling fire and smoke. My target crumpled facedown, plugged through the lungs and heart. His last wish had been to slaughter me. Instead, death came for him. I wondered if he knew what had hit him.

"What the Hell?" my second target hollered. I ran my iron gun sights in a 180-degree sweep, but that Kilby no longer stood there. I fired anyway to make some noise.

Spent cordite poisoned the air. I gritted my teeth, my eyes moistening and my nose burning to stifle convulsing coughs. I sank down, a shotgun discharged where I'd just stood. Double-ought buckshot splintered the pews behind me.

I did the arithmetic in my head: eleven rounds left in my magazine, two in Kilby's. Unless Pettigrew had modified his Mossbergs—that would make four. A grim realization hit me. It was less and less likely that I'd ever capture Kilby alive. We'd both hoisted the black flag – yield no quarter. We were vying for who'd stumble out still upright.

Protected in his pew, cursing, Kilby lodged a shotgun blast at the crucifix. To me, it was a wasted shot. I scuttered off the center aisle and moved deeper into a pew to squat under the "Jesus Falls a Third Time" Station of the Cross hanging on the wall. My mind wrapped around a plan. Rearward at the door was where any advantage now existed. I had a worsening dread that Kilby, given a head start fleeing from the church, might slip through my fingers.

I scooted between the rows on the far aisle. Stealth was less important now. I detected movement along the other side. Had we both devised the same strategy? At the last row, I poked out my head. Hello. Kilby did the same. We traded eye blinks.

Kilby racked in a new shell. Boo-yaa! He bored out the drywall where my head had just been. He pumped and pumped the Mossberg with metallic precision. Pumped again. Nothing. He'd shot his wad.

"Johnson!" he said. "A-yo, Johnson! Can you hear me?"

I identified him as the munchkin Kilby.

He bellowed, his volume hoarser. "Johnson, I want to parley."

"No parley. You throw down your weapon. Inch out with your hands up high," I said. "We can walk out of this together."

"Okay, okay, damn it, okay."

I figured he was pulling some stunt until I heard the thrown shotgun thud near me. Peering over the pew's ledge, I saw the short Kilby taking measured steps, hands interlaced behind his head. He was surrendering. Self-preservation offset his bloodlust. Better a live chicken than a dead duck. That childhood saying was made clear to me. Arising, I trained the 9 mil at Kilby. Bile seeped at its blackest through me.

He laughed uneasy at seeing my crazed face.

"I'll take my lumps powering through a stretch at the super max."

"Sure. Our governor goes begging to fill those cages," I said. "That's far enough. Stop, face the door."

Kilby did as I ordered. "A Kilby posse is there," he said. "Funny, they claim the wind never stops rustling over that mountaintop."

"No shit," I said. "The whistling wind."

The black bile inside me brewed dark intent.

"I'll get a little OJT there in painting walls and picking up trash." Kilby slobbered a laugh. "But the road to this crime was paved with gold. Pure gold. Closer the bone, sweeter the meat. Eh, Johnson?"

A distant siren pricked our ears. The black bile surged through my shoulder, jolted my biceps, and grafted my fingers. The thorny moment fell away and I accepted what I had to do.

"It's the place the baddest of the bad go." My voice coarsened to a gravelly monotone. My trigger finger twitched.

The bandy-legged Kilby unlimbered a cocky strut to the vestibule. In my mind's eye, I saw him in one of those bright orange scrubs. He was strolling the exercise yard or pumping iron to beef up for his next rape victim. Concertina razor wire and guard towers and 50,000-volt stun guns wouldn't be enough. Not for this devil's cum.

"Fucking-A. The baddest of the bad. That's me."

"Only thing wrong with that is you might come out again."

"What?" Kilby ceased his strut. "I'd didn't dig the sound of that."

I talked over him. "Decisions, decisions. I can march you off to jail. Or I can smoke your ass here and now."

"J—J—Johnson," said Kilby. "Can't we rap this out?"

"What's the point?"

"All right, now. Easy does it. I'm about to turn around real slow."

"Don't bother," I said.

My first shot impaled his shoulder blade under which I judged his black heart gave life to his evil. Two rounds peeled back his cranium, white scraps of bone and brains spattered into a satanic halo.

The Zapruder film clip was replayed right before my eyes.

As Kilby convulsed on the church floor, I emptied my full magazine into him. He didn't move, not even involuntarily. Police sirens cranked up the street, too little and too late.

I staggered into the restroom, retched into the commode, and flushed cold water on my bloodless face. My pupils were garbanzo beans. More cold water rinsed out my mouth. Rinsed again. The bitter aftertaste wouldn't wash out. Never. These violent acts were layered on the hellish core too many years in police work had stacked on me. I hated it all.

Before stepping through the heavy oak door, I blessed myself with holy water.

Kaiser was a dirty little town. Dirty little people ran it. Its dirty little people crawled all over my back. This hit me yet again. Thornbird had pleaded my case with passion and eloquence. He'd make a professional's professional. The murky chill this hour before dawn made me appreciate not to be in shackles and manacles.

Sure, a few pissant criminal charges were "pending." Obstruction of justice. Trespassing and destroying private property. Unlawful discharge of a firearm within town limits. For that last one, I had had to cough up my 9 mil. Sheriff Pettigrew, now back in town, put it with my .357, another freebie for his collection. Complying with that had grated. I expected further questions between more mugs of creosote coffee. No damn matter. The facts didn't alter. No criminal charges had been filed against me.

Good, bad, or indifferent, the Kilby shootings had been in self-defense. A justified use of deadly force to protect myself. My gun permit was legal as was my right to fire it whenever I was jammed with imminent danger. Imminent danger meant any bastard training a loaded 12-gauge shotgun on me.

I sat buckled up inside my car, and just breathed. A free man breathing free air in our democracy. A local newspaper box on the bus terminal docks would hawk its lurid headlines. Headlines to stories how in an old-fashioned Wild West shoot-out, I'd mortally wounded two home boys. Mortally wounded them in a neighborhood church, no less.

A tap came at the glass. It was Thornbird. I rotored down the window.

"How are you fixed for leaving Kaiser?" he asked me.

"Why? Is that an invitation?"

"The sheriff is incensed," said Thornbird. "He's spoiling to arrest you on whatever load of hooey he can fabricate."

"I figured as much," I said.

"You have an attorney?" asked Thornbird. "I'm talking a street savvy lawyer. Not your Gucci loafered tinkerbells practicing over in Middleburg."

"Yeah. Robert Gatlin," I said half-aloud. "He's a shitkicker, filthy rich, and the last white knight left in the world."

"If this Gatlin is any good, I'd get him on board pronto before you've got no more wiggle room," said Thornbird.

I peered around Thornbird. "You see a pay phone?"

"Here go," Thornbird said. "Use this cell phone."

Chuckling, Thornbird had to demonstrate how to work the gizmo and patch through my call. I'd forgotten. Buttons and all, it still impressed me. I cranked up my window for some privacy, and let it buzz seven times.

"Hello...Robert Gatlin," answered a sleep-thickened voice.

"Mr. Gatlin," I greeted him. "Frank Johnson here. Hi."

Ponderous breathing. "Johnson. Tell me it's a bad dream. Please. Tell me I'll roll over, fart out a horny toad, and it'll end."

"Can the jive ass crap," I said before explaining to him my predicament.

"Good Lord, I didn't have a clue about Mary Taliaferro." Overplayed astonishment infused his speech. "It would be a cakewalk for you is how I figured it. Well, well. What to do now? Well, at the risk of stating the painfully obvious, Johnson, get the hell out of Kaiser."

"I got a few more stray ends."

Gatlin's tone grew earnest. "Stray ends? If you're arrested in Kaiser, you'll never be granted conditional bail. Even if I put up a million dollars of my money or try to bribe a dozen judges."

"Give me a day," I said. "If I'm not home, come fetch me."

I punched off, before Gatlin could scream some sense into me.

After putting down the window, I handed Thornbird the cell phone. "I can see you're not about to make yourself scarce," he said. "I half-expected that."

I flipped the key, my engine fired. "I'll be around. Could be once Pettigrew calms down, he'll lay off me."

"Look. If the sheriff orders me to haul you in," said Thornbird, "I'll have no choice but do it. Nothing personal."

"I understand," were my parting words to Thornbird. "Head on back inside, kid. You never saw me here today."

I rolled down Main Street and accelerated pulling onto the road to Mary Taliaferro's ruined mansion. When a critical insight hit me, I jounced into the first driveway I came to, socked my car into reverse, and swung around to make tracks back into Kaiser.

At Sally's Nails, I shoved my tires against the curbstone. The salon's blinds were drawn. The street was vacant. The windows above the salon were impenetrable. So too were the dark windows into Sheila's darker soul that compounded my present woes. It'd taken me until now to cobble together what she'd damn near pulled off. Now the "why" had me tied in knots.

I crossed the street, entered the stairwell, and ascended two steps at a clip. The hallway was dirty and little. Pounding on their walk-up door, I hollered. "Open up! Open up in there!"

Mrs. Hamilton, tugging on a red terrycloth bathrobe, cracked the door. "Franklin, are you out of your gourd?"

"Round up Sheila," I said.

"You hush. Sheila is still asleep."

"Send her to the damn door," I said. "Or I'm barreling in there after her."

Mrs. Hamilton paled. "Calm down, Frank. What's bitten you?"

"Mom, who is it?" asked a sleepy person shuffling into the kitchen.

"Frank Johnson acting the fool he is," Mrs. Hamilton replied over her shoulder.

I said. "Damn you, Sheila."

"Frank," she said from behind her mother. "You go away from here."

"You double-crossed me!" I said. "Why did you fall for what lies Mary Taliaferro fed you?"

Mrs. Hamilton started to close the door. My foot wedged into the narrowing space.

"What about Mrs. Taliaferro?" Sheila's face passed me a puzzled look.

"You unlocked the sheriff's office and freed Kilbys from jail," I said. "You told them where to run, knowing I'd be right behind them. Why?"

Sheila edging better into my sightline, shook her head, those long blonde braids swishing. "No, that wasn't my doing."

"Don't deny it. Liar!"

Mrs. Hamilton shoved the door harder, leaning her weight against it. "Frank Johnson, you'd be smart to leave us be. Go on. Do like Sheila tells you."

"You're the only one who could've helped them." My anguished shout hit a raw nerve. Sheila winced. I couldn't tell whether she regretted being exposed now or felt remorse because her stab at vengeance had failed.

"Frank, you march on downstairs," said Mrs. Hamilton. "Leave us be. Off you go. Sheila, phone Sheriff Pettigrew."

"She can't deny it. I've got a right to know why."

Sheila broke down, hands smothering her wet eyes. "I did nothing wrong," she said.

"Bullshit!"

Mrs. Hamilton's liver-spotted arm stiffed me in the chest. I was forced to step away. "Frank," she said. "You best go on back to your Mary Taliaferro or Susie or whomever now warms your bed."

Alone on the pre-dawn street, I dropped back my head and ripped out a maniac howl, one that hyenas raise on the star-crazed veldt. For once Mary Taliaferro had told the gospel truth. She really had telephoned Sheila.

Chapter 17

Saturday 9 AM, April 22nd

I loafed near Kaiser the whole day Friday and then Friday night. It was garbage time like in a basketball game. What did I do? After the ER dressed my bullet nick from Mrs. Taliaferro's .25, I wrote them a check. I also made an executive decision to retain Mrs. Taliaferro's $200,000. Shit, I'd earned it.

Later, after gassing up at a BP station over in The Plains, I hammered down rural roads throughout Kaiser and over in Fauquier County, grooving on the springtime's beauty unraveling in the horse squires' Eden. It was great, weather and country. I drove and drove, my head humming with thoughts. Hellbent was Black Fury, not Misty of Chincoteague. Where was he? An image swept through my imagination—a wild stallion blitzed through rolling acreage of sweet clover. Freedom, sweet freedom, let it ring out.

Pettigrew didn't sic his deputies on me. No, he was tap dancing for the Mayor and Town Council about his Poconos jaunt with a married lady. They hated even the scent of scandal in the horse country. Someone in the know had tipped them off about his skipping the Roanoke convention. I never did catch nor care what his lady's name was. I only described her as a squat, dirty blonde.

Mid-morning, Deputy Sheriff Thornbird had the joy to transport Mary Taliaferro to the women's lockup in Middleburg. I waited parked on the street corner when they escorted her out the prison door into the waiting cruiser. The sun had broken through the clouds. She was shackled three ways, wearing the orange jump suit outlaws are compelled to endure.

Head erect, shoulders high, and breasts jutted, she played it with perfect cool. The lady was vain as she was evil as she was crazy. Carrying herself as if accepting a Grammy Award, it was a game she got off on. It wasn't so much a smirk as a profound satisfaction knowing that she looked ravishing, despite her reduced circumstances. As much as I detested to admit it, she was right.

Her future was predictable as it was tragic. Her initial trial would culminate with a guilty verdict. Subsequent appeals would litigate out over the next few years. Mary Taliaferro would die via lethal injection on Death Row at Jarrett. The needle, the big jab. It'd been done to her sex before. The Governor, according popular will, wouldn't commute her death sentence. Two murders exceeded the bounds of any executive mercy. The fact I was almost Number Three gave me pause. One thing got decided—I'd no plans to attend her execution.

After the prisoner was tethered in the rear seat, Thornbird walked down to me. His swagger was sure-legged—he had it down like a seasoned cop, his elbow pressed against his weapon, his hand left unencumbered to draw down. The homegrown deputy had matured over the past few days. A recent raft of wrinkles creased his baby face. He'd collect a few more if he continued in police work.

"You ain't hit the trail yet," he said in a mock drawl.

I hawked out the window. "Too much excitement here."

"I might be soon unemployed."

"You might end up top dog," I said.

"That's possible, too. We'll see. By the way, Susie got back to me with the DNA results. Emily's blood was on the ashtray stand. Her mother's partial prints were lifted off it, too. Joyner also extracted microscopic metal slivers in Emily's skull."

"Even with F. Lee Bailey, Johnnie Cochrane, and all the Dream Team on her side, Mrs. Taliaferro will never get off."

"The damn trial promises to be a freak fair," he said.

"Did James Martin leave town?"

"Yeah, he did. If I know Martin, he'll be in touch with you. He's always good for a drink or a joke. Stanley Pettigrew left to begin his drying out."

"And Adam?"

"He put in an application for Deputy Sheriff. Now ain't that some shit for you? Anyway, I shouldn't be seeing you again." Thornbird extended his hand.

I accepted and we shook it like true Southern gentlemen do.

"Frank, it pains me to say this, but don't ever come back here."

That he didn't bring up our manhunt for the bastards who killed his dad surprised me. Tossing him a nod however, I granted him the favor. "Did the Dawson girl get discharged?"

"She was and is back with her dad and sisters," said Thornbird. "I'm being bandied as a hero for arresting the Kilbys. Isn't that a kick in the head?"

"Your head is pretty hard."

"You were the Good Samaritan," said Thornbird.

"Fuck it. Like Carole already agreed to, that stays between us. Always."

"Sure, Lone Ranger. Here you go." Thornbird presented me a cell phone. "Pettigrew won't miss it. It's got four million free minutes or something like that. It's a lopsided swap for your personal firearms. Still, it might prove more valuable to you some day soon."

"Later, Thornbird."

"Have yourself a nice Easter," he said.

My car coughed to life and I headed to the center of town, took a right, and disappeared into the hunt countryside under the Blue Ridge Mountains. While driving away, I remembered the Kilby fray wasn't yet resolved. A pair of overfed cousins in a Willys Overlander had claimed the Kilby corpses.

They'd left ugly threats against me with Joyner. Fine. I'd be in my town expecting them. All other accounts had been settled. I'd compensated the damages to the Charismatic Catholic church and the tow truck's owner, the old man at the garage.

Money erases most ill will.

Acknowledgements

Thanks are extended to Joan Davidson for insights about equestrian matters.

The horse riding accident was suggested by the tragic death of Shelly Malone who was supposedly trampled to death by her own horse. Source: "The Horse Whisperers" by Peter Slevin, *The Washington Post*, May 2, 1999.

About the Author

Ed Lynskey's fiction has appeared in *Mississippi Review*, *HandHeldCrime*, and *Plots With Guns*. A short collection, *Out of Town a Few Days*, appeared in 2004 and a novel titled *The Blue Cheer* is scheduled for 2006.

Ed's flash fiction titled, "Referee Gone Wild," appears in the October 2005 issue of *Alfred Hitchcock Mystery Magazine*.

Ed's next PI Frank Johnson novel, *Pelham Fell Here* is scheduled for release in 2007 from Mundania Press.

Printed in the United States
91579LV00003B/123/A